TRUTH IN
FICTION

TR_TU_H_ETH
IN
FICTION

A COLLECTION OF SHORT STORIES

PETER CRAWLEY

Matador
9 Priory Business Park,
Wistow Road, Kibworth Beauchamp,
Leicestershire. LE8 0RX
Tel: 0116 279 2299
Email: books@troubador.co.uk
Web: www.troubador.co.uk/matador
Twitter: @matadorbooks

ISBN 978 1784625 368

British Library Cataloguing in Publication Data.
A catalogue record for this book is available from the British Library.

Printed by TJ International, Padstow, Cornwall
Typeset in 12pt Centaur MT by Troubador Publishing Ltd, Leicester, UK

Matador is an imprint of Troubador Publishing Ltd

For Emma

From the Mountains of the Moon to the Sea of Marmara,
'cross the shifting sands of Sinai, by the Gulf of Aqaba,
a young woman pauses in the shade of an Acacia
and recalls the many strangers who have shown her kindness.

Jim,
with best wishes,
Peter Crossley

The first person:

The views and attitudes expressed in these short stories are in no way to be confused with those of the author, even and especially when written in the first person. They are merely the voices and views of the fictional characters as featured in each story.

Contents

Preface

A couple or three years ago my niece flew over from San Francisco to go interrailing around Europe. She and her two companions enjoyed a few weeks bathing in history, absorbing culture and sampling the local alcoholic beverages of each city they passed through. Why wouldn't they? At eighteen, back home in the States, they could do just about anything they wanted – join the army, carry a firearm, drive a car and smoke pot, though apparently not all at the same time. Actually, I'm not sure that isn't feasible, but let's not mix polemics with possibility and percentage. However, back home neither my niece nor her friends could enjoy the simple pleasures of conversation over a glass of wine until they turned twenty-one, so this was probably where Europe edged it over home as a suitable venue for exploring the attendant consequences of liquid refreshment. Before flying back, and to keep her out of mischief on the long flight, I gave her a book of short stories by *Hemingway*.

Recently, my niece came by again to check in with friends and relations, and I asked her if she had read many or any of Hemingway's stories. She bridled a little and moaned that she'd spent too many hours being lectured by her college English professor on the merits of short story writing: how each line had to possess its own weight and significance relative to the story, and how she was supposed to read what was going on between the lines and not just the lines as they sat on the page. In being spoon-fed, or rather force-fed, all this mumbo-jumbo she had lost her appetite for the genre. Surely the fundamental reason for reading short stories, she argued, was simply to enjoy them, not necessarily to anaesthetize them, dissect them and work out how they are constructed. "The idea," she concluded, "is to appreciate the beauty of the animal, not tear it to pieces simply to find out what makes it breathe."

My niece has a point.

Many great authors have waxed long and lyrically about how to write short stories. Some quote specific rules that must be adhered to, but then hurry right along to praise those writers brave enough to disregard them. From a purely personal perspective, I like to think each short story possesses its own very individual form, and to suggest there is a formula that must be applied to the writing of a short story is to suggest that one only has to queue up at the factory door in order to collect one. This is, in my experience, not the case: we all think differently, which is why we all enjoy a variety of tales.

In medieval times, a wandering minstrel would earn his board and lodging by entertaining his hosts with the union of his voice and his lyre. The *Scéalaí* of Ireland earn theirs in much the same fashion, but without any musical accompaniment; they simply tell stories. Their rule is that there is no story to be told unless there is a person to listen to it in the first place. I like the simplicity in this logic; it is the reason why we write stories.

In *The Truth in Fiction* I have assembled a collection of some of the short stories I have written over the last ten years. Some are written in the first person, which permits the reader to assume the identity of the narrator, thus reading the story and appreciating what goes on through his or her eyes: others are written in the third person, which permits the reader to appreciate what goes on from a distance and therefore to interpret the events as he or she sees fit. However, if truth is the main ingredient, then fiction is the flavour conjured by the author.

In the Appendix, I have tried to pass on the origins of these stories; where they were born, if you like, why they were written and the contributions of the many people without whom this collection would not have made it into print.

Finally, I must thank Pete Darby for the time, care and imagination he put in to the extraordinary cover image of The Truth In Fiction. He is without doubt a gifted artist and worthy of recognition.

Two Books

South Island, New Zealand

It must be just after ten, for down the lane and around the corner the Lady of the Lake has slipped her moorings and is, in her customary and curiously unladylike manner, smothering the town with the acrid effluvium of her morning's exertions.

"Excuse me," the girl asks.

He'd noticed her, sitting there reading, whilst deciding on a table. There had been other tables free, as most of the tourists were down at the quay watching the old Lady belch her way out from the Queenstown dock into the opalescent waters of the lake, but at first glance he'd thought her pretty, so he'd taken the table next to her.

"Sure," he replies, turning to face her, "how can I help?"

"The Earnslaw. The TSS Earnslaw. I mean I know that SS stands for Steam Ship, but what does the T stand for? The?"

She has strawberry-blond hair, tied back, and a lean face which is frowning in query. Her straight nose extends in one uninterrupted slope down from her high forehead and her eyes are grey; grey like the morning light on cloud before the sun creeps over the horizon.

He doesn't reckon her for the hardier variety of backpacker: not for her the all-weather jacket and pants and mud-encrusted boots. And yet she sports a light-blue hybrid jacket and cross-trainers, so maybe she is one of the new breed of designer backpackers he's grown accustomed to seeing about the town. It is, after all, summer.

"Screw," he replies. "The first S stands for Screw and the second for Steamship. The T stands for Twin; Twin-Screw Steamship, hence TSS."

For a moment her frown deepens as she debates whether he is being either clever or vulgar, or both. But when she's made up her mind that he is being straight with her, her face colours a little and she looks back down at her book.

"What that means is," he explains, vaguely amused at her discomfort, "she has two propellers, one on either side."

After a pause, she says, "Smelly old thing, isn't she?"

The girl is British.

"Yes, she burns a lot of coal. Launched the same year as the Titanic sank."

"Which was?" she asks, looking up, challenging him.

"1912."

"So it was," she replies, her slightly cocky, confident smile suggesting she'd been ready to correct him if he'd got the date wrong. She buries her head back in her book. "Where does she go? I mean, on the lake. Up or down?" she asks, without looking up.

He likes it that she doesn't seem backward in coming forward with her questions. "Across," he replies. "She crosses the lake to Walter Peak."

"Worth the trip, is it? Walter Peak?" This time she does look up.

"Gardens will be at their best and you'll definitely lower the average age at the lunch, but you'll be a captive audience for nearly four hours and the lake can chop up a bit in the afternoon."

"Mmm. Thanks, might duck that one then." She pauses, studying him, not in any critical way, more in the sense that she is trying to place him.

When she's reached some agreeable decision about him, she closes her book, sets it on the small round table and sits up.

"There's just too much to do here," she states, "I'm almost blinded by the choice. I haven't the first clue as to how to decide what to see and what not to."

"Depends what you want to get out of it, doesn't it?"

"How d'you mean?" she asks, clearly confused.

Now it is his turn to make his mind up about her. Is she the kind who answers every question with a question; one of those who can't see for looking? Or is she, could she be, one of that rare breed who actually want to get to know the locale rather than merely observe it?

"Well, if you want the thrill of the bungy, the Ledge up there," he points up over his shoulder, "is one of the best places to do it, though some prefer the experience over water. You can tandem paraglide or mountain bike down from the top, too. There's a luge up there as well, but that's really only for kids – big kids, if you like. Then there's jetboats up the Shotover, light plane or heli trips to Milford Sound or Lake Manapouri – where they filmed the Lord of the Rings, vineyard tours on the road to Wanaka or, as your nose has just informed you, Lady of the Lake cruises across Lake Wakatipu."

He pauses and glances to see whether he still commands her attention.

"But if you hunger for a more spiritual experience," he adds, "the view from Bob's Peak is as good a place as any to start."

He is right, she has glazed over.

"You've read about that, then?"

"Yes," she replies, hauling herself from her daze and holding up a fistful of leaflets, "I have. And that's what I mean. I'm spoilt for choice, but the choice doesn't do it for me."

He chuckles. "So reading a book in a café does?"

"At least this way I get a feel for the place."

He chuckles again and is pleased. "The only feeling you're going to get reading a tome like that is the one that tells you your bum has gone to sleep. By the way, what are you reading?" He leans over to look at the cover of her book.

It is his way when he meets women for the first time. He takes a curious delight in standing them up to see if they can take his raw South Island humour. If they don't get up and walk away – or run in some cases – he figures they might be worth the investment of his time.

"*San Miguel, TC Boyle.*" She flashes the cover at him; the title and author's name are set in a ruby band across the middle of a picture of a dark-haired woman in a white dress, striding away through tussock grass. "A friend gave it to me in case I got bored with the airline movies on the way over," she adds in a tone that leaves him in no doubt she is about to walk.

Of course, she walked. Possibly it was simply because she'd finished her coffee or possibly it was because she'd got somewhere else to be, something like that. And yet more probably it was because his line of approach was, for her, a shade too direct. Whichever it was it didn't matter, the result was the same: she walked.

But, the cover of the book she'd been reading stuck with him. He is sure – as sure as anyone can be from a brief glance – that he's seen the picture of the dark-haired woman striding away through tussock grass before.

Tuesday sees Fin back behind the counter of the *i-SITE* on the corner of Shotover and Camp.

"No wonder you were able to quote the visitors guide to me," she says, playfully.

He hadn't seen her come in; he'd been busy repelling a gaggle of Japanese tourists.

"So which of the many activities and adventures did you choose?" he asks, coolly.

He decides she looks even better than the first time he saw her. Her face looks more relaxed, less tight about her cheeks, and her smile seems even brighter, as though before it was constrained and now it is given over to the full range of its lively expression.

"Strangely enough, only one."

"How's that?"

"I spent the weekend in Wanaka," she replies, grinning, but she holds his eye contact, goading him to quiz her a little further.

He doesn't mind her game. Like the colour of her cheeks the first time they met, her mischievous smile draws him to her. "And you stayed where?"

"At the Wanaka Bakpaka."

"Good place?"

"Oh, I wasn't there much."

"Finish that book?"

"Not yet. Been busy," she replies, and smiles another one of her broad, mischievous smiles.

"So, what did you get up to that kept you from your book?"

"'Bit nosey aren't you?"

He notes for the second time her propensity for answering one question with another. "It's my job to ask. That way we get to know which activities you day-trippers like most."

This time she snorts with amusement.

But Fin chooses to ignore her scepticism, deciding instead to leave her to run with the ball.

"Okay," she yields. "What did I get up to?" She puts her finger to her lip and glances at the ceiling in mock contemplation. "Let me see: a little swimming, a little bicycling, and a little running, quickly followed by a lo-o-ot of sleeping."

He winces: "Challenge Wanaka?"

"Right first time! Give the monkey a banana." She raises her arms in triumph: "Challenge Anneka."

"Sorry?"

"Don't be," she encourages, "it's an old and completely ridiculous television programme I'm only just old enough to remember." She stands back and smiles at him, waiting to see if he can take her jibe about him being a monkey.

"I'm Fin," he says, holding out his hand, "short for Finlay."

"I'm Amy," she replies, "not quite so short in heels."

His day off just happens to be Wednesday, the next day.

When he asks her what she wants to do, she says it's up to him to choose. So he does, and suggests she bring walking shoes.

Amy is staying at the youth hostel just along the esplanade. He picks her up at nine and drives out through Frankton up over the Crown Range back to Wanaka.

She is bright and breezy, like the day, and they resist the temptation to taunt, preferring to find out what there is to know about each other.

Amy is twenty-six; a lawyer from London. If he didn't already know she is a triathlete, Fin might think her a trifle bookish.

He is reluctant to admit his age at first. But, after she pushes him gently, he admits to being twenty-five. He works at the family vineyard along the valley from Cromwell: Pinot Noir, Pinot Gris, a little Riesling. But for the moment he is at loggerheads with his father over some issue he is keen not to discuss, so he has decided to take some time away; the job at the information centre is really only a fill-in. Fin also tells her he has a crib on Thompson Street just up from the lakefront, "One of those quaint, clapboard bungalows that boasts a coal range amongst its luxuries."

He is both pleased and relieved that Amy resists the temptation to compare the local geography to some part of the world she's previously visited. He's grown weary of tourists telling him how much the Mackenzie Basin resembles the Cairngorms of Scotland, or Central Otago the Nappa valley. He doesn't know whether she is alive to it or just doesn't think that way, but with each kilometre he drives, he feels himself relax more than he has at any time over the past few months.

He turns left at the lake and drives round the south side, passing the campsite at Motutapu and on up the Matukituki valley beneath the soaring flanks of Treble Cone and Black Peak. The road soon turns to gravel and, when it eventually runs out, he pulls up in Raspberry Flat car-park. Ten or so other cars litter the paddock and a couple of climbers, leaning on enormous packs, wait patiently for a heli-transfer up to French Ridge Hut.

"They'll be going up to Mount Aspiring," he tells her. "It's not as easy an ascent as some think." And, as if to make a point, he adds that of late the mountain has developed something of an appetite for Australians.

Amy wears a fleece vest, shorts and Berghaus Explorers. She has, as he'd expected, well-toned legs.

He offers her some homemade fly repellent, but she doesn't think she'll need it and Fin isn't about to try and convince her otherwise. He has already worked out that Amy does what she wants, not necessarily what others recommend. He is, he knows, much the same, particularly when it comes to dealing with his father.

The Matukituki riverbed is wide and pretty much dry, and as they cross the swing bridge a dust devil blows up and consumes them, forcing them to close their eyes and hang on to each other for a moment.

He carries a modest backpack; first aid kit, space blanket, water and a handful of high-energy oat bars. It isn't exactly a picnic they are setting out for, but he reckons they'll need a little sustenance by the time they reach their destination.

Fin leads, pausing every now and then to check his pace isn't too rapid for her.

It isn't. He didn't think it would be as he's checked her time for the Challenge, but he wants her to know it has crossed his mind. A shade over eleven hours for an Iron Man – 4.8 km swim, 180 km bike ride and a full marathon – is a very respectable time. He tells her so, but she replies that she would like to have been nearer ten than eleven.

They traverse the right-hand side of the valley, gaining height all the while before entering the gorge that leads them up to the foot of the glacier. As the gorge narrows and its slopes steepen, so the roar of the stream below them makes conversation impossible. The air through the forest remains cool and damp, and their path, which winds like a lazy snake – except, he says in case she is concerned, there are no snakes in New Zealand – is shaded by tall silver beech, their limbs garnished with straggling grey beards. Up the path winds, higher and higher towards a bright white wall gleaming through the leaves.

Then, very suddenly, the trees give way to open scrub and before them hangs a vast and magnificent curtain of ice. Countless waterfalls trail off from where the glacier halts abruptly halfway down from the peak and away to the left a solitary cascade of water plummets down a sheer face, dispersing into a mist that bears a permanent rainbow. A muddy-coloured *Kea* struts about waiting to be fed, its hooked beak intimidating.

Amy sits down on a smooth grey rock to marvel at the immense panorama of ice spread high before her. Every few minutes a slab breaks away from the pack and thunders down the face, splintering and smashing as it tumbles and bounces off the ridges into the valley below.

"Come on," Fin orders, "let's go down to the stream. The nearer you get to the base of the glacier, the better the view up to it." And he leads her down through the gorse to the blue-white meltwaters flowing out down through the gorge.

The stream runs fast, swirling and coursing with considerable force along a narrow, twisting bed strewn with rocks and boulders.

Amy looks up at the fine spray of the tall waterfall to their left, "Can we make it over to that face? I fancy a shower."

Fin shakes his head in disbelief and sets out to find a way across. But every time he thinks he's discovered a succession of stepping stones that might help them over to the other side, he is faced with too long a leap for them to make it safely.

"No matter," she says, removing her boots and socks and sitting down to dangle her feet in the cool water. Amy unties her hair and shakes it out so that it hangs straight down. She leans back and closes her eyes to the sun.

Fin sits down beside her and does the same, except that he glances at her now and again, deciding he has rarely if ever met someone to whom he is so drawn.

"Bloody hell! That's so cold it hurts," she squeals, lifting her feet clear of the water. But immediately she's said it, she bursts into a fit of giggles.

"Sorry," she says, rubbing her feet and looking somewhat sheepish, "that wasn't the smartest observation, was it?"

"Odd, isn't it?" he replies. "It always seems colder than it has a right to be." But then Fin can no longer keep the lid on his amusement and he too surrenders to the absurdity of her reaction. "Believe it or not," he continues, chuckling, "I've seen people bathe in this stream. Not for long, mind you. Just a quick immersion, you might say."

"You've got to be joking?" Amy suggests.

So he stands, strips off his shirt and shorts, and clad only in his briefs he walks down to a calmer backwater and eases himself into it.

"Fin?" Amy shouts in terror. "What the hell are you doing?"

And with that, he slides down until the blue-white water closes over his head.

Fin counts to three and that is as much as he can take. He stands up and calmly steps up onto the rock beside her.

"Well," he says, casually wiping the icy water from his face and hair, "that was bracing."

"Bracing?" she repeats, laughing. "Aw, Fin, you're such a boy."

Fin grins and sits down, hoping his briefs will dry sooner than later. He knows his display is a little cheesy, but for some reason she unhinges him.

Amy looks around, stands up and quickly removes her fleece, vest and shorts, and lays them carefully beside him.

He looks away politely. "Oh, no—"

But when Fin turns his head back, to his amazement Amy pulls her sports bra over her head, rather daintily removes her knickers and throws them on top of the rest of her clothes. She presents her lean buttocks to him and steps very gingerly into the pool, crouching down until she is completely underwater.

Fin begins to count, but doesn't even get to two.

Amy shoots out of the pool, like a cork out of a shaken champagne bottle. A stream of expletives issue from her hair-covered face and she stands seemingly paralysed for a few seconds, completely and beautifully naked.

But, she realises he is watching her, so she covers up with her hands and stumbles behind a boulder.

"Was that everything you feared it might be?" he asks.

"W-worse!"

"Said it was bracing, didn't I?"

"M-m-m," she mumbles.

"Oh, and Amy," he pauses.

"Y-yes, F-Fin?"

"You're such a girl," he declares, adding, "and as fine a looking lass as has ever been seen naked below Rob Roy Glacier."

––––––––––

The bars and cafés in the small warren of streets in Queenstown are humming by the time they get back. He treats her to a Fergburger, after which they bar-crawl for the rest of the evening, laughing and giggling like schoolchildren who've written something rude on a blackboard.

When time comes to pull the plug on the evening, they have both drunk more than is healthy for their navigation. However, Amy seems reluctant to call it a night, so they lurch and stumble over to his crib which is, he points out, marginally nearer than her hostel.

They sit out on his front step and Amy says she's never seen so many stars; says she's never seen the Milky Way so clearly.

Fin shows her how if you draw a line through the Southern Cross and the Pointers, where the two lines intersect, about halfway between the Southern Cross and Archenar; that is where you find the South Celestial Pole.

Some time later they see a shooting star which causes them both, in their own way, to wonder.

Then Fin asks Amy what it is that has made her return to Queenstown. He isn't fishing for compliments, or so he says, it's more that he's got the strangest feeling there is more to her return than merely his vibrant, animal magnetism.

Amy laughs and slaps his shoulder in mock disdain, but then she falls silent. Even in the dark he can see her biting gently at her lower lip.

"Sure, okay, there was," she begins. "It was after I met you at the café. Or maybe it was what you said. I don't know." She pauses, marshalling her thoughts. "As I remember it, after you'd given me that list of all the activities on offer, you said, "if you hunger for a more spiritual experience, then start up at Bob's Peak," or something like that. So I did. I took the gondola up to the Skyline and found a quiet spot to sit and take in the view. I saw the Lady of the Lake cruising across Wakatipu. I saw the jagged peaks of the Remarkables standing tall behind the Heights. And I saw this enormous sky that seemed to go on far, far away beyond the horizon. And the weirdest thing happened. I don't know if I was over-tired, or nervous about the Challenge, or if it was any number of other things, but the lake — look, I know it's late and I know I've had far too much to drink and I know this will sound perfectly stupid, but the lake seemed to be looking back up at me and it seemed to be alive, as though it was sleeping or resting or waiting for me to do something."

Fin goes to interrupt, but she cuts him off.

"No, wait, please. Give me a minute. I don't know why, but it set me to think about everything I've accomplished in the last few years. And it suddenly dawned on me that the weight of my achievements was holding me down, as though each and every degree or diploma I've worked so hard to achieve is pegging me back and reducing any chance I'll ever have of getting off the wretched hamster's wheel of my life."

Fin tries to interrupt again, but Amy holds up her hands in appeal.

"No, one last thing. Please. Just one. And it's this. Afterwards, when I came down the mountain, I felt curiously unchained, like I'd been turned loose or been released or something. I didn't really understand it until I was running the marathon leg of the Challenge.

"Just around the distance I was expecting to hit the wall, my legs assumed this extraordinary lightness, as though some wizard had lifted all the weight from me. It was like — like I was running on the air. There, I said it was weird. That's it. Your turn?"

This time Fin waits until he's absolutely certain Amy is finished.

"You're right, in a way," he says quietly. "It was the lake. Or rather it was the giant." He pauses. "You remember how the lake is shaped like a man lying on his side; sleeping, almost foetal, but a bit more stretched out. Well, the *Maori* legend has it that a giant from the mountains in the west, *Matau*, made off with the beautiful princess *Manata*. But, while the giant slept, *Manata's* lover, *Matakauri*, rescued her and in the process tied the giant down so that he would not be able to pursue them. It is said that the giant still sleeps, here, and that the lake has been formed by his great weight. We believe that he sleeps deep in the green waters and that the level of the lake rises and falls in time with his breathing. What you saw was the rhythm of the lake. What it was telling you was that it is time for you to leave the giant to sleep and for you to go your own way. It was suggesting to you that it is time for you to be free from whatever it is that holds you down."

Amy shows no reaction to his conclusion, and for a second he thinks she might have drifted off to sleep with the giant, *Matau*. But Fin notices her eyes are glinting in the starlight and wonders if she, too, is moved by the legend.

Then she snorts in exactly the same way she had snorted the day before. "Aw, Fin," she giggles, "and there I was thinking you were too grown up for fairy tales."

He chuckles. "Oh, let me tell you, we too like our fair share of omens and fairy tales."

———

Amy is due to fly out of Queenstown back to London on the Friday afternoon. She asks him not to see her to the airport, so they meet at the café.

Both, they agree, have had a good if rather brief run together and he tells her he looks forward to seeing her again whenever their paths cross.

"Not before too long, I hope," he adds looking deep into her morning-grey eyes. "Oh," he continues, pulling a brown-wrapped packet out of his pocket, "I got another epic for you. Didn't know whether you'd finished the other one?"

"San Miguel? Yes, I have." Amy removes the wrapper. "*The*

Parihaka Woman by *Witi Ihimaera*," she reads. "The cover," a dark-haired figure, in a white dress, striding away through tussock grass, "I'm sure I've seen it before somewhere. It's strangely familiar."

Just for the most fleeting of moments, he thinks he sees her eyes water. But, not wanting to provoke another of her snorts, he ignores the temptation to comment further and says simply, "In case you get bored on the plane."

Amy reaches over, puts her hand behind his neck and pulls his face to hers. She kisses him softly and just long enough for him to appreciate the warmth in her lips.

"Bye, Fin," she calls as she walks away. "And, thank you for the book."

––––––––––

Snow comes early to central Otago.

Fin's self-imposed exile extends and he spends the winter teaching skiing up at Coronet Peak.

However, spring and his mother herald a thaw in the relationship between Fin and his father, so he moves back to the vineyard.

By Christmas the new restaurant Fin has always wanted to run in tandem with the wine tasting tours has taken off and even his father has been overheard to mumble a grudging recognition of his son's more entrepreneurial abilities.

One late January morning when his father is away for the day, Fin strolls up through the vineyard.

"Chris? How's it going?" Fin asks.

The winemaker bends to examine the white rose blossom at the end of a row of vines: "Coming along well. Could do with a bit more rain," he adds, rising, "but then, when couldn't we?"

"Good crew this season?"

"Most of 'em, yes," he replies. "New girl down there says she's met you before."

"Me? Where?"

Chris frowns. "Yes, Fin, you! And, how would I bloody know where? In case you haven't noticed I've barely had a moment to scratch my backside these last few weeks. Anyway, why don't you go and ask her yourself? Tan sunhat, blue shirt and jeans." The winemaker points away down the hill. "And don't go taking up too much of her time, mate. We don't stop for brandy and cigars up here, y'know."

Intrigued, Fin wanders down between the rows of vines to where a group of viticulturists are leaf-plucking.

Like many of the labourers, the girl wears a wide-brimmed hat and long-sleeved shirt, buttoned to her wrists.

"Excuse me," he starts, "but—"

She turns and smiles: "Hello Fin! Two books, same cover. Omens and fairy tales! Who's a clever boy?"

I Know

London, England

"I loved him, you know."

"Yes," I reply, and without thinking add, "I know."

She pauses and her expression stiffens, the muscles of her neck tensing so that her mouth pulls down fractionally at the edges, opening just enough to reveal her even, pearl-white teeth.

She stares back at me, wondering; no doubt rapidly assessing the potential damage from her admission of such a personal detail.

The celebration of the deceased's life, as it has been dubbed, is being held in the garden room of a hotel overlooking Hyde Park. A celebration it may be, but a wake it most definitely is.

I know some present; not many, but some. Every now and then, across a sea of faces, someone mouths a *hello* or smiles sympathetically or nods discreetly. However, having merely skimmed the outer atmospheres of the deceased's planet means that although acceptable, I am not worthy of the attention of his nearest and, as so many of them like to think of themselves, dearest. The insignificants, like me, have to content ourselves with permanent orbit as opposed to being recognised and ushered to an official berth down on planet condolence.

It is very obviously how it is with the woman standing next to me. Like me, she is revolving silently. Two forgotten satellites, our trajectories destined to collide.

My new acquaintance wears a black, tweed tunic dress over a cream silk blouse and silver mesh necklace. Her hair is dark brown, bob cut, and her figure a shade over petite, except for her bust, which might in real terms as against political be defined as liberal. I put her at forty, but perhaps that too is a feline estimate. She is a popular commercial artist whose work I have seen in the glossies.

Coraline sweeps her hair back from her face and attempts a resigned smile. But her effort founders in mid-formation and the pain of regret infects her look.

"You know? How the devil d'you know?" she clips.

I colour at her response. It seems that in trying to apply a gentle balm to the singed heart on her sleeve, I have laid it on too thick.

Mourners in my experience — and thankfully at thirty my experience is limited — are not prone to confess to relative strangers their innermost feelings towards the deceased. They might think the departed an absolute shit, but the chances of them actually saying it are truly remote, for that would be bad form. They are, though, far more disposed to declare a gentle affection, coming to understand that if they don't speak of it, the affection that existed between he or she will, likely as not now that one of them has died, evaporate as rapidly as warm breath on cold glass. But to confess love?

"I saw it in your eyes when I sat next to you at the service," I reply. "I don't know how, but I got the impression you cared for him very deeply, that's all. I don't mean to offend." It was during the eulogy: two lines of tears trickling down her cheeks and her muted, stifled sobs between long held breaths. They told me all I needed to know. But to mention the depth of her distress seems, now, unkind.

This time the smile breaks through; a combination of relief, appreciation and surrender. "It's so unfair, being taken so suddenly. And only just forty. Not right, is it?"

She seems to want to talk and I am more than happy to listen. Others seem intent on lightening the atmosphere by making faux-upbeat conversation. In my experience it is not only a deflection of the pain of sorrow, but also a mechanism by which mourners attempt to hurdle the awkwardness of the occasion. People employ this type of forced levity at wakes, the upshot of which compels them to relate the more comical moments from the life of the deceased. It convinces them they have contributed to the easing of the soul's passing; a blithesome send-off, one might say.

Standing in the crowded yet deserted room, the two of us are drawn towards shared intimacy.

"How long did you…?"

Coraline sips her champagne. "Know him? Oh, ten years, give or take. I met him at a charity dinner. He bought a painting of mine; one I had donated to help with his fundraising. I wasn't doing so well at the time. My work wasn't selling and I was at a bit of a low ebb. He told me how much he admired me. His affirmation provided me with the injection of confidence I so desperately needed. Shortly after that, everything changed and my paintings became fashionable. I suppose I must be grateful to him. Stupid really! It was timing, nothing more. Good or bad timing, I'm not so sure." She quiets, reminiscing.

"It so often is," I agree. "Timing, I mean. Bumping into someone you once knew: at the airport, in the bank, in a shop. It doesn't really matter how it happens; it just happens."

"Fate? Is that what you mean?"

"Mmm, possibly," I muse, "or simply a coincidence. It doesn't need to be predestined, does it?"

"No, I suppose not. Perhaps it's that we're more comfortable with assuming it is. Perhaps fate provides us with an excuse; makes us believe there is nothing we can do about something because it was always going to happen anyway. That it's not our fault, whatever the fall-out."

The fall-out! I nod, thoughtfully. "Comfortable. Yes, you're right. That's a good way of putting it; comfortable."

A large black man, embarrassed, tentative, presents himself. He apologises and explains that he would like to be introduced to the unfortunate widow. Coraline and I stare blankly at each other. It isn't that we don't understand the man's West African Pidgin English; it's more that neither of us is in a hurry to step forward. And when, eventually, neither of us volunteers, he reverses reverently back into the crowd.

This curious incident whereby both of us have shied away from his request, binds us. We are, or so it must appear, strangers to the family. And now that Coraline is more certain I am not related to the deceased, and therefore not such a close friend that I am inclined to introduce others to the widow, the tension slips from her shoulders. She finishes her champagne and grabs another from a passing waiter.

We stand for a minute and sip in silence, alone-but-together with our thoughts. Pictures one would expect to find in the study of an ex-public schoolboy grace the tables: callow youths wearing blazers over puffed-out chests in cricket and rugby teams; black-tie ball revellers sitting arm-in-arm, alcohol infused smiles, laughing; and celebrities posing with the deceased outside the Houses of Parliament or his constituency office.

"Do you know many here?" she asks, still not one hundred percent sure of me.

"No, not really. I recognise a couple of faces from a few years ago, a couple more from the European parliament, but I doubt they'll remember me."

"Not from the press, are you?" The champagne has emboldened her; her tone is subtly laced with aggression.

"Most definitely not. No, it's as I said. It was a long time ago. I was an intern, fresh out of university. Worked for him for six months; research, that sort of thing. Rather honoured to have been put on the list, really."

"What do you do now? Still in politics?"

"Good grief, no," I reply, though immediately wonder why I should feel the need to give her the impression that I look down on the denizens of Westminster. After all, there was a time when I had yearned to be one. "I'm an interpreter: French, German, Italian."

She baulks momentarily. "Clever girl! Where?"

"Oh, Brussels."

Coraline glances nervously towards the door. "Do you think they'll mind if I smoke?"

I glance down at a photograph of the deceased and think aloud, "Well, you wouldn't, would you? Hated all that legislation about people not being allowed to smoke in hotels, pubs and restaurants, didn't you? Thought it all a gross violation of the common man's rights. Always said the choice should lie with the establishment. Believed people should be allowed to vote with their feet, not be nanny'd by the state."

She giggles behind her pack of cigarettes. "Of course, none of them knew he smoked. Not even his wife. Crazy, huh?"

"Is that so?" I reply, knowing full well that he did.

"When was the last time you saw him then?" she asks, looking round nervously.

"Oh, fairly recently, I bumped into him in Brussels. What about you?"

"Not for a while." Coraline leans forward as though she is about to divulge the plot of some menacing conspiracy. "I used to see him quite regularly." She pauses and flashes me a craven, wanton look, one designed to leave me in no doubt that their relationship was, to say the least, carnal. Her behaviour is wholly inappropriate for a wake, but again I can see how her brazen side would have attracted him; he liked it raw – sometimes.

"Strictly between you and me," she whispers, looking about theatrically, "we didn't part on the best of terms. Called him some wretched names that last time. Wished I hadn't, of course. Made it terribly difficult when we met socially, later. Mind you he could summon the most wonderful poker-face, couldn't he? I remember once, we were in a restaurant playing footsie under the table – stupid really, juvenile even – and I thought I could've told him his wife was standing at the bar and he'd have looked back at me and said "So?", as though it was perfectly natural for her be there and what the hell was I doing thinking it might be strange. He could turn the tables so quickly."

Her appraisal of one of his many talents makes me smile.

"He was a very practised politician, wasn't he?" I press. "That look went with the territory. What about you? You said you fell out, but when did you last see him?"

Coraline rocks back on her heels and examines the ceiling. She is attractive; her neck shows few lines and the crows feet at the corners of her eyes suggest laughter rather than wear and tear. He would like her shorter hair, too; he would be happy with the way she looks now.

"Oh, about a year ago," she sighs. "We used to meet at this flat in Fulham. Wasn't his flat, of course. Even I could see that. The décor was all wrong. He liked warmth, heavy curtains, thick carpets, dark furniture; not blinds, a parquet floor and beige minimalism. Still, I never let on, even when I saw it up for sale." She purses her lips.

I thin mine in order to preserve my straight face; a similar face to the one he used to reserve for those awkward moments he was so good at sliding out of. I know the flat to which she refers. It lies down a side-road off Parson's Green. "What drove you apart?"

She fumbles with her pack of cigarettes, but then thinks better of smoking and takes a healthy slug from her glass. "It all started about a year ago.

"You see I was always very careful not to demand anything from him, and I mean anything," she arches a carefully appointed eyebrow, "I knew our time together was... finite, if you like. I knew it wasn't forever. Only a fool would have thought that way. But, you see, I'd always imagined his wife would take him away from me or that his work would separate us, him going away on business, something like that. I never thought he'd tire of me."

"What made you think he did?"

"Signs. Small things. He started to get a little short with me; our meetings rushed. Haste, I suppose. Less time for conversation; less time together. I could see his mind was elsewhere. It wasn't work, I knew him well enough to know that. Even during elections, even when he was under the cruelest pressure, he'd never hurried with me. Towards the end," Coraline pauses, remembering, "it was as though he couldn't wait to be gone. Then, when he went and became an MEP the opportunities to get together fell fewer and farther between. In the end I found out he'd been back to London a couple of times and hadn't bothered to call. I knew then that my days, or should that be our afternoons, were numbered."

"Perhaps he did go back to his wife," I offer, feeling oddly obliged to ease her pain. "Apparently, she's the most wonderful woman. Always has given him the best possible support."

Coraline screws up her face. "And don't I feel like a heel talking to you like this, here, now, with that adorable woman over there glad-handing people she's never met, half of whom are only here because they think they ought to be?"

"Do you ever think his wife knew?"

She examines her fingers as if she expects to find dirt beneath her nails, but they are beautifully manicured and lacquered in bright crimson. "If she did, she never showed it. She's never been anything other than perfectly polite to me; never cold, rather too charming really."

"So you think there was someone else?"

"Oh, for sure," she sighs. "He never lost his appetite. It was one of the qualities that attracted me to him; his voraciousness. Us women find that irresistible, don't we? It's a challenge. We like to think we can satisfy any man's appetite; doing so lends us a sense of worth, makes us feel good about ourselves; this power we have over a man." She sips again. "But let's not fool ourselves, it's only ever temporary."

"I never looked at it that way." I reflect for a moment, wondering whether there is any truth or sense in her verdict that the strength of a relationship can be gauged by measuring the distribution of power within it.

Coraline sips again and her glass is now empty. She looks around for the waiter as though ours may be avoiding us intentionally. Her lips, I notice, share a similar fullness to that of her breasts and her calves are toned and tanned.

Once the waiter has provided her with a fresh glass, she focuses her attention back to me.

"Why would you look at it that way; you're young enough," she makes a play of appraising me, "not to have to worry if you let love slip through your fingers."

I am vaguely insulted. "Surely, it's not the frequency with which one loves but the intensity?"

She watches me again, still appraising. "Yes, dear, you make a good point. But forgive me for pointing out that love is like a London bus; if you stand at the right stop, there's bound to be one along sooner or later that'll take you where you want to go. Particularly one as young and as pretty as you." She sighs and sips. "No, as sure as God made little apples I'm sure he ditched me for a younger model. Can't blame him, really."

"You think he was that vain? That shallow?"

"It wasn't his vanity, dear, though every man likes to be flattered and rewarded, let me tell you. It was his appetite. His palate told him it was time for fresher fruit. He'd grown tired of the same old menu."

I resent her callous view and yet I understand it in the context of the bitterness of her rejection. However, I am trying to like Coraline and she is not making it easy for me. Instead of the warmth of common sympathy one would expect to meet at a celebration of the life of someone who once was, all she would appear to crave is the sympathy rightly or wrongly due to the spurned lover.

"As to his depth," she continues, surveying the crowd as though they, too, are guilty of being shallow, "who knows? How does one ever know?"

"I perceived a depth in him," I state, all too quickly leaping to his defence. "He felt deeply about many things."

"Did he, indeed," she says, throwing down the gauntlet.

Though I know I should let her denunciation go, I cannot. Her assertion that he was shallow has pricked me and pricked me as though she has jabbed me with a similar needle.

"Yes, he did: healthcare, education, the minimum wage, refugees. He cared deeply. Not so much about regulation, fracking and the privacy of celebrities. He had no time for that — the way celebrities trade off their fame whilst all the time moaning about their lack of privacy. He hated the hypocrisy of that."

Coraline finishes her drink, places her empty glass on the table and picks up her handbag. She bridles her mouth, frowns and arches her left eyebrow. "And yet he espoused the virtues of the happy, unified family, didn't he? The foundation of a good upbringing, as he liked to call it."

"Yes," I reply, "that was exactly the phrase he used to use, *the foundation of a good upbringing.*"

25

"Whilst all the time risking the demolition of his own happy, unified family?" she scoffs, though curiously without malice.

"Perhaps," I am dreaming as I speak, "though I'm inclined to believe that over-simplifies it a little. He wasn't a bad man."

Coraline fixes me with a knowing look; one that I cannot pretend I do not recognise. "I never said he was, dear," she replies. "I never said he was."

She makes to leave, but I have to stop her. I have to tell her, but I know I shouldn't. The tide of my emotions — the hurt, the sorrow, the abandonment, the loss, the guilt, the fear that no lover will ever again make me feel so special — overwhelms me and I am abandoned to a sea of sadness.

I touch her arm. The words slip from my mouth. "I loved him too, you know."

"Yes," she replies, "I know."

A Propitious Epiphany for Padraig

Santiago de Compostella, Spain

There were times that had been good and there were times that had been not so good.

And Padraig O'Rahilly considers himself to be a lucky man. Not necessarily because the good times have outweighed the not so good, but because when it comes to thinking about the past, the curiously illogical allotment of Padraig's lucid mind always moves him to remember only the very best of times.

Some people have told him he got the right breaks. Others say he worked hard. Padraig, or so he is telling me, likes to think he's worked hard *and* has been fortunate enough to get the right breaks at the right time.

"Surely it is down that road a man makes his own luck, is it not? Once or twice," he adds, "I have even been down on me luck."

The white light thrown down by the street lanterns sparkles in his rheumy blue eyes. He pauses and leans forward as if he is about to surrender a long-harboured secret.

"But, I'm glad to say that whenever I've been down, there's always been someone there to help me back up."

Padraig squints ever-so slightly. He is watching for something in me, watching probably for my reaction to his subtle prognostication that there is a greater authority who decides which of us deserves to be helped back up off the floor.

His rather saintly expression is one I am accustomed to. It is not uncommon for the *peregrinos* – the pilgrims who flood into Santiago de Compostela every day – to feel close to their deity. Some *peregrinos* hobble the entire seven hundred and thirty kilometres from St Jean Pied-de-Port beyond the Pyrenees. Some stride. And some come singly and others in groups. Some cry when they arrive and some laugh. But to a man and woman they all know why they have walked their part of the Camino de Santiago.

Some even cycle the fourteen hundred odd kilometres from Le Puy-en-Velay, but my business is not with them. The cyclists are not like the *peregrinos* who walk, though they like to think they are. They are separate. Like sharks, they nose their way stealthily through the shoals of humanity passing beneath the *Porta do Camino* into the city.

"Was *He* there to help you when you stumbled on the trail, Padraig?" I smile, hoping he will not mistake my poking fun at his belief for something less genuine.

"That he was," he replies. "That he was."

"How did your legs hold up, if you'll excuse the pun?"

"Can't complain," he says. "Wouldn't do much good if I did, now would it?" Padraig is a considerable trunk of a man; walking such a distance must have involved enormous effort and no little articulation. He wears a cream short-sleeved shirt and shorts, and even though the evening air has turned cool he shows no appreciation of it. He has his foot up on the seat beside him; his sock and sandal by his chair. His ankle is red and swollen.

I shake my head in agreement. "It is one of life's stranger ironies, wearing out one's body in pilgrimage; a bit like fighting for peace or shouting for silence."

Padraig chuckles and rubs his foot. His grey hair is big, like his forehead and his shoulders and hands, and I can imagine him fording a river with a child on his back.

We are sitting in the narrow alley of the *Rúa de Troia* near the *Praza de Cervantes*, where the paving slabs have over the centuries been worn smooth by the soles of so many *peregrinos*. The particular *peregrino*, or pilgrim, opposite me I have met earlier in the evening.

Padraig was reeling from the attentions of the hard-sell waiters in the *Rúa do Franco*. Like many, he didn't know one restaurant from another and when I approached him and suggested he looked a little bemused, he replied that all he wanted "was some good, honest, local food in a good, honest, local eatin' house". I said I knew a place, and he said he'd "be happy to stand me dinner" if I would be kind enough "to get him the hell off this kip of a street".

I was hungry: the *Bierzo Enxebre* was just the place.

"Is that what we're drinking, *Bierzo En*-whatever-it is?" he asks.

"No, it's not beer. Sounds like it though, doesn't it? But *Bierzo* is a wine growing *comarca* – a district, in the province of Leon. Ponferrada is the market town. It's one of the last big towns you would have come through, probably about a week ago."

Padraig searches the wall opposite as though it is a map. "Got it," he says, looking pleased. "I remember it now. And *En*-whatever-it-is?"

"*Enxebre*," I pronounce the *x* as a *z*; it's not completely accurate, but it will have to do. After four years of living in Santiago I like to think I've mastered the Galician tongue, but I know I haven't. The dialect is like the view from a misty hilltop: one moment you glimpse it, the next it disappears. "It means something somewhere between tradition, soul, heart and embodiment; each individually and yet all at once. Essence might be the easiest way to understand it."

"Essence," he repeated, "like a concentration. Distilled, you might say, like *Poitín* – our moonshine, the very essence of Ireland." Padraig studies his non-existent map again, no doubt recalling the last time he tasted his precious *Poitín*.

As if to demonstrate the manifold likenesses between the Irish and Galician peoples, a pipe-band starts up around the corner in the *Praza de Cervantes*. Padraig grins. "I'm beginning to like this city." He nods his head in the direction of the sound. "Do you fancy a walk and a listen?"

I advise him to rest his foot. "They'll be along in a minute or two. They quite often play in this alley. I was hoping we'd see them. The seventeenth of the month is a local bank holiday; a sort of vague tilt at independence dressed up as a fiesta for the literary heroes of Galicia. They like a party this lot. They'll be along."

We eat and we eat well. Padraig tucks into asparagus with goat's cheese while I'm happy with the *pimientos de padrón* – the grilled small green peppers. For main, he asks for something just as local but more substantial. I recommend the *Zorza* – diced pork in paprika doesn't get much more local and I've seen few clear the plate – and I plump for the steak with pickles.

He does, though, clear his plate and he follows it up with a flan. We drink *Ribeiro*, the smooth local red wine. The meal is exactly what Padraig wanted; good, honest and local. He insists on buying us each a *copa* of brandy. Who am I to refuse?

I am hoping that if I show Padraig a good time he will want to make use of my services as a guide tomorrow. Experience has taught me people, especially loners like Padraig, are better disposed towards strangers when they have a happy stomach.

The Americans are not difficult; initially they are very

distrusting, but they always end up wanting you to be their NBF – their New Best Friend. The Germans don't need any help: well, not until they need your help, then they adopt you as they would an orphaned *dachshund*. The French never need any help: how far from France does one think they are? The Japanese look at you deadpan: they don't understand Santiago – why should you understand the place any better? And the British: well, they like a little assistance; a little, but not too much, not so much that there's a risk they might be suspected of being in some way inadequate.

The Irish, on the other hand, travel better than all the other nationalities put together. Whilst other creeds, colours and tongues bask in the triumph of their pilgrimage to the great cathedral, the Irish casually permit St James to bask in the glory of their presence; almost as though it was merely convenient of him to billet his bones at their journey's end, but not necessarily a prerequisite.

As we finish our meal the band turns the corner into the *Rúa de Troia*. Because the alley is narrow and the pipers, their elbows extended and drones swaying, occupy enough space for two, the ensemble follow on behind. The stubble-chinned pipers sport *boinas*, the Galician flat cap, and collarless white shirts and waistcoats. In fact the whole troupe dresses as though they have just been persuaded from dozing at the family hearth, which many of them have. Even though it is well past ten in the evening, a dozen children old enough to give voice skip in tune behind the pied pipers.

The troupe comes to a halt beside the restaurant. Padraig's eyes are wide in appreciation and his smile is keen. Clearly this is the kind of party for which he has been searching.

He turns my way, catches me watching him, and winks. We are friends. I am glad.

Then, exhibiting one of his many genial talents, he quickly attracts the attention of the busy waiter and orders not just a glass, but another bottle of *Ribeiro*, and I realise it will be my head which in the morning pays the price of his company.

The melodies are soft and lilting, but underpinned by a latent energy that increases with each tune: a layer of Irish brogue straining to bridle a Highland Reel. The joy, the gaiety on the faces of the musicians is infectious. The temptation to frolic and gambol and spin and whirl and prance and whirl is irresistible. Those who recognise the music leave their tables and dance with the children, arms raised and rounded, toes tipping, legs jigging. *Peregrinos* with weary limbs are drawn in and tourists, encouraged beyond their rhythmic limitations, join in too.

Eventually Padraig succumbs, and for a big man he dances well. His movements are deft; they betray a confident agility and, in spite of his swollen ankle, his feet are far more nimble than his ample proportions suggest they have a right to be.

The drummer, the clarinettist and saxophonist respond to his enthusiasm and step up the tempo; scallop shells, the traditional symbol of the *Camino*, are scraped like skiffle boards, and a small sea of youth and age sways back and forth and round and about.

Suddenly the pipes silence and the adults give voice. When their verse is over the children give greater voice, repeating the verse. The adults respond with another verse, this time louder than the children. But the children come back again and so the volume grows. The clarity of diction, the synchronicity of timing, the union of the acapella are all mesmerising and beguiling: joy is celebrated through the union of generations.

"Like *Uilleann* pipes – Irish bagpipes," Padraig says, when eventually he sits back down, "only different. These fellas are playing thirds and sixths; our fellas would use a grander scale."

"They're called *Gaitas* – the Galician pipes," I reply in an attempt to conceal my ignorance of the Irish pipes. "They used to make the whole instrument out of one goatskin."

Padraig laughs. "Makes a damn sight better sound dead than

alive, I'll say." He raises his glass to me. I raise mine and we touch. "'Tis a fine place you've brought me to."

Much later we move on from the top of the town and people-watch in a pavement café down by the entrance to the *Parque da Alameda*: people watching people stroll by; people watching people, who are watching us, watching people.

Padraig is nursing yet more wine and I am wondering when he is going to call a halt to the evening. He may not, of course. He doesn't appear remotely the worse for wear even though he has drunk enough *Ribeiro* to fell a mule.

He turns to me, sweeps back his grey hair, and blinks. "You haven't asked me why I've done it," he says.

"Done what?"

"Walked the *Camino de Santiago*? What else, ya stupid eejit?"

"It's not a question one asks, Padraig," I reply politely. "People do it for all sorts of different reasons and a lot of those reasons are intensely personal."

"Personal," he repeats as though it is a word foreign to him. "What's personal about doing something hundreds of other people do? There were so many pilgrims waiting outside one hostel, it was like queuing for a bus in O'Connell Street."

Now it's my turn to run my fingers through my hair. "It's not that hundreds of others have walked the *Camino*, and yet it is. That is the point. You can make the journey either on your own or in the company of others, but your reason for making the journey — your motivation, what drives you to make it, whether it's in search of God or yourself or to atone for past sins, or perhaps to reach an understanding with yourself or others, or of something that has happened in your life — this reason is intensely personal. I've met mothers and children walking in order to come to terms with the loss of husbands and fathers. I've known priests walk to regain their faith. I've known philosophers walk because they believe the physical effort engenders a purity and clarity of thought." I draw breath. "And so it goes on."

Padraig studies me. His expression is set. His rheumy eyes are unblinking and locked on mine, and he is not inclined to speak.

"But everyone walks for their own spiritual reason, because it is *spirit* that is required to complete the pilgrimage, whether you walk from St Jean Pied-de-Port to Santiago de Compostela or from here to Finistere. What is required above all is *spirit*."

"And St James?"

It is a question I am often asked. Now it is my turn to assess the man before me. I have to tailor my response carefully otherwise I risk offending his beliefs and so risk losing the chance of a day's wages.

"Wherever you look you will find a similar theme. Perhaps the apostle St James did preach in this part of the world. Perhaps he is buried in the cathedral. Perhaps he was first buried in Jerusalem and some shepherd dug up his bones and brought them here to be buried. But perhaps it is the Christian heretic Priscillian who is buried here and not St James. We really only know two things for sure. One: St James the Apostle is deceased. And two: people like to believe he is buried here. Beyond that, what more do we need to know?"

For a moment I fear Padraig is going to ask me if I believe it is St James and his disciples, Anastasius and Theodore, who are lying in state in the silver casket in the lower chamber. But, thankfully, he doesn't.

And then, like the hermit Pelayo who saw the shining light in the field of stars, the *Campus Stellae* from which the city takes its name, I see that which is all too plain: neither I nor any of his fellow *peregrinos* has as yet asked Padraig why he's walked the Camino. And it is this secret — this motive — that is weighing heavily on him now.

Cars and buses glide round the elegant facade of the *Colexio de San Clemente* and tulip vendors wearing intricately embroidered frocks and round hats ease between the tables. A blanket of coffee and cigar smoke separates us from the cold night air.

Padraig is a sleepy child too tired to know he'd be better off in bed, but he will not surrender.

I refill our glasses and sit back.

"I was a bit of a corner boy when I was a lad," he begins. "Not much for the hands to do and not the hands for doing much. Spent the first years out of school on the scratch – the dole, that is. Started out knick-knacking, you know, ringing the door bell and running away: ended up most nights riding around in a jammer – a stolen car – waiting for the razzers to chase us. I was pretty handy behind the wheel and could be trusted not to make a right hames of it, beg pardon, a right mess of it. Never got caught, mind you."

Having seen how light he is on his feet, I can understand why.

"Don't get me wrong, we weren't gougers; not dangerous like the career criminals. But neither were we as thick as a ditch, like some of the other young fellas. We knew we had to be lively or we'd be left behind. I had a job delivering the bread round even before I was old enough to hold a driving licence. Can you believe that? But the baker wouldn't pay me more than a couple of nicker because he said I was too young to drive and if I got caught he'd be out of pocket as he would be the one to pay the fine, which would've cost him more than he would've had to've paid someone old enough to hold a proper licence in the first place." He grins and drinks his wine, hoping I can follow the rather Irish irony of his employment.

"In fact I had a load of different jobs. I worked as a fairground boxer and a bouncer bashing red necks in a bar in Blanchardstown. So it was only a matter of time before I fell under the wrong influences.

"My youngest sister attended a local convent. In fact all of my four sisters attended the same run down dump of a place. But

Siobhan was younger than me by five years, so, what with my Da being God-knows-where and my Ma passed away, I used to pick Siobhan up when she came home at weekends. They would never let me into the place of course. I used to ring the bell and wait for the sister on door duty to put her book down, get up off her chair, stagger to the door, open the door, see it was me, close the door, and stagger back to the Mother Superior's office and so on. It used to take forever. After an age the Mother Superior would appear with Siobhan. The mother Superior was a right heifer of a woman, a hard-faced old cow. Used to look at me as though she knew I was up to no good. She never gave out to me, mind; she'd just look at me as though she knew. That used to rile me, I can tell you.

"Well, one weekend I went to pick Siobhan up from the convent and while I was waiting I noticed that one wall of the chapel had collapsed. There was scaffolding in place, but I could see right up to the altar. The convent may have been run down, but on the altar stood the most magnificent crucifix I'd ever seen. If it wasn't gold, it was probably gold plate and underneath the plate was probably copper, so it would be worth a few nicker.

"Now, I wasn't much of a one for religion at the time and I needed a couple of extra bob because there was a girl I fancied worked behind the bar in the pub. And," Padraig tries his best to suppress his very cheeky grin, "in those days I could resist everything except temptation."

He pauses, I think probably because he is waiting to see if I display any horror at what I think is coming next. I can't keep a straight face and I am not sure if my smile is appropriate, but having spent the last few hours with him I am confident there will be some redemption in his tale.

"So that night, after I've finished up at the bar, I return to the convent, park the van a mile or so up the road, slip up to the convent and climb up the scaffolding and the mound of rubble into the chapel. It's not easy, the bricks are loose, but I am, if you'll excuse the expression, as quiet as a church mouse. I creep up to the altar. The crucifix is sitting far higher than I had at first thought." Padraig pauses. "I am on tip-toe…"

He stands up. Others around us have noticed his mime and are entertained.

"I reach out towards the crucifix…" He lifts up his hand and stretches it out, straining as if he is trying to pull something out of the air high above his head. "I get my fingers around the shaft…" He closes his fist. There is a look of religious desperation on his face. "It is heavy, but I can just lift it enough to get it off its mounting… I hold it aloft with my hand tight around it…" Padraig smiles, like a man who has just got his hands on the Gaelic Football trophy. "And then…"

He pauses for dramatic effect. People are laughing, but carefully, unsure as to whether his mime is serious or humorous. I, on the other hand, am confident the chapel at the convent will turn out to be his *Campus Stellae*.

"And then… I get a couple of hundred volts through my right hand and a disembodied voice says, "That'll be ten Hail Marys and I'll thank you not to set foot in this place of worship again, Padraig O'Rahilly"."

As he sits down he runs his fingers through his hair so that it stands straight up as if electrocuted. He shows me the scar on his right palm, and his expression adopts a divine astonishment.

It is true. He is Pelayo. He has seen the light.

When I have calmed down and Padraig O'Rahilly has finally finished his fabulous theatre, we convince the waiter that he should allow us just one more glass of *Ribeiro*. In a rare show of gratitude to Padraig for encouraging others to stay on and order more wine, Pepe brings us two complementary glasses. He winks at me and I hope the cost of this *free* wine will not reduce my usual commission.

"And that's why you've walked the Camino; to atone for the sins of your youth?"

"Not exactly," Padraig replies.

"There's more?"

"Indeed there is." He takes a pull from his glass. "As you can imagine, after an epiphany of this nature and with such a sore hand, I slept little that night. By Sunday evening I am convinced of the need to change my life. Monday morning I get up early. I say ten Hail Marys, drop Siobhan off a discreet distance from the convent and get straight to the FÁS office – the employment office. I reel off a list of talents; well, both of them, driving vans and knocking heads, that is. And the man asks me if I can start straight away and if I mind working nights and long hours.

"Of course I don't," I says.

He says, "You say you have some experience in the security trade?"

I nod enthusiastically.

"Well, we have just the thing," he says, "only temporary, mind. Come in right this morning, it has. Wait outside, I'll come round the front, pick you up and run you over."

Padraig pauses and drinks his wine.

"We start driving through Blanchardstown. I am relieved when we pass the bakers and even more relieved when we pass the door of the bar where I had recently been working. But I begin to feel uneasy when the man turns down the road to Siobhan's convent. And you can imagine my horror when he pulls up outside the door."

His eyes are wide now. He is watching the ghost of his youth.

"I am white as a sheet as the man rings the bell. Eventually the door is opened and the door sister, wrestling with an expression of dismay and perplexity, says, "You've come for Siobhan? But it is Monday?"

"The man says, "Please tell Mother Superior that Mister Hennessy from the employment office is here to see her." A year seems to pass until we are ushered inside the heavy door and along the cold cloister to Mother Superior's office.

"The hard-faced heifer doesn't rise from her desk when we step in. The man coughs politely. "Mister Hennessy," he says by way of both attracting her attention and introducing himself. "Mother Superior, I have very promptly found you a man to solve the problem of your security. Mister O'Rahilly, here, has some valuable experience in the security trade."

Padraig grins mischievously.

"Mother superior looks up at him, then at me, then back at him. Mister Hennessy is almost as uncomfortable in her presence as I am.

"He leaves me standing in her office, like an orphan at the workhouse gate. It feels like a further year passes, during which time Mother Superior attends diligently to her paperwork.

"Just as I am about to faint beneath the weight of her silence, she asks in a voice that makes the open sore in my right palm itch, "Would it be too much to hope you've said your Hail Marys, Padraig O'Rahilly?

———————

The next morning dawns bright; the thin clouds are high and the swifts dip and dive as they catch insects born of the recent rains. As instructed, I meet Padraig O'Rahilly outside his hotel on the *Rúa do Vilar*. Judging by the deal we strike he is no longer short of a bob or two and readily agrees to pay me what I consider to be a very fair day's wage for shepherding him around Santiago de Compostella.

"But," he says, "I'm a bit of a *curamach*. I'm cautious with money, which is why I'm not staying in that ridiculously expensive *Parador* opposite the cathedral."

I lead him up the hill towards the market, stopping along

the way for a *café solo* and a slice of *bica* – a half-cake half-biscuit guaranteed to gird the loins of any sightseer.

"What I didn't tell you last night," Padraig declares as he tucks into the *bica*, "was that Mother Superior never mentioned my misdemeanour again, and when the builders finished rebuilding the chapel wall she paid me very handsomely for my nightly vigil. After that, and to my great surprise, she introduced me to other convents, schools and businesses that required a similar service. Soon enough I was employing my chums to cover the jobs I couldn't manage on my own. One thing led to another and after forty years in the business I've now passed it over to my son." Padraig knocks back his *solo* as if to signal he is about to pronounce the last word on the matter.

"It's just that I can't for the life of me work out whether it's all down to that hard-faced, old heifer of a churchwoman or the hand of the Good Lord Himself."

Once in the market he marvels at the enormous turbot and ray hanging above the fish counters. At *Carmen's* I describe how the fishermen lower their women down the rocks to the waterline in order to collect the *Percebes* – the Goose Barnacles. The *Percebes* are expensive: their collection costs many lives each year. We sample slices of *Serrano Ham* at *Lolita Cardelle's Carniceria* and Lolita explains that *Serrano* comes from the thigh and that *Lacon* comes from the top, inside part of the hind leg, nearer the belly of the pig, which is why it is fatty and more like bacon. Pensioners with faces lined from squinting in the summer sun are selling their vegetables outside the market halls: anyone with an allotment can grow *Grelos*, broccoli or turnip leaves and everyone outside of the city has an allotment.

When Padraig's taste buds have been sufficiently confused by the varieties of food on offer, we head down to the cathedral.

We begin at the *Puerta Santa* in the *Praza da Quintana* – the square behind the cathedral. If the twenty-four Apostles and

Prophets who flank the great gate don't inspire awe in a *peregrino*, then Mateo's *Pórtico de la Gloria* at the entrance to the central aisle surely will. The sight of Jesus, wounded palms raised, Matthew, Mark, Luke, and John seated either side, is enough to humble even the hardest of hearts.

I leave him staring up at the fourth station of the cross, wherein Jesus meets his mother. There are tears in his eyes and his hands are trembling ever so slightly. I have given him a guided tour of the cathedral and he is best left to his own devices for the moment. In the great church, before the golden High Altar, I am sure this warm, charming and genial man is reliving the startling epiphany of his youth. For this *peregrino* – this pilgrim – the last few steps of the Camino may well be the hardest. Whether the curiously illogical allotment of his lucid mind will permit him to believe St James lies at his journey's end is not of paramount importance, for Padraig O'Rahilly goes not to pay homage to the long dead Saint, rather he goes to pay his respects to his Mother Superior who, surely, made Padraig the man he is today.

A SHOT IN THE ARM

Chamonix, France

They meet, literally, by accident. It isn't a train wreck or accident of birth – it isn't that kind of bad luck. It is simply a slight slip of Matthew's fingers; an accident, nevertheless, but one which might have gone on to bear far graver consequences were it not for Hoyt.

They are queuing at the ticket window for the cable car up to *Plan de l'Aiguille.*

"Hey, buddy," the stranger says, tagging his arm. "You must have plenty to throw about. You dropped this."

Being English, and therefore not at ease amongst foreigners, Matthew tries his best to ignore the American.

But then the fellow shoves a piece of paper in his hand and when he looks down, Matthew realises he must have dropped the hundred Euro note.

"Sorry. Yes. Gosh! Thanks," is all he can think of to say, as the blood swells into his cheeks.

He stuffs the note in his pocket and turns away from the stranger, trying desperately to recall the correct French for '*one-way ticket, please*' so that he doesn't have to make an even bigger fool out of himself.

"You going all the way?" the fellow asks from over his shoulder.

Matthew sighs and for the *n*th time wonders why it is the god-given right of every American to think he's entitled to make conversation with anyone who happens to speak a vaguely similar language.

"No, I'm not," he replies, without turning round.

"Guessed not!"

Now, he does turn round. The American is short and squat, like an oak tree trunk cut off to a stump; and one which is, judging by his unruly mop of black hair, trying its best to sprout again. He is wearing the trademark attire of one who walks: check shirt in the manner of a lumberjack, shorts and well-worn boots. His calves are bulbous and knotted, and he sports a saggy rucksack, walking poles and a genial smile.

"How so?" Matthew asks. "I mean, how did you know I'm not going all the way?"

"What you're wearing, buddy." He looks Matthew up and down. "The guys at the tourist office told me it's minus fifteen up at the top – and that's without the wind chill. You ain't wearing enough clothes for that kind of cold."

Matthew glances first up at the broad flank of *Mont Blanc* towering away into the clouds and second up at the sky. There are odd patches of blue, but they come and go quickly, which can mean only one thing: the wind is much stronger higher up.

"No, you're right. I'm only going as far as the middle station."

"Walking back along the *Balcon* to Montenvers?"

Matthew hesitates, quickly realising that if the American intends the same, it will be foolish of him to lie. And, though he is content with his own company, perhaps he's endured it enough of late, so he says, "That's the idea."

"Done it before?"

"No."

The yank scratches his stubbly chin. "Me neither. Perhaps we could walk along together. The name's Hoyt." He holds out his hand.

Matthew takes it, shakes it and introduces himself.

And that is how they meet.

The red cable car deposits them at the midway station and fortunately for both first-timers, the trail is signed.

Hoyt, who has already proved himself honest in returning the 100 Euro note, now reveals his competitive nature by taking the lead, setting a swift pace and talking as he walks.

Matthew, though, is happy to listen and, with his much longer legs, amble along in Hoyt's wake.

Over the preceding weeks Matthew has hiked and climbed up many of the mountains in the Haute Savoie and so is no stranger to spectacular views. Yet, the front face of the *Aiguille Verte* away across the glacier looks steep enough to intimidate even the most experienced climber and he feels strangely dizzy imagining what it must be like to swing from a rope in the narrow *Couloir Cordier*.

Towards the end of the trail they discuss their options and decide to take the spur over to *Signal Forbes* so that they can take in the view of the *Mer de Glace* far below. They sit and discuss the silence and the majesty of the mountains; though Matthew had already noticed that silence is peculiarly anathema to Hoyt. And when the jagged peaks of *Les Drus* appear framed by the roiling clouds, Matthew remarks that the scene reminds him of a painting he's seen: an island floating in the sky.

"Jeez," Hoyt grumbles beneath his breath, but just loud enough for his companion to hear, "a romantic."

Matthew thinks Hoyt a shade free with his observations, but he doesn't find his new acquaintance as much of a pain as initially he thought he might be.

Hoyt is impatient and without subtlety, but he makes a steady walking companion.

When they arrive at the little train station and café in Montenvers, they agree to walk the rest of the way down to Chamonix rather than take the train. Hoyt thinks the little rack and pinion train *cute* but Matthew, mildly irritated, demurs, pointing out that *quaint* or *charming* might be a more elegant and therefore a more appropriate representation.

They are both pleasantly weary and in need of refreshment, so they wander over to the imposing stone edifice that is the *Grand Hotel du Montenvers*, perched precariously high above the glacier.

Matthew hesitates at the entrance, thinking to take his soiled boots off but, after checking the flagstone floor and seeing it is not freshly mopped, thinks better of it.

However, no such consideration occurs to Hoyt, who marches right in, accosts the waitress and demands two beers. "Guess we are a long ways up the hill," he mumbles, when presented with the bill.

Once they are seated in the conservatory Matthew asks the American what has brought him to Europe or, more particularly, to the Haute Savoie.

Hoyt sighs. Having come through college he landed a first-rate job in a textile business on the East Coast. Things worked out well for him for a while, then life "bit him in the ass" when he wasn't paying attention. He fell head over heels for a local cocktail waitress.

"She was... wow, well, I'm not sure how to describe her; she was..." But, after a long and turbulent relationship the Bitch from Boston had thrown him over.

He declares that the waitress who's just served them reminds him of her; though her "tits don't come a close second." The rejection, he adds, hit him hard.

"And why wouldn't it? Let me tell you, buddy, she was something else. I went completely nuts, right off the scale; couldn't help myself. I went to the bar every night just to get served by her. I worked my way through the entire cocktail and shot menu. Jeez, I gave the bitch my heart and all I got was arrears and a PhD in hangovers."

Hoyt subsequently lost what little bearings he had left and, not long after that, his job. So, he's come to Europe to get his life back on track. Physical exercise is, he maintains, good for the soul and he hopes a good dose of it will repair the hole he has dug in his.

"Yeah, buddy, let me tell you, she did me over big time."

Matthew smothers his slight amusement at Hoyt's rendering of the tale, but then loses control and chuckles at the idea of having to sit and listen to such a vulgar story in such a refined setting.

"Something funny, buddy?"

"No. Forgive me, Hoyt. It's just that us sitting here reminds me of that film about those two strangers waiting for a plane. You know, the one where they end up with nothing better to do than tell each other their darkest secrets."

"That's funny?"

Matthew glances out the window and chuckles once more, "Well, we are at altitude."

"So, why are you here, Matthew," Hoyt asks in a tone that suggests he is hoping his new-found companion will have a more engaging excuse for wandering the mountains.

"Oh, I'm taking a gap year before starting university. I enjoy hiking."

They walk back down through the forest to Chamonix. Old man's beard clings to the branches of the pines, fly catchers swoop and dip, and out in the open sections the spring perfumes of buttercup and rock-rose fill the cool air.

"Take my picture by the old steam engine?" Hoyt asks, as they stroll back through the two stations.

"Thank you for that, buddy," he says once the necessary photo has been taken and then taken again to be sure Hoyt doesn't look too square against the tall iron wheels. "Say, can I buy you a beer? I know a great little place round the corner? The waitress is to die for."

Matthew, though he's avoided alcohol over the past few days, finds the idea appealing. The hostel at the far end of town is not exactly blessed with any great social dynamic and the one beer he's drunk has roused his taste buds.

The café is cosy and warm. Black and white photographs of climbers from a bygone era dot the wood-panelled walls and the scent of cooked food and coffee hangs thick in the air.

Once they are seated at the bar, Hoyt says, far too loudly, "The girl behind the bar sure is pretty. What I wouldn't give to..."

If she hears him, which Matthew thinks she must have, she doesn't react. "My shout," he says. "What'll you have?"

"A Guinness," Hoyt replies.

"In the Alps?"

"Irish-American," Hoyt states, as though that plain and simple fact explains all the mysteries of the universe.

The waitress looks over at Matthew and waits.

What Hoyt has said is true: she is incredibly pretty. She reminds him of Cosette from *Les Miserables*. Her long straw-blond hair falls straight either side of her face, except for two slender, plaited strands laced with gentian blossoms, which trail from her temples and tie up behind her head. She is Cosette, but without the fear Hugo forced upon her.

"*Une biere,*" Matthew hesitates, "*et un Guinness.*"

She waits a little longer and then replies in a tone that suggests he ought to know better, "It is *Une biere et 'une' Guinness,* okay?"

Matthew colours as she turns away and begins pouring their drinks, although he isn't sure whether it is her looks or her admonition that make him react so.

When she returns with their drinks, she simply places them on the bar without looking at him. He is vaguely offended.

Hoyt begins talking about another walk, above Passy. He took the bus up the winding road to Plaine Joux, where he watched the paraponters take off. And later he hiked over to *Lac de Pormenaz* and back to *Lac Vert*. . .

But, Matthew isn't really listening; he can't wrest his attention from the waitress.

She doesn't smile much, if at all, but that isn't to say she looks sad or depressed. Her expression hints more that she might find the world trivial and her tasks menial and therefore not worthy of her talents. She has delicate cheek bones, broad but slightly downturned lips, and startlingly beautiful eyes the colour of the sky in the seconds after the last of the early morning mist has been driven away by the sun.

"It's a helluva hike and the lake is not much," Hoyt is saying, "but it's the best spot to watch them take off."

"Who?" Matthew asks.

Hoyt frowns, "The paraponters. Who else?"

"Sorry. I wasn't concentrating."

The American chuckles, "Oh yes, you were, my friend. Only you weren't concentrating on what I was saying." He pauses. "I said she was pretty, didn't I? She looks like that girl from the movie. . ."

"The Glums?"

"Pardon me?" Hoyt frowns again.

"*Les Miserables*," Matthew replies, forgetting. "Yes, I couldn't agree more. She looks like Cosette from the novel, only she's neither so thin nor as pale as Hugo wrote her."

Hoyt's face suddenly lights up. "Yeah, you're right; Amanda Seyfried. I knew she reminded me of someone."

Of course, that isn't what Matthew means at all, but he decides to let it go.

"Hey, Cosette," Hoyt calls, fracturing the tranquillity of the café like a clap of thunder, "can my British friend and me have another round?"

She makes him wait just long enough. And when she sets their drinks before them she again shows no reaction to the American's lack of manners.

But Hoyt is not to be deterred, "My friend here says you remind him of Cosette from *Les Misérables*. I know this sounds ridiculous, but is it possible your name is Cosette?"

The waitress shrugs and pouts. "Sure," she replies, "why not? Of course my name is Cosette. Your friend is very perceptive." Her English is softly French-accented and, it seems to Matthew, rather sensual. She looks at the American as though he is carved from cheap pine and turns away to serve someone down the bar.

"Man!" Hoyt observes, "She's even prettier when she's angry."

Matthew shakes his head, slowly.

Cosette wears a denim jacket over a rara skirt and, when she leaves the bar to serve at table, he realises there must be a step up behind the bar, for she is petite like a ballet dancer.

Hoyt talks and he listens, patiently. And every time Matthew tires of the conversation and risks a glance at the waitress, she seems to sense his scrutiny of her and she pauses in what she's doing to look over at him. Sadly for him, though, hers is not a response that offers any encouragement; it is purely a look that suggests she was aware of his attention, nothing more.

Matthew is not good at reading the signals of women. He knows it and knows it is one of the reasons why he is still — he shudders to think — a virgin. And this unfortunate state of mind and body bothers him so much that recently the issue of his virginity has assumed the significance of an albatross around his neck; the consequence of which being that whenever he finds himself in the company of attractive women, he feels dreadfully self-conscious. It is why he colours so whenever he is spoken to.

Two men come into the bar and sit down at a table at the back. They exchange small talk with one of the other waitresses and when she returns to the bar to collect their order, she very obviously relates their conversation to Cosette, who smiles and whispers her reply, concealing whatever it is she is saying by raising her hand to cover her mouth.

One of the men squirms in his seat, evidently embarrassed that the waitress should repeat to Cosette what he's said.

She proceeds to giggle and tease the man wickedly. Her eyes sparkle and her lips turn up at the corners; her face is a picture of cynical amusement.

The men do not stay long and after they've left, Cosette continues to whisper about them to her colleague. It is only this once during the evening that Matthew sees her smile and he wonders whether she is the sort who smiles only when taking pleasure in the discomfort of men; more than a few of whose kind he's had the misfortune to get on the wrong side of at school. Curiously though, this thought – this stinging memory – doesn't lessen his attraction for her.

They sit and drink several more beers and by the time the street lights come on, the American has stoked the fires of his ego sufficiently to get up a full head of steam. And judging by the increased frequency with which he insists on describing to Matthew exactly what he will do to Cosette if he manages to get his hands on her, Hoyt has made up his mind he is going to make a play for her.

Matthew is intrigued; intrigued and fairly sure he now understands, given Hoyt's all too colourful description of his crude designs, why the Bitch from Boston threw him over.

"I'm a little tired of all this beer, my friend," the American decides, "why don't we move the night along with a couple of shots?" He winks somewhat conspiratorially and nods towards the menu of shots written on the blackboard behind the bar: "What do you reckon?"

For Matthew, the reckoning is simple: adding shots to the swamp of beer swilling in his stomach is not a good idea: he has yet to walk back to the hostel. But, and although he finds Hoyt rather too loud for his taste, he's enjoyed the evening and is reluctant to call a halt to it.

The list of shots is both extensive and highly imaginative, and some are so obscure he's not come across them before.

"Sex with an Alligator?" he asks.

Hoyt nods: "Melon, raspberry and Jägermeister – all over too fast. Wouldn't recommend it."

"A Double Pucker?"

"Yeah, that one lingers," he replies, as if recalling the exact moment: "Apple and watermelon schnapps."

"A Shit on the grass?" Matthew counters with a liberal dose of incredulity.

Hoyt chuckles: "Had one of those last night – coffee liqueur on melon. Sounds awful, but you feel a whole lot better for it afterward."

Matthew laughs too. But also he realises that he will not be able to keep a straight face if he has to order any such shot from the pretty waitress. "You choose, Hoyt. But be gentle with me."

The American grins mischievously, "It's your funeral, buddy." He turns his attention back to the bar: "Hey, Cosette!"

She looks up briefly, but then returns to drying and then polishing a glass, which she holds up to the light several times to check her work is perfect. Eventually, she steps over and inclines her head.

Having been made to wait, Hoyt too drags out the moment.

"Hurry, please," Cosette suggests, "I'm off duty in five minutes."

"Okay, my friend here would like a Slippery Nipple and how about a Quick Fuck for me?"

Cosette doesn't blink; she stands stock still, completely unfazed by the American's assault. In fact Hoyt, Matthew decides, might as well be asking her for the time of the last bus to Argentiere for all her wan reaction. After a few seconds, she steps back, pulls a couple of bottles down from the rack and begins to make up their shots.

Hoyt, on the other hand, cannot contain himself and erupts in a fit of laughter.

Others at the bar look over to see the cause of his amusement.

Matthew studies the many gaily coloured bottles on the racks and the thought comes to him that poisonous plants bear red berries as a warning to birds and animals not to eat them, and that if one applies the same theory to the multi-coloured bottles, surely many of them would remain forever unopened.

Cosette sets two shot glasses on the bar before them and turns back to the till for the ticket.

"Hey, wait a minute," says Hoyt, studying the glasses as if they contain some lethal liquid, "this is nothing like a Quick Fuck. A Quick Fuck is Baileys, Kahlua and Midori. This is triple-sec, Bailey's and Chambord." He studies Matthew's glass. "Hey, she's mixed up our shots, buddy. Looks like you've got the Quick Fuck."

As Hoyt reaches over to take the shot Cosette has placed in front of Matthew, she slaps the plastic saucer with the bill on the bar and pushes his hand roughly away.

"*Non,*" she says, loud enough to attract the attention of those sitting around them, "for you, tonight: a Wet Crotch. It is all you deserve."

Cosette smiles at Matthew, "Come on kid. Put your coat on. We are leaving."

PUDDACIARI

Lipari, the Aeolian Islands, Italy

The shutters opening out on to the alley are pulled to, but the atmosphere in my living room is far from cool; it is heavy and musty with the odour of middle-aged men who've only recently found respite from the Aeolian sun. And there is no breeze from the alley; the white heat of afternoon has driven all before it.

My room is dark, as they all are, but not so dark that I cannot help but notice my guest's shirt is slowly drying on him.

The Caravaglio, if I raise it to my nose, provides a brief distraction. The grapefruit and melon perfume more than adequately compensates for our own less savoury but just as natural fragrance, and the pale, straw-green of the wine is brindled by the condensation on our glasses. Caravaglio comes from Salina, the next island to the north, and I suspect it is my very ready provision of shade and wine that draws Sandro to the narrow confines of my quarters in the *Vico Giraffa*. It certainly isn't my knowledge of Italian football.

"Andrea Pirlo, Gigi Buffon," he says, puffing out his

chest, "the best football players in the world– Okay, maybe the best football player in the world is Messi, eh? *Ma*, Pirlo and Buffon, they 'ave place on Panarea. Armani, Dolce and Gabbana also. *Ma*, IL Cavaliere – Berlusconi, he 'ave one, eh! Nice place, lot of monies," Sandro blows on his finger tips as though he has singed them, and adds, "*Ma*, you cannot choose who live next door," as if he can choose who beds down next to him.

He's talking about the island of Panarea, a fashionable holiday spot for celebrities and Milanese bankers: white-walled villas, bougainvillea, views of Stromboli the volcano on the next island up the chain, and Raya, the nightclub with, or so I'm told, even better views than those of Stromboli.

But instead of cradling cocktails and picking at plates of *prosciutto* by the pool, Sandro and I are grazing on salami and sipping wine in my *monolocale*.

"You see the Carabinieri this morning in the Marina Corta?" he asks as he chews.

The Marina Corta is Lipari town square; the old fishing harbour below the *cittade*, the Castle Rock. In the Corta the couples take their *passeggio*, their evening stroll, and families sit out on the low harbour wall to talk and watch their children gambol, play hide and seek beneath the statue of San Bartolo, and kick at empty plastic water bottles. It is the meeting place, the heart of the town. It's also where by day Sandro plies his trade, hustling tourists into boat trips around the islands.

"Uh-huh," I reply, as I try to de-stone an olive in my mouth.

I had been sitting in one of the cafés taking breakfast as the blue uniformed policemen strong armed their catch into their launch. Clearly they felt the need to put on a show even though the sad strip of a felon didn't look up to any meaningful resistance. "Know him?"

"No. I not recognise him. From the mountains," Sandro

56

dismisses, which in local parlance means he was from across the water; from Sicily.

"On the run, huh."

He glances at me straight and hard. "Probably drugs," he suggests. "Beginning of season Carabinieri always like to make drugs bust. They think it teach us *Terroni* to be'ave properly." He pauses. "As if *Terroni* need lesson from bloody *Polentoni*, eh?" he scoffs and sprays me with Napolitano Salami. Sandro raises an eyebrow and wipes his mouth with his handkerchief; an apology that smacks more of acknowledgement than it does contrition.

As far as Sandro is concerned, he is *Terroni*, which means he is from the south, and I don't feel inclined to embarrass him with the information that my grandfather was born in Florence, which makes me *Polentoni*.

It is hot, some days cruelly so for the *Polentoni*, but that doesn't deter them. The *Aliscafo*, the hydrofoil, brings the day-trippers in from Milazzo in Sicily; they swell the population of ten thousand to more than double in August. And the *Nave* brings the day trippers in their hundreds from Taormina. The *Romanacci, Catanesi, Calabresi, Milazzesi*, and this year a hatful of Australians are all manna from heaven for the likes of Sandro.

"You know," he begins, "four thousand years ago they used to mine Obsidian here. The black glass was used for cutting; now it makes for a pretty souvenir, eh; a paperweight, perhaps a necklace. And *Pomice* too, eh."

The pumice mines, the great scars in the coastline at the northern end of Lipari, have long since closed: *Pomice* is now mined much cheaper in other, further, parts of the new world. The locals will tell you proudly that much of it was used in the building of the skyscrapers of New York, but it was more likely used in the less enchanting manufacture of detergents, glue, sandpaper, and polishing materials. These

57

days the drying houses of La Cava overlook the beach of Pietra Lischia, like old men waiting for the return of the good old days: the good old days when children as young as five worked the mines.

"Obsidian and Pumice," he scoffs again. "They are like sunshine; everyone sell them, but you can find them on the beach without having to put hand in your pocket."

"You're English is good Sandro," I suggest.

He beams. "Last year I work in London. You know Manor House and Plaistow in London? Oh yes," he adds with a knowing smirk, "I work in, what you would call, the highest quality places."

I nod. "Out of season?"

"Of course! The season here is only three months; June to August — very short. Out of season there is no work here. I mean," he leans forward to emphasize his point, *"no work for anyone."* He shrugs. "There is work in Messina, in Catania. There are universities there. But here there is nothing, just a few volcanoes that sleep like old women."

"Stromboli doesn't sleep. I've seen it from the beach at Porticello. Blew quite a spout the day before yesterday."

"Okay." He shakes his head as if to forgive Stromboli's occasional tantrums. "But we 'ave saying: *When the volcano is quiet, the tourists do not come.* Maybe the tourist office provoke these little displays of emotion. I don't know."

"Didn't take you for a conspiracy theorist, Sandro."

He shakes his head again and sighs, "I am not. I don't believe it. But the tourist office is not stupid. You know what *Romanacci* call a Sicilian with an IQ of one hundred-eighty?" He doesn't wait long enough for me to confirm my ignorance. "Someone from Lipari!"

He grins. His teeth are long and there seem to be more of them than any man has a right to. "But, what else is there to do here but talk?"

It is true. I have noticed where there is no work, there is always talk.

"You like it here?"

"Sure," I reply, "I think it's as close to heaven as one can find."

"No." He grins. "If we were that close to heaven, Stromboli would not disturb the peace by make eruption so many times. You know the dead volcano on Vulcano? They say it is the entrance to hell. This, I believe. Maybe this is why the place stinks so much. You are staying long?"

"A while."

"Holiday?"

"Tell me about the families, Sandro?" I cut him off so rudely and abruptly that he cannot be left in any doubt that I have done so intentionally.

He sits back, considering, guarded.

"What about them?" he asks, "Which family?" The corners of his mouth turn down. It seems Sandro doesn't like being asked questions any more than I do.

"The old lady who has the vegetable shop on the Emanuele — the shop at the bottom where it meets the Marina Lunga?"

He screws up his face and sits forward, unsure of where I mean.

"The short woman with a voice like gravel? She sells everything from bergamot oil to caper plants? The one next door to the yellow people office?"

"Ah, *Popolo Giallo*," he replies.

Popolo Giallo, Yellow People, is one of the tour companies that run the small boats, *barcas*, around the islands. Portelli Sonia, Regina, Aliante, and da Massimo are others. At first I thought they were run by families in the way that most people think Sicily is run by Mafia families. Partly that's because so many of the *Escurzionisti* wear sunglasses, which lends them a vaguely sinister look; then again, why wouldn't you wear sunglasses when the Aeolian sun can bleach the back of your eyeballs by lunchtime. But, Sandro tells me, the tour companies are all franchised and endorsed and regulated by the council, so I guess I'll just have to believe him.

A light switches on in his head and with it comes a look of relief. "*La Papela?* You mean *La Papela?*"

"Why do you call her that?"

He laughs heartily, rocking back in his chair. "She has a voice like a machine gun. You know, very... how you say... staccato, like Rossini. She growl like dog, but very fast, very short."

"Yes, that's the one. Always has a broom in her hands."

Sandro nods and grins again, "Anna-Maria Li Donni. Old family; like Zagami, Rastuccia, Biviano."

These are names I have seen on the war memorial plaque outside the Municipio in the Mazzini; lean sons of Lipari driven to their death by fat cowards in cockerel uniforms.

The Caravaglio is nearly done and beyond the shutters a mantel clock chimes four.

Sandro's eyebrows arch in union. He hauls his creaking frame upright, and yawns and stretches. "I have people coming from Vulcano," he says through the end of his yawn, "I must go. I say thank you for your wine and your hospitality." He reaches down and we shake hands. His grip is limp; it betrays no promise of the strength his rangy torso suggests.

"Anytime."

He hesitates. "*Alla prossima. Domani* — tomorrow, you want to go to Stromboli, maybe Salina?"

I stifle my chuckle. I have learnt it is not wise to laugh at such men too openly.

"Maybe Alicudi, Filicudi?" he asks.

"Thanks, Sandro, but no. I'm either going to take a *taxi mare* up to one of the beaches or maybe hire a scooter and ride up to Four Loaves if it's too hot for the beach." It's my idea of a gentle joke. I hope it doesn't offend.

"Four Loaves?" The cogs whirr and the gears grind. "Oh! *Capisco. Quattropani. Si.* Four loaves. And *Quattrocchi* is Four Eyes, eh?" He grins. "Ah yes, perhaps it is cooler on the other side of the island. You need a scooter?"

He makes me smile, does Sandro; he doesn't stop trying. "Thanks, but no. Do you know a guy by the name of Tonio," I struggle with the pronunciation, "Sciacchitano?"

"Sure! Who doesn't? Old family too, eh! Big interest in the Marina Lunga. They say he is trying to get permission for big pier in the harbour, big pier for the big boats; bigger than the pier where the water and fuel ships come. *Si,* of course, everyone know Tonio Sciacchitano."

"You pronounce it better than I do," I reply. "Yes. Tonio. He says if I need a scooter he can let me have one. I'm going fishing with him tonight."

Sandro blinks. I guess it's not so surprising that in an island of only ten thousand people everyone knows everybody. But what does surprise me is the speed with which Sandro's normally genial expression fades as if a clown has nipped out of the sideboard and thrown a bucket of water over him.

He backs up and turns, "Okay. Maybe see you tomorrow. *Grazie,* eh! *Ciao, ciao — ciao,*" he calls over his shoulder.

Sandro steps out into the *Vico Giraffa* and closes the door very quietly, almost reverently vacating my confessional.

Tonio's little fishing dinghy is tied up in the Porto delle Genti, a small bay a few hundred metres to the south of the Marina Corta. He has a man: Salvatore.

Whereas Tonio is medium height and medium build, except for the all too obvious evidence of his appetite, which protrudes from below his chest like the body of a busker's mandolin, Salvatore is short and perhaps a shade too thin for his own good, a little like a man boiled down and beaten. But Sal's teeth and eyes shine white in the half-light, and when he shakes my hand it is plain he is no stranger to manual labour.

Sal has already brought the dinghy to the pebbly beach. It is a plain wooden row boat, a skiff suited to four oarsmen at most, but with a small outboard fitted. Just forward of centre Sal has rigged a slender but adequate mast and crossbar, from which hang navigation lights powered by a car battery. He holds the boat steady while Tonio and I clamber in, and then slides in himself and with his right arm snatches at the starter handle of the outboard.

We whine our way a mile east off shore. The water is flat and oily, and, as the sky ripens like a plum, the island behind us is robed in crimson.

When Sal is happy, sniffing the air and searching for reference points from the hills, he cuts the motor and hands us coils of fishing line each of which is attached to small cylinders not much longer than a hand and no wider than a thick finger. The cylinders have a light at one end, the end to which the lines are tied, and at the other an assembly of hooks. The eight or so hooks spread out from the shaft like the spokes of an upside-down umbrella, curving back up towards the end with the light.

"*Ontreto*," Tonio says when he catches me examining it. He pronounces the word with soft vowels, without inflection or accent; just plain *ontreto*. It seems an unassuming word for such an unpleasant looking implement.

"Squid-jag, I think they call it," I reply, mesmerised by the tool.

Sal bids us drop the *ontretos* over the side. The moment they hit the water the white light in the top begins to blink slowly, rhythmically.

"Like this," says Tonio. He measures and counts off twenty-five sections of line between his outstretched arms and allows his *ontreto* to sink beneath the boat.

62

The lights from onshore twinkle and glitter in the warmth of evening, the giant radiator of rock releasing the heat retained from the day. And apart from the distant drone of the late *Aliscafo*, the odd waft of music from the Marina Corta, and the gentle lap from an occasional weakening wake, all I can hear is me counting out the sections of line as I sit in the prow and watch the light from my *ontreto* dim as it descends into the inky black beneath.

Tonio shifts to beneath the navigation lights on the crossbar. "Like this," he repeats. He lifts up his right hand so that I can see he is holding the line across his palm through his closed fist. "When you feel playing, pulling, then you bring back up, but not too fast, no jerk, eh."

The only other time the silence is broken is when they talk, or rather when Tonio talks. Tonio is not given to long conversation. He is prone to pauses similar to those favoured by modern playwrights, as though the pauses are strategically implanted into his response to make you think, rather than to imply he is doing the same. Merely asking after his health can often elicit a thought-provoking and unsettling silence. But if Tonio is selective in his conversation, Salvatore is cheeseparing. He speaks only when he cannot avoid doing so, and though his dialect is Sicilian in essence, I cannot penetrate it.

"You meet Alessandro Tartaro today?" Tonio asks quietly.

It is too dark for me to weigh the significance of his question; even with the light thrown from the crossbar I can't see his expression. "Sure," I reply in all innocence. "Seems like a decent sort."

"Alessandro is what the *Messinesi* call *puddaciaru*?"

"Meaning?"

"It is a name the *Messinesi* have for the people from Lipari. It is a name they give for people who talk too much. The *Messinesi* says that in Lipari there is nothing else to do but talk." Tonio

63

employs one of his theatrical pauses and then continues, "You have a saying in English about lips and ships."

"Loose lips sink ships," I prompt, "But that's an old war slogan."

"It is *logica fondamentale*," Tonio concludes.

Sandro is a talker. I consider myself told.

After what I can only guess to be fifteen minutes — for it is difficult to gauge the passage of time when sitting out in the middle of a silent, unmoving sea — Tonio says, "Bring it in."

I draw my line up smoothly, trying to lay it in a tidy coil at my feet. The blinking light ascends towards me and when I pull it clear of the water there is nothing hanging from the hooks of the *ontreto*.

"More line," says Tonio, "Try maybe thirty."

This time I try to keep a more accurate count of the lengths I pay out.

After an age in which I study the myriad stars and play hostage to the whistling tinnitus in my head, I sense a small aggravation on the end of my line.

I look up at Tonio and Sal. They don't see me look up; rather they sense the shift in the attitude of the boat as I tighten.

"Pull. Not hard," Tonio orders calmly. "Now bring in."

Trying to pull up arm over arm as gently and regularly as my enthusiasm will allow, and after what I am certain must be more lengths than I paid out, I see the *ontreto* flickering eerily in the deep.

Gradually it comes to me. I can feel the hairs on the back of my neck stand in a frisson of anticipation. I have no firm perception of what it is that I am about to draw from the darkness of the deep — no real image in my mind, but my naivety, my inexperience, my virginity is overwhelmed by my desire to know what might be at the end of the line.

The closer it rises towards me, the greater grows the curious, fumbling aggravation until I can feel the impatient tug of fingers on the line. By the time the light from the *ontreto* breaches the surface, there is an urgent and frantic struggle against my draw.

I haul the line into the boat and drop the *ontreto* and the thrashing *totani* into the bottom of the boat. Attached, writhing on the end is a small flying squid, baby pink, tubular, ear-winged, and just longer than the length of my hand. It trails long sinuous tentacles which are fighting desperately to extricate its torso from the hooks on which it is impaled.

Sal eases forward round Tonio. He bends and grasps the line at the lighted end of the *ontreto*, jerks the squid off the hooks, and chucks it unceremoniously into the white, plastic bucket at my feet.

For some reason I had expected to see him dispatch the squid with some hooked lance or pointed blade; some swift coup de grace, some mark of respect for a life taken to nourish the lives of others, or perhaps even a prayer offered in appreciation. Instead Sal merely returns to his perch at the stern.

Tonio says simply, "Now we will take more," and the equilibrium is returned as though little worth remarking has taken place.

The squid lays on its side, struggling like a thin, angry newborn in the bucket, its small black pupil in its large white eye staring up at me, uncomprehending. After a minute or so it gives up the fight and is still; strangely relaxed in its dying.

"Thirty again," Tonio prompts. "Maybe little more this time."

We fish for what seems to me like all night. Thirty lengths, around sixty metres, would appear to be the depth at which the squid are feeding. Some of them are smaller than my first catch; these Sal throws back. Some, however, are larger, as long as my forearm, and violent and aggressive in their submission. And it is only when Sal has to grapple to extricate the larger *totani* off the *ontreto* that he displays any real emotion, chuckling with whoops of delight.

When both our buckets are full Sal starts up the outboard, the nasal whine resonating in the night air, and we cruise back into Porto delle Genti. We unload onto the beach.

"*Bene*," says Sal, holding out his hand for me to shake. He squeezes my hand firmly, holding on for longer than I expect, and his eyes gleam with what I can only interpret as some form of gratitude.

I cannot see why he should be grateful. "*Grazie, Salvatore*," I reply, "*Grazie, molto gentile!*"

Sal doesn't offer me any of our pink, staring catch. He simply returns to packing up the boat, removing the delicate mast, the navigation lights, and the outboard. As Tonio and I walk up the hill, Salvatore is rowing the small boat out to its mooring in the bay.

"Do you have the time, Tonio?"

"You can't afford a watch?" he replies. There is sufficient inflection in his tone to know he is poking fun at me.

There are no street lights and Tonio could probably read his watch by the ambient light supplied by the stars, but he doesn't need to. He looks up briefly and considers his response: "Close to one o'clock."

"You can tell the time by the stars?" I don't try to conceal my admiration.

"No," he replies in a flat, matter of fact way, "The band in the Marina Corta has finished playing."

I can feel his smirk in the dark.

At his modest but detached house on the edge of the Diana at the back of town, we sit out on his veranda and Tonio pours us both a glass of Malvasia. The golden brown liquid is sweet like dessert wine, but thicker, sweeter, and with a slight hint of orange.

"We must be quiet, eh," he whispers, "I have guests."

Rather strangely, there is no sound from any cicadas to mask our conversation. "You run a bed and breakfast?"

"No, I look after a couple for a week. Houseguests you would call them."

"A week?" My turn for a pause, "You know what fish and houseguests have in common, Tonio?"

He thinks for a moment. "No. What is it they have in common?"

"After three days, they go off!" I reply.

"Go off? You mean *è andato a male*, like go sour?" he chortles.

"Exactly!"

He pauses, reflects, "No. This one will not go bad. Well, not soon. She is pretty, eh, but she is with her fiancé, and she is the daughter of the chief in the Capitanerie de Porto in Milazzo. No, my friend, she will not go sour. Everyday, Salvatore takes them to the Piano Conte. It is quiet there. There are some secluded beaches. They like to sunbathe naked. *Aie-yaie-yaie!*" he whispers and sighs.

We sit in silence for a while. Before us the Lunga, the Corta and the proud *cittade* rising between them, are at peace. Lipari is sleeping.

"Salvatore keeps all the squid?" I ask him.

He pauses as though the answer to my question will come to me if I think long and hard enough.

"*Si,*" he then replies.

"So he sells the squid, takes his fee out of the proceeds and gives you the balance."

Tonio bridles at my guess, hunching his shoulders and shaking his head slowly from side to side, "Something like this."

I try harder to work out the sequence of connections that tie the two of them together. "He works for you?"

Tonio considers. "Work?" he turns the word over in his mind. "Something like this also."

I can feel Tonio's eyes watching me in the dark, but I cannot tell whether he disapproves of my impertinence or whether he is encouraging me to work out the puzzle for myself. I think out loud: "He takes you fishing. You catch the squid. He keeps the squid. He sells them. He keeps the money. When you need him to work for you, you don't have to pay him because you have helped him with his fishing."

It seems that my rather logical progression is correct, as Tonio only replies when I require shepherding.

"No money passes through your hands," I continue, "so there is no tax, no paper trail. Therefore apart from living in the same town, there is no evidential connection to you. There is no trace."

His teeth shine in the starlight.

"So how do the tax authorities think Salvatore earns a living?"

"We are a World Heritage Site," he announces, "UNESCO has given us this honour. UNESCO, not Rome! Salvatore is very old. How old, I am not sure. I don't think even Salvatore knows how old he is. The *Guardia Finanza* is not interested in Salvatore. They have bigger fish to fry than mere scraps like Salvatore. They like to prey on the big Russian yachts. Last year they confiscate a grand, very grand, motor-yacht in Lipari. They were provided with information that a notorious Russian gangster was on board. When they put everyone ashore on the little pier in the Lunga, they discover a member of the Russian Parliament is on board. Big diplomatic incident! Many red faces." Tonio chuckles the way a magician might after discovering a new and potentially wonderful trick.

At his mention of the word pier, I recall the conversation I had with Sandro earlier in the day. "I gather you are trying to get permission to build an extended pier in the Lunga."

I feel Tonio tighten the way I tightened when I became aware of the squid aggravating the end of my line. We're not on a boat and so there is no change in attitude beneath our feet, but the sudden shift in atmosphere between us is palpable.

He is silent for as long as I can hold a breath.

Then, very quietly he says, "It is true. To do this I need some permissions from the *Capitanerie* in Milazzo."

Tonio is silent a few seconds longer. I sense his agreeable mood becoming restive, as though his thoughts, once directed towards me, are now turning away from me.

I make tracks for the *Vico Giraffa*, thanking Tonio for taking me fishing and for standing me the bottle of Malvasia on his terrace so late into the night.

As I close his driveway gate behind me I hear him mutter, "*Puddaciaru!*"

The next morning I am up with the swifts. My head is a little heavy from too much of Tonio's Malvasia, but there is little point in staying inside after the Aeolian sun has risen so high. Early on, the air in the *vico* is cool and fresh, but with every minute it heats and stales, thickening like soup left in a bowl.

In the *Corso Vittorio Emanuele*, the town is waking and making ready for the day, but slowly. Though the cool of dawn is retreating into the foothills of Monte Pelato, there is no profit in haste. The shopkeepers are methodically laying out their stalls: postcards, guide books, fridge magnets of fish, crabs, moons and fruit, and hats, and necklaces, and T-shirts are hung up high beside the door by means of a long pole and a steady hand.

In the small *piazza* beside the post office Maurizio is filleting fish and flapping at flies with a rolled-up newspaper. Of course he's not cheap! Why should he be? His *Mupa* and *Dentice* are fresh off his boat this morning. Maurizio's careworn *Ape*, his three-wheeled open-sided van, creaks beneath its cargo of tuna, swordfish, and bream. And Maurizio is always out so early some suspect his *Ape* doesn't actually run at all; some prefer to believe he freewheels it down the Emanuele every morning and cajoles it back up each afternoon in much the same way his father would have cajoled his donkey.

Further down the road, but not so close that he encroaches on *La Papela's* turf, Mario is touting the very reasonable price of his home-grown pale apricots, yellow melons, light-green grapes, mauve plums, and deep red tomatoes. Trays crammed with deep green watermelons slope down from the eves of the little van, and music speakers and a jumble of empty boxes are piled haphazardly on its roof. His smartly sign-written, bright red *Ape* stands up well considering its mighty load.

Up in the cemetery the stooped Natalizia Fighera is placing a water bottle over the flowers on her sister's grave. She has punctured the bottom of the plastic bottle so that it will drain drip-by-drip into the vase over the next few days. An image of her sister Antoinetta is set in bas-relief in the headstone. Natalizia has worn black ever since the day her sister disappeared on Monte San Angelo sixty years ago. She has never married, but neither is she one of those old maids made over to Christ; she is not what they call hereabouts *bizzocchi*.

The first *Aliscafo* of the day drones into the Lunga and the *Capitanerie de Porto* barks its onward route, "Salina, Panarea, e Stromboli."

The *Escurzionisti* are out and about, organising day-trips to climb the volcano on Stromboli or preparing for the day-trippers from Taormina. I search for Sandro, but he is not amongst them this bright and sunny morning. One of the yellow people thinks he may have gone to Milazzo for a few days.

I See Him Coming

Porto, Portugal

I see him coming. He doesn't know I am watching him, but I do see him. I see all of them, even the ones who are convinced they are already invisible. Even *they* do not escape my attention. To my practised eye, they are all too obvious.

He is walking – no, strolling – towards me as if out for a Sunday promenade. He is good looking, though not my type you understand. I don't allow myself an eye for aesthetics; they are a luxury to me, but they distract me from my goal and remind me of what I miss so much.

"Hello," I say, as he goes to pass me.

He half turns and glances back the way he has come – from the city – and when he realises there is no one behind him and therefore I must be speaking to him, his pale complexion reddens.

"Oh, I'm sorry." His face colours the crimson red of a schoolchild who has been noticed engaging in a deeply personal act. "Do I know you?" he asks.

"I've seen you here before," I reply, casually. "Here on the *Dom Luis Bridge*, the last couple of weekends?"

If it is at all possible, his face is now a similar hue to the port wine, which is ferried down the *Douro* in the wooden *Rabelo* boats, a handful of which lie moored in two neat lines below us; one line beside the Gaia bank, the other on the Porto side.

"You've no need to be embarrassed," I offer, in order to stem the swelling of blood in his face. "I've seen you, but there is no reason why you should have seen me. You've been watching the water."

Some of them have already made their decision before walking onto the bridge and some of them will never be dissuaded from their path no matter how positive, lucid, logical or long-winded my argument. I use the term *long-winded* because I have learned that time and energy are intertwined.

Like two lovers who walk hand in hand, time and energy are connected. On the one hand, though time is the fourth dimension and therefore intangible or, if you like, of no physical substance, I have learned it is perhaps the most precious commodity of all. Energy, on the other hand, can be generated, depleted and regenerated either in an instant or over varying periods of time; it therefore has physical substance. However, they are both joined in as much as when one runs out of energy one also runs out of time and this is the moment when people, like the young man now standing before me, are at their most vulnerable. It is the moment when all things hang in the balance.

My idea is to wear them down so that they haven't the physical or mental energy to continue with their undertaking. Then, if I do not win in the long term, at least I have won in the short term — the day, if you like — and to win the day buys both of us time.

The Taoists taught me this — their *time strategy* — and over the years it has proved most effective. They practice the art of delay, reasoning that if one persuades the soul to hesitate or pause, however briefly, then there is a better chance of turning the soul from its path.

You might regard this as obvious and you would be right. But only partially so.

Of course, if they do not pause and I am not sufficiently swift, then there is only one end. But sometimes I have been able to head them off before they reach their platform – their launch point or their point of no return, to put it in real terms.

I have many wiles. An unexpected gust of wind brings with it a sudden chill which elicits a brief awareness. A tram leaving the *Sao Bento* passes at the critical moment, allowing the passengers to become spectators to an intimate process which, being no longer intimate, is therefore ruined. Or I have been known to hustle a family of tourists to stand beside the poor wretch, so that the smiles of the children tug sufficiently on his or her heart strings. This last has worked for me on many occasions; it is my most common of tricks.

The soul before me is little different from the rest, even though he fervently believes he is. Unique and exclusive is how he sees himself. They all do, but even I can see this one is ordinary; if ordinary any of them are. However, there are slight and subtle differences.

For a start his physical appearance sets him apart from so many others. More generally, they are unkempt, deciding as they do that there are more weighty aspects of their intention which require their attention rather than simply their dress. Most are unshaven, sometimes unwashed and more often than not underfed: they have had neither the time nor the energy for that kind of detail. But this one is not one of those.

He is clean and clean shaven, and carries just enough form at his waist to suggest he hasn't gone without these past few days, if ever. His rich, collar-length auburn hair curls in waves, but in an organised and ordered fashion, not unruly. He sports a tan jacket over a check shirt and tailored jeans, and his moccasin-style shoes are clearly not long out of the shop. And with all his smartened attire and easy gait, he is trying his best to look like one of many who walk across the *Dom Luis Bridge* everyday.

But, I see him coming and I must set to it. Although he strolls to all intents and purposes as though he has not a care in the world, his direct line towards a point above the central span of the bridge betrays his purpose. Some stagger, reluctantly, as if they are being drawn by a powerful magnet. Others stride as if they are on their way to a business meeting, which is often exactly how they perceive their task.

He doesn't display openly any of the symptoms of depression; though depression does not always manifest itself through a haggard expression or a darkening around the eyes. And he doesn't show any of the classic signs of the psychotic; though again psychotics are, more than anyone, extremely proficient at concealing their psychosis. But this one possesses neither the thousand yard stare nor the trademark-tell of a twitch. His step is measured, suggesting he is neither whimsical nor unpredictable; suggesting there are no rogue electrical impulses racing round his cerebral circuitry.

That is good. That is a relief. That suggests he is in control of his faculties. And his smart-though-ordinary appearance indicates he is not one of those crying out for either help or recognition, as so many do.

No, this one is a philosopher of some nature. He is a thinker and they can be the most trouble.

My mind races through a glossary of religions and their cultural stereotypes. He is not wearing the orange robes of a priest and his countenance exudes no loathing, fear or anger, such are the customary motivations required for a Buddhist to breach the First Precept. Neither is he wearing a *keffiyeh* or *bisht* or a *boubou*, the cloth headdress or black or grey robes of Islam. But then, like the

Christians and the Jews, Islam believes one's soul is not one's own, but owned only by God: the soul is merely on loan, as it were. He is not a Sikh, for he wears no turban and doesn't look the sort to interfere in a greater plan or purpose. And neither does he appear to labour under the burden of shame, which his intended actions would bring to the family of a Hindu. As for the Zoroastrians and the swelling congregations of the Baha'i? Well, I cannot remember when I last saw one of either of their creeds, so he is unlikely to number amongst their community.

No, this one is everyman. He is a philosopher. A nightmare! The worst! They answer questions only with more questions. They are never satisfied and it is irrelevant whether they are theologians or Philistines, atheists or agnostics. Philosophers, I don't argue with. They hide behind the veneer of their philosophising, believing that process is all and common sense is immaterial.

I have seen him coming and have already dredged the ocean of my wiles dry. If I cannot appeal to him on any religious or racial ground, then subterfuge is my last resort.

"I like to watch the water too," I say.

"You do?" he replies, surprised to learn he is not alone in his fascination.

"Yes, I find it mesmerising; the constant motion and yet the sameness. It makes me forget why I come here."

He pauses, deliberating.

I smile self-consciously at him to let him know that though shy, I would like him to respond.

"Why do you come here?" he asks at last.

"To watch the water."

Like the fly-fishermen, I have cast my bait. And like the hook that hangs below the counterfeit fly...

"But," he hesitates, "if all you do is watch the water when you get here, why... why *do* you come here?" he interrupts, the frustration of innocence and confusion creeping into his tone.

"I don't know really. It's a bit of a trick," I point out. "It's my diversion. Why are you here?"

He looks down at his recently acquired shoes but, it pleases me to see, not down over the rail which separates us from the fifty metres straight down to the flat grey surface of the *Rio Douro*.

His eyes tear and he wrinkles up his nose and grimaces in an attempt to drive the water from the corner of his eyes. "I don't know," he says, his voice drying and cracking a little.

But I know why he is here. "If *you* don't know why you come here, why do *you* come?"

"I don't know," he repeats. And in the moment of his denial he lifts his hand to his face and wipes his eyes. It is as if he is wiping away his motivation for his coming to the *Dom Luis* in the first place.

It is now my turn to fill the silence. "Most people come here because they think this is the bridge that was built by Gustave Eiffel. But they're wrong. The *Ponte Dona Maria Pia*," I point the way we are facing, upstream, "is the bridge built by Eiffel. You can see it just there, beyond the turn. There's a train running across it now." There isn't, of course. The bridge is out of sight round the corner and the trains have not run across it for over twenty years. I just want him to focus his eyes for a second.

"Sure," he replies, still wiping them.

"It's the height too, isn't it?"

I wonder if I have broken him too early. Experience has taught me that if they reach their surrender point too quickly, the shock of it can be difficult to recover from, leaving them only dazed and yet more muddled.

"What is?" He sniffs, inelegantly.

But this sniff is manna from heaven for me. The sharp intake of air wakes him, enlivening his nasal cavity like snuff sniffed from the back of one's hand. He will be able to smell now, which is a step in the right direction. For I have noticed that when people make up their mind to embark on a certain course, smell is the first of the senses to be lost to their wake. Reviving it so means the oxygen supply to his brain has been restored.

"The *Ponte Dona Maria Pia*, the *Dom Luis* and the *Arrábida* bridges here in Porto; the *Golden Gate* and the *Brooklyn* bridges in America: they all share between forty and sixty metres clearance in their centre span."

He is leaning against the railing now, staring down at the seemingly concrete surface of the *Douro*. His amber eyes are glazed: he sees everything and yet he sees nothing.

"Hey!" I shout, to haul him from his stupor. "I'm talking to you."

He flinches and turns to look at me. "Sorry, I must have drifted off. I didn't mean to be rude."

The flinch and the fact that he has heard me are better omens too. His reaction implies his hearing is still functioning.

"That's okay. I said it is mesmerising. I just sort of hoped in a silly way that you might find me more hypnotising than the water, if you know what I mean."

Talking of water, I know I am fishing shamelessly, but you must understand it is not because I crave his attention; what I crave is his attention for himself.

We are standing on the upstream side of the bridge. A breeze blows down the *Douro* from the vineyards surrounding *Pinhão* and *Tua*. Trams run either way across the centre. Tourists loiter on the downstream side, gazing at the rows of terracotta-roofed Port Wine warehouses, the gaudy yellow and red façades of the balconied houses lining the *Cais da Ribeira*, and the cobbled alleys of the *Sebastião* and the *Sao Domingos*, which trickle down from the high city like tributaries feeding the broad river below the bridge.

"There is a nice breeze today," I say to rescue him from his discomfort. "When it comes from the sea," I indicate over my shoulder, "you can taste the salt water from the Atlantic. Today, you can taste the grapes from the vineyards." I wait and watch.

He glances self-consciously at me.

"Go on, breathe in. See if you can taste the *Bastardo* or the *Barroca* on the wind. Strange name for a grape, don't you think, *Bastardo?*"

Like you cannot see the *Ponte Dona Maria Pia* from the *Dom Luis*, you cannot smell the grapes of the *Douro* either; I just want him to try. "They taste good, eh?"

He looks at me as though I am mad, which I suppose I must be to put up with my current employment.

"Funny thing," I add. "This banister which keeps us from falling off the bridge," I tap the flat, metal rail which runs just above hip high along either side of the bridge, "it's always so cold to touch. You'd think it would feel warmer on a sunny day like today."

He grasps the rail tightly. The cramped muscles of his arms bulge as he steadies himself. A wave of nausea, vertigo or perhaps the beginnings of doubt, wash through his form.

"So, how come I haven't seen you here before?" he asks, to divert his mind away from his sudden sea-sickness.

"Oh, you probably haven't looked for me. I shouldn't worry. I'm not offended or anything like that. You've probably had other things on your mind. Like today. You've got a lot on your mind today. Leastways I think you have. I could be mistaken, but when I've been watching you before, you've seemed to be up to bearing whatever the load is you are carrying. But today, it's different. This time you've got more on your mind than when you were last here."

He frowns, not adequately grasping what I am on about. He is uncertain, unbalanced. He is swaying like the metal-arched bridge beneath our feet when the wind gets up.

"I shouldn't worry," I repeat, anxious now that I have pierced his lacquered shell to press further into him. "Lots of people come here when they've got too much on their plate," I shake my head at him, "No, that's not fair of me. Some people come here because they have too little on their plate. But that's the problem with plates, isn't it? You've either got too much on them or not enough. One day they're too light and the next too heavy. It's difficult to see how one can win some of the time. Do you know what I mean?"

He hesitates and I hold my breath.

After what seems a lifetime, which is most appropriate when I come to think of it, he sighs, "Yes, I do. I know exactly what you mean."

His shoulders sag. The tension in his face falls away; not in any kind of landslide way, not as though the braces behind his façade have snapped or as though the muscle responsible for smiling – the muscle they call the zygomaticus – has let go. Not like that, no. It is the kind of relief that comes from being informed that the results of your last exam are not as bad as you had once feared they might be or the kind of relief you feel when the surgeon tells you your mother will suffer no lasting side-effects from her life-saving operation. The loosening of his deportment, the slackening of his poise and the easing of his posture suggest he is in the process of laying his burden – his millstone – down.

For how long, though, I never know; but it is a start and like all things, there must be a beginning.

A gaggle of far-eastern tourists approach us. I have to be careful. They crowd in on us, offering him their cameras, pressing him to take their picture. They grin and nod in encouragement.

But, he is not in the mood. He is still busy, quietly untying the rope which connects him to his millstone. He does not want to make a noise and in so doing broadcast to the strollers of the *Dom Luis* that this is exactly what he is doing. He looks at me, a little like a puppy wanting to be taken for a walk.

They plead with him, cackling. They beseech him with their silver boxes.

He looks at me, hoping upon hope that I will wrest their cameras from them and do their bidding. But, I cannot. They are looking at him, not at me.

Eventually, he re-engages his zygomaticus, not much but just enough to let the toothy ensemble know that, reluctant though he is, he will comply with their wishes.

They band together, hands on each others shoulders, hips against hips, grins outshining grins, and he takes their photograph.

I am rewarded, not only that he is busy untying the cord which connects him to his stone, but also that he is not so busy that he can refuse the reasonable request of his fellow beings. It is a small sign that the seed of confidence I have sown in him is already germinating. Yet I must not be complacent. I have known them pause to take another's photo before suddenly hurling their stone over the parapet, only to follow it down towards the flat grey waters below. From fifty metres up it takes less than three seconds to arrive at the horizontal veneer of the *Douro*. Another nine seconds and they would be falling as fast as anyone can fall. But the flat grey water interrupts their progress before they ever get to reach that terminal velocity.

"You're very pretty," he says.

They remark this often when they have made up their minds to defer their action; it is part of the substantiation of their decision.

I could look like Medusa the Gorgon or Cruella De Vil or even the Wicked Witch of the West, it wouldn't matter. They all think I am beautiful when they have allowed themselves the gift of time.

"Thank you. You don't look too bad yourself."

He hesitates, "The... those tourists?"

"Yes? What about them?"

"I guess they asked me to take their picture because I am a man. It was strange how they didn't even look at you."

I chuckle, but not so that he may misconstrue my amusement as being directed at him: "No, they wouldn't. Cameras and me? Not good bedfellows. I have a kind of photographic memory. It's all I have ever needed."

My attention is drawn away down the bridge: a man has shuffled onto the *Dom Luis* from the Gaia side. He is dishevelled in appearance and his body is thin to the point of emaciation. Even at this distance I can tell his breath reeks of alcohol. His eyes stare as though he is oblivious of the world. That is my cue. He is a seeker after oblivion. He has come to the *Dom Luis* to find it.

The bridges are a tough environment in which to labour for one's salvation. Each month sees two souls leap from any one of the six which span the *Douro* in Porto. I should be grateful, I suppose, the Golden Gate witnesses up to thirty a year; the Brooklyn even more. Numbers like that are too much for one to handle. So, to watch all the bridges of Porto is all at once time consuming, rewarding and depressing.

But it is my choice.

"Now, I must be going," I say, looking deep into his amber eyes. "I may be up at the *Majestic Café* next week. Do you know it? It is in the *Santa Catarina*."

"Of course I know it. Who doesn't?"

"Perhaps I'll see you there."

He smiles. He has a nice smile. It is far too nice a smile for him to go depriving others of its warmth. I am glad.

"I'd like that," he replies.

A tram is exiting the *Sao Bento* and starting across the bridge. It moves steadily, silently, towards us.

I look down to the man who is stumbling along towards us.

I must go.

The tram is coming: 50, 40, 30 metres... I get ready.

"I don't know your name," he says.

"No, you haven't asked."

...20, 10 metres... I lean away from him.

"What is it, your name?"

...5, 4, 3 and—

"My name is *Consciência*." I step back.

The tram glides between us and I am gone, keeping pace with the tram until I am close enough to my next assignment to slow down and present myself.

I sidle up to him, the old new man.

This one, I recognise. He is Deprivation and Depression: two evils who grow more powerful in each other's company. For this one I must alter my appearance; older and wiser might be more appropriate and, perhaps, masculine.

"Evening, my friend."

"What do you want?" he responds, aggressively.

I glance back down the bridge. The young man is looking everywhere for me; not frantically as though his life depends on finding me, but calmly as though he would like me to have stayed a while longer.

But I cannot. For I am not only Conscience; I am Patience, too. I am both the Angel of Squandered Opportunity and the Angel of Hope. My duties are many, time is short and yet my day is never done.

MAURICE AND MIKE

Cannes, the Côte d'Azur, France

In the cool of the early morning the old man sits so still and for so long that I am sure he has frozen to death.

He looks to be fused to the bench, like one of those bronze statues I have seen in the coastal towns of Cataluña. Usually the statues are of old men rather like this man, who stares out to sea, waiting patiently for the fishing fleet to come in. Either that or they are sculptures of small dogs, tongues hanging down, watching the children play on the esplanade. I guess they're not made of bronze these days or someone would steal them.

Every half an hour or so the old boy must lose the feeling in his backside – he cannot be much more than a bag of bones, judging by the way his clothes hang on him – because he shifts his weight to alleviate some numbness. It isn't much of an adjustment, just a slight swaying; a gentle rocking from side to side, as though a wave has pitched hard against his boat and he is leaning to counteract the swell. And if a couple of tourists are standing near, or even sitting beside him on the bench, they will startle at his sudden motion and then giggle behind their hands at their own stupidity in mistaking him for a statue.

I think it is a game he plays, sitting still there like that and then moving. I think it amuses him, even though he never shows any sign of it.

From where our boat is moored, stern on to the dock, I can see the old boy come shuffling up the *Jetée Albert Édouard* between the *Casino*, the *Palais Club* and the *Vieux Port*. He wears a heavily creased and faded Panama suit and hat, and he holds his hands low and out front as though he has forgotten his belt and is permanently trying to hold his pants up with his forearms. His gait reminds me of that of a felon, hands tied, feet tethered.

I am the boat-boy, deckhand, book keeper, and caretaker of the Lord Jim for the summer. There must be worse things to do with your gap year than get paid to slum it in the high spots of the Côte d'Azur, but nothing comes easily to mind. My boss has gone — for now. He'll no doubt be back later in the summer, and so for the moment I am hostage to a twelve metre sports cruiser in the *Vieux Port*, Cannes. A hardship — it isn't.

I'm always up early washing the boat down, which is when I see him coming down the quai. I wave to him on occasion; not much more than a raise of my hand to touch my forehead, as I have seen some of the other port workers do. But, so far, my acknowledgement has drawn no response.

Most mornings I walk down to the public gardens by the *Hotel de Ville* and pick up a *Pan-Bagnat* for breakfast. I split the enormous, round sandwich in two and save the second half for lunch, and when I get back to the boat, the old boy is still there, sitting, watching. He stays until late morning and I never seem to be around when he leaves. He's just there one minute and gone the next.

Berthed beside us on the *basin à flot* — the wet dock — is a ketch, the *Tangaroa*. It looks a bit Jerry-built — as though it started out a bad idea and got worse — and Mike, the New Zealander who owns it and crews it, looks about the same. I wouldn't say the sailboat is untidy. That would be unkind. Accurate, but nevertheless unkind. Assorted scuba diving gear is draped haphazardly over the rails, and a splicing spike, parrel beads, whipping twine and rolls of tape are spread out on partially repaired sails. Mike sports sun-bleached, unruly hair and is, like his boat, a collection of sharp angles, a few of which combine to form a nose which has very evidently been broken on more than one occasion. He is slim, perhaps even a shade underfed and he flaunts a passion for mockney, or what he thinks of as cockney. Tonight we are going to the *Cercle des Marins* in the newer port of Canto at the eastern end of the bay. Apparently it's cheap and cheerful and exclusively for *nauticos*.

"Well, and the yachties like you and me, mate," or so Mike boldly proclaims.

I make a mental note to say *oué* instead of *oui* in the hope of sounding more native.

I've held back from joining in with the local yacht-crew's social excitements. Cannes can be cruelly expensive. But my own company and a succession of early nights are beginning to bore me, so I guess an evening out with Mike won't hurt.

———

Sadly, it does!

The mussels were delicious and the *Kronenburg* refreshing. But the *Pernod* was unnecessary, particularly the second bottle, and I have little recollection of when or how I must have staggered along the *Croisette* to get back to the boat. Surely I didn't manage it all on my own?

This morning I am awash with alcohol, and when I clean my teeth I feel giddy.

It is blazing hot on deck. The sun is arcing towards its zenith and the old boy is exactly where I would expect him. I open hatches and portholes, in an effort to disperse the cloud of aniseed, and grab a bottle of *Evian* out of the fridge. Perhaps the old boy won't mind some company?

I park myself clumsily beside him, observing a very necessary quarantine separation, and struggle with the plastic bottle top. There is little-to-no breeze and the surface of the water appears to be sprinkled with flakes of aluminium.

"*Une belle vue de la mer*," I offer for the want of anything more complex to construct.

He glances at me out of the corner of his eye. His face is lined, like his suit, and his bulbous nose suggests he is no stranger to liquor.

"It is the same view," he replies. His English carries only a vague trace of French.

His logic is unarguable and draws whatever wind I may have hoped was lying idle in my sail. I nod slowly.

"In the morning you pay the price for the night before," he says. Though his face betrays no emotion, his tone suggests he is amused at my abused state.

"Feels that way," I reply.

"*Cercle des Marins*, eh?"

"Mmm." I wonder how he knows it was there that I'd slipped disgracefully into a sea of *Pernod*.

"It is sometimes necessary to wash off the salt," he replies, as though his metaphor belies a deeper meaning. "Your friend, Mike, he likes to enjoy himself."

He doesn't say much more and our conversation, if it ever was such, dries up. The old boy is miserly with his words.

At midday, as usual, he disappears.

I take my troubled head for a stroll down town, keeping an eye out for the old man in case he merely vacates one bench in favour of another. I don't see him. I guess he's probably over in one of the other ports keeping up to date with all the scuttlebutt.

After the previous evening's excitement I'm not minded to revisit *Port Canto*, so I turn about at the end of the *Croisette* and head back to the boat.

When I get there, Mike is standing on the quay, wiping paint off his hands with a rag all too liberally dosed with thinners. The fumes are overpowering, and for a moment I have to fight to keep hold of my stomach.

"Clears more than the head, doesn't it?" He grins. "Ready for a hair of the dog?" he asks as he struggles into a collarless shirt which, like his face, is in need of ironing.

We walk round the harbour to the *quai Saint-Pierre*. The *Voile au Vent*, halfway along, would seem to be the local church for yacht crew. Early diners are picking their way through local fish and duck from Les Landes. I get the feeling I've swapped one boat for another as the interior is decked out like an old skiff: varnished planks and beams, and bits of tired sail and brass porthole-surrounds decorate the ceiling. The flank wall opposite the bar is painted with a full length landscape of the bay of Cannes from two hundred years before; *Cognac* and cigarettes have dulled its detail. There is a small huddle of yacht-crew at the bar. Some sport pin-sharp whites, others grease and caulking.

Mike is generous in his introduction, as are the assembled company in their welcome. I don't suppose a boat-boy from a Sealine Sports Cruiser ranks very high amongst the smart white-sock brigade, but they all display an appetite for my circumstance: where have I come up from, and when and where am I going next.

The evening flows by like the azure sea of which I feel I am now a part, and people come and go like small boats from the port beyond the glass doors.

A good few beers and a spread of seafaring tales later, a

brunette joins our company. She is shorter than the men in the group and most of them seem to know her, judging by the ease with which they accept her into their fold. She is wearing a floral patterned skirt and a plain cream blouse. She is pretty in a modest, school-principal sort of way and her eyes are deep pools of chocolate.

"Evening, Celeste," Mike says as he turns to order her a drink.

Celeste accepts a glass of *crème de menthe* with ice, but I don't get the sense there is any great familiarity or bond between them; she doesn't greet Mike with any noticeable affection.

She sips the green liqueur and turns to me. "I think we met briefly in the Cercle des Marins last evening," she says. There is a soft rounding to her pronunciation, but her French accent is otherwise pressed almost flat.

"How could I forget?" I ask. But I have!

We shake hands; hers is small and soft. Her lips are full, her cheek bones proud and her nose delicate. But it is her brown eyes and their gentle warmth that captivate me. The ready gift of her company is so empowering I quickly convince myself there is no one else in the bar she would rather talk to.

We make small talk. I confess to feeling like Conrad's Marlow, which is easy when I am living on a boat christened Lord Jim. I wax lyrically about how much I love the sharp air of dawn and how I believe that if I had to choose one part of the day in which to live, it would surely be that hour in which the sun first appears crimson above the horizon. I know I am running off at the mouth, but I am desperate to avoid even the slightest suspension of our conversation in case it results in my losing her attention.

"There's this old guy," I tell her. "He walks up the *quai* every morning, sits on the bench above the breakwater and watches the bay until midday. I've only been here a few days, but as far as I can make out, he follows the same routine every day."

Celeste raises an eyebrow: "On the *Jetée* by the *Palais?*"

I nod. "He wears a summer suit and a Panama hat. He just sits and watches the maritime world go by."

She doesn't respond, but her eyebrows furrow fractionally as if to say "so".

"Seems to know Mike," I say. "In fact, he seems to know everything that goes on in every harbour between here and Nice."

"Oh," she replies slowly, as though I am talking of someone everybody in the room already knows, "Maurice."

"I guess so," I reply, embarrassed at my ignorance.

Celeste falls quiet. The silence between us is awkward. She looks at the floor and then glances at Mike and the other men standing around her.

"Maurice is..." begins Mike.

But Celeste cuts him off: "He used to be a chef...on the yachts. A day chef, very much in demand; not a Michelin-starred chef, but very popular with many of the very wealthy yacht owners." She looks nervously around our assembled company as though she hopes her explanation will suffice.

"There was this yacht..." Mike prompts her again.

She is not pleased with Mike but, fortunately for me, not too displeased to carry on.

"There was a motor-yacht – one of the big new boats. Not like the Camper and Nicholson old-style motor-yachts, more sleek, like the Feadships. It was built in an Italian yard for a very high profile Saudi businessman. People say he was a fixer, a go-between, an intermediary: arms, aeroplanes, real estate, computers for defence systems, anything and everything, and on an international scale. Well, whatever he was, he had this boat, the *Jawhara* – the gem, named after his daughter. It was bigger than the biggest motor-yachts. Bigger even than King Khalid's *Al Riyadh*. It was like *Karina* and *Lac II* joined together. The motor-yacht had a helicopter landing pad, two made-to-measure Rivas for tenders, gold plate where there should be brass and silver plate where there would normally be chrome. But this yacht was too long to berth here or in Antibes or Beaulieu, so this Saudi, he enters into negotiations with the port authority to have a finger quai built in the *Vieux Port*." Celeste tries hard to focus on me; others in our group are leaning in on her. She takes a long sip of her drink and replaces her glass on the bar, forcing the group to stand back.

"In the meantime he has to anchor in the bay where it is not always calm. The authorities argue that his boat is too valuable to be berthed here, what with all the gold and silver plate on display. But the man argues that they have extended the *quai* in Port Canto especially for the *Karina*, so why not for his boat? The story goes that on board he has a priceless chess set, a gift from one of the Khans of Pakistan for some dark service. It is said the white pieces are fashioned from solid silver, the black pieces from solid gold, and all the pieces have hand-crafted, miniature heads. The rumour is that in the face of each head are set two precious stones for eyes: diamonds for the queens, sapphires for the kings, emeralds for the bishops, rubies for the knights and black opals for the castles. The authorities understand that this chess set will provoke an irresistible longing in the heart of every cat burglar on the Côte d'Azur." Celeste empties her glass and it is immediately refilled.

"Who knows," she says playfully, "perhaps a prize of this extraordinary magnitude will start a contest between the local cat burglars to see who would be the first to steal such a fabulous collection?"

Drinkers at the bar, noticing our group has gone quiet, quit their conversations and tune in to the pretty brunette's tale.

I am lost in her every word. *Peachey Carnehan* she is not: she is far more attractive. And the night outside is not *pitchy* black and there is no burning *loo* blowing and the constant hooting from passing cars provides a much livelier accompaniment than the hooting of night-jars. We are very definitely somewhere other than Lahore. We are in the *Voile au Vent*, on the *quai Saint-Pierre* in Cannes, the air is thick with garlic and *Gauloise*, and the bubbling melodies of an accordion drift in from the street. But, I suddenly see Mike as *Daniel Dravot*, a raffish exuberant, a man who would, given half the chance, marry a local girl and become king. And, just like Kipling, I am drawn to his light.

Celeste continues, "This man – the businessman, is selling military jets for the newly formed SNIAS, the company which is now Aerospatiale. But, what he doesn't tell them is that some of the jets he is selling are going to Algeria, which, as you can imagine after the war of independence that has brought down the Fourth Republic, does not please the government. When they find out, they tell him he is not welcome in the Côte d'Azur. But, this man thinks he is a bigger man than President Pompidou. Maybe he is? All things are possible." She pouts and shrugs. "But Pompidou is de Gaulle's puppet, and no one is bigger than de Gaulle."

We are all waiting to see where the old man who sits each day out on the rocks is going to fit into this tale when Celeste says: "Maurice is working on the *Jawhara* as a chef for a special occasion. On this evening, with many guests on board, there is a fire on the *Jawhara*. It spreads very fast and the guests have to jump into the water to escape. There is no time for lifejackets and the tenders are busy rescuing the guests and ferrying them to shore. The Captain, instead of beaching the boat, takes it out of the way, out to sea, out beyond the Îles de Lérins. But very quickly the *Jawhara* is consumed by the flames, a great heat that melts the boat like candle wax. Of course! It would! It is very combustible. It does not take very long before the boat breaks up and sinks.

"Fortunately no one is drowned or injured. The next day Maurice is fêted by the press, because in spite of the flames he went back on board the *Jawhara* to look for his young *sous-chef*. But the next day, happily, the sous-chef is found drunk in a bar in

Golfe Juan; he had swum ashore in the night." Celeste takes a quick sip of her *crème*.

"There then begins a long investigation into the cause of the fire. The insurance company suspect government agents have perpetrated this crime, but they cannot prove it. The press like to promote the story that the fire was started as a diversion for a burglar to steal the chess set. Others suggest the boat was not properly trialled, that the wrong materials were used in construction and that an electrical fault was to blame. And some people say it was because the cigars the man smoked were too large for his own good.

"After many months the Marine Accident Investigation Bureau concludes that the fire was an accident. The chef Maurice was cooking *Steak Diane* for the guests in the stateroom and unfortunately, between the pitching of the boat and the flaming of the steak, Maurice accidentally set light to the table cloth. This, the Bureau decides, was the combination of factors that led to the great fire that sank the *Jawhara*: Maurice, Steak Diane and the rough waters."

"Steak Diane? Maurice?" My voice sounds overloud against the quiet of those hunched around. "Sounds more like something the *Deuxième Bureau* would dream up!" I suggest, rather over-pleased with my knowledge of French literature.

"Yes," Celeste bridles, "I agree. It does sound like something from a Simenon novel, although they no longer call the Intelligence Service the *Deuxième Bureau*."

Mike is still grinning. There must be more to come.

"So what happened to Maurice?" I ask. "Surely he would never get work again?"

"It is true," Celeste says. There is a hint of both sadness and resignation in her tone. "Of course no one will hire a chef who is considered to be a liability – a chef who sets fire to a dining table is naturally discredited and impossible to insure." She raises an eyebrow and inclines her head, considering. "Or, who knows, perhaps this is not the case. Perhaps a chef like Maurice – one who it is whispered has committed a selfless act of bravery on behalf of his nation – can expect to be more in demand? Perhaps he is the first of a new kind of chef, a chef who enjoys a celebrity status. But it was towards the end of his career. It was not long before the time came for him to retire."

"And the chess set?"

Now Celeste rolls her eyes and scoffs. "Oh, it has never been found. No one has ever seen any of the pieces. Sometimes someone will say they heard someone else say that a jeweller somewhere has brought a piece of melted gold containing two precious stones and that it came from the *Jawhara*. But, the insurance company sent divers to the wreck and salvage companies also searched for this treasure. But they all came back with the same answer. The heat from the fire was so intense that nothing worth recovering was left: no gold taps or portholes, no silver chess pieces or hand rails. There is an exclusion zone around the wreck of the *Jawhara* now. The port authority in Nice has designated it a dangerous site; no divers are allowed near the wreck."

Mike is still grinning like a naughty schoolboy. "Don't we all just love a good buried treasure story," he says. "Makes all that foul water in the *Vieux Port* smell vaguely perfumed."

I check Celeste's fingers in case they are decorated with any precious gems.

She catches me looking and shakes her head. "So that," she says, "is why Maurice sits and watches the bay all day. He is thinking about the chess set that lies beneath the wreck of the *Jawhara. Voila! C'est fini!*" She laughs a little nervously.

The assembled company all thank Celeste for her tale. Some embrace her, some lean forward to kiss her politely: first her left cheek, then right, and then left again. The steady hubbub of conversation resumes and I can see one or two wondering if the denizens of the deep are still playing chess with a row of pawns that would fund their retirement.

By now, Celeste has been bought so many drinks the patron has poured them all into a much larger glass: a pack of small icebergs jostle in a broad, green sea.

"You're very good at telling stories."

"I get all the practice I need," she replies, and when I rather obviously don't understand why, she continues, "I am a school teacher at the *école élémentaire* on the other side of the *Carnot*. My children are mostly between nine and eleven years. The ability to tell stories is a *condition* for school teachers, is it not? And," she winks, "good for children of all ages, eh."

"And your English?"

"One has to teach something," she replies, deadpan.

I get the feeling Celeste is not comfortable talking about herself, so I change tack. "Mike's quite a character."

"You could say that," she replies as though I don't know the half of it. "How old are you, kid?"

Suddenly I'm struggling. I'm taken with the idea that I should lie, say I'm older. I don't know why, as I am under the impression that the age difference in affairs of the heart doesn't matter in France. But, being a school teacher, Celeste will almost certainly guess my age correctly. I colour at my hesitation.

The delayed effects of the night before, not to mention the accumulation of the evening's beers, begin to take their toll. My compass goes a little haywire and my gyro seems curiously out of kilter.

When I return from my voyage to the incommodious commode out the back of the bar, Celeste is deep in conversation with a *plaisancier*. I've learned to spot the weekend yachtsmen. They wear striped sweaters and matelot's caps, their skin is pale and their nails are clean. It's not just the depth of the *seasonnaires* suntan or the tar beneath their nails that marks them out, there's a studied insouciance to the way they hold themselves, a bit like the seagulls that strut about the *quai*.

The evening kind of freewheels along. It's all too easy to wallow in the calm yet heady atmosphere of the bar. The world outside is irrelevant, so far away, and I am happy to imagine that later I might walk Celeste home.

As luck would have it, it happens — but not in the way I was hoping. Mike points me at the door and once outside I tack round the harbour on a rising tide of Belgian beer. Celeste glides close on my port beam — the road side, and Mike cruises along to starboard — the port side. The idiosyncrasy of my observation amuses me, but my escorts do not share in my humour and their bemused expressions cause me to giggle all the more.

This is pretty much how the rest of the summer goes.

Whenever I'm back in the *Vieux Port*, Mike and I go out and paint the town our own distinctive shade of salmon pink. More often than not, Celeste tags along, and though I suspect there is something going on between them, I never witness any intimacy. Mike is a bit of a cove when it comes to women and public displays of affection, I learn, are not his style.

On my days off he teaches me to scuba dive. We borrow an inflatable and whine our way out to the Île Sainte-Marguerite, where the man in the iron mask was supposed to have been imprisoned. It takes me a while to get the hang of clearing the water out of my mask and I am too fascinated by the flat, silver discs of air floating up to the surface to pay proper attention — or so Mike insists on telling me. One time I ask him to show me where the *Jawhara* went down, but he just grins in that *Daniel Dravot*, exuberant sort of way and steers our little boat into a tall wave.

I slip up to the breakwater when I can to chat to the old boy, Maurice. He never misses a morning, except when the *Mistral* blows that is. He teaches me to recognise the sharp air that heralds its arrival, and he helps me to realise the value in sitting and watching the world whir by.

September comes too soon and three years of reading English at university beckon. Mike and Celeste see to it that my departure is properly celebrated in the *Voile au Vent*.

On the last morning and with my last dull head of the summer, I make sure I am up on the breakwater waiting for Maurice to come shuffling up the *Jetée*. I try to burn the image in my head.

We say nothing at first. We just sit and watch the seagulls reel in the breeze. I want to ask him about the *Jawhara*. I've wanted to for some time, but somehow felt that it is the one question he's been waiting for me to ask, so I haven't — until now.

"Celeste said..."

"Yes?" he interrupts.

I see the crow's feet deep at the corners of his eyes, the creases and crumples in his summer suit, and the loosening straw in his hat. "Celeste said..." I start again.

But this time, too, he interrupts me and says, "Celeste tells me you are leaving today. If she says this, it must be true."

I turn his words over in my head: "*If she says this, it must be true.*" I have learnt that Maurice is very selective in his choice of words. He speaks rarely and when he does whatever he says is usually intended to shepherd me towards the conclusion of our conversation.

"Celeste is your daughter?" I ask.

A horn hoots behind me; the taxi is waiting to take me to the airport in Nice.

Maurice turns towards me and winks. And the way he winks, so slowly and with such a flourish, suggests he is embracing me, taking me right into his being, letting me know I am now his friend and will be for all time.

Being so touched with his display of affection, I do not notice that he has smuggled something out of his pocket. He glances down and my eyes follow his.

Maurice chuckles and opens his hand. In his palm lies a smooth cylindrical lump of gold, a long nugget wider at one end, and shaped like and no bigger than my middle finger. In the top of it are set two large white diamonds which sparkle beneath the azure sky.

He chuckles so much his laughing makes him cough.

———————

That was a good few years ago, and I am sure the ease of my existence was not as comfortable then as my memory now likes to suggest. A year or so after I left, I received a letter from Mike. He married Celeste and set up his own mobile chandlery business – I guess I know where he got his start-up funds from. In the letter he also told me that Maurice died not long after I left, but that an anonymous organisation commissioned a bronze statue of Maurice, wearing his trademark Panama suit and hat, sitting on his favourite bench, looking out towards the Îles de Lérins. He was, after all, a fundamental element of the *Vieux Port* and, supposedly, a courageous and loyal patriot too.

I looked up the *Vieux Port* on Google recently and navigated the little gold figure around the *quai Saint-Pierre*. The big boats have all gone to the new harbour in Antibes and the *Voile au Vent* is now an Irish bar. At the end of the *Jetée Albert Édouard* the bench is still there, but Maurice is no longer in residence. I can only imagine that someone has stolen him.

The Longcase

London, England

A young man is invited to dinner, at the last minute and alone.

His presence has been much in demand over recent weeks, so much so that a couple of invitations he has had to decline: that warms him. He has always remained reasonably popular, but over the years he has grown to understand that his popularity depends on a number of factors, the most important of these being whether he is or isn't in a relationship.

At the moment, Lucas occupies that curious no-man's land of being between partners; a geographical *heimat*, or homeland as you might call it – one whose male citizens are entitled to a passport permitting them access to social events often off-limits to married or partnered men. He is, in short, a spare pair of trousers; that rarest of dinner guests who can be summoned at the eleventh hour to sit next to the friend whose husband has recently run off with – well, in this case the barman from the local cocktail bar for example.

This dinner party is happening in Hasker Street, Chelsea, a

stone's throw from Harrods and round the corner from the John Lewis depository. The house is one of those ludicrously expensive, Cadogan estate terraced properties that are all stairs and cupboard rooms. There are eight of them seated round the Regency dining table in the kitchen-basement and the hostess is, because Lucas is spare, flirting with him.

He often finds himself ill at ease with such a socially sophisticated set, but on this occasion he could find no good reason to pass up the invite and, secretly, he finds the hostess' attentions diverting. And yet... and yet her behaviour is pretty much par for the course for the bored *hausfrau* who throws a midweek dinner party in order to drag some much needed colour into her life.

The woman for whom he has been imported to play consort, perches opposite him. She doesn't like him; that much is obvious. That she has only just met him is irrelevant, but he represents the available male brought in, in emergency, to accompany the suddenly single woman; an act committed purely out of pity and one which is, to the beneficiary because it can only be interpreted as patronising, deplorable and therefore to be resented.

Robyn twitches like an irritable blackbird, her concentration flitting from one conversation to the other, as though she is nervous of missing some scrap of gossip that might have a bearing on the folly of her spouse's rejection. Lucas' oblique and subtle humour is carefully designed to calm and reassure her that even though she has been tossed aside in favour of some more attractive morsel, she is still worthy of his attention. But Robyn's wound is not yet sufficiently healed for her to appreciate such subtlety.

The hostess however, the aptly named Apple, a luscious and voluptuous woman with rounded, rosy cheeks, has spotted this and in an effort to persuade Lucas that his evening will not be wasted, is making eyes at him and playing footsie under the table.

The assembled eight are discussing *feng shui*, two words none of them can agree on how to pronounce. They look to Lucas for some kind of arbitration, but–

"Sorry, I wasn't in on that. What was the question?"

Apple's husband, Giovanni – an hotelier from the Amalfi Coast – is pointing to the longcase clock which towers imperiously over them: "This magnificent timepiece should stand on the landing, not here in the kitchen, don't you agree, Lucas?"

The grandfather clock stands tall and proud and seemingly aloof, like an offended butler, and in spite of its height there is still an inch of clearance below the low ceiling.

"That depends," he replies and returns his attention to his fillet of bass, playing for time.

"It should most definitely be on the landing," Giovanni maintains, asserting his authority. "That is where a clock of this size should be. It is too big – has too much presence for the kitchen. It is like being spied on by one of her elderly relations, eh." He hurls his pronouncement down the table as though he has discovered a bone in his fillet.

Apple scoffs, "And where, if you have your way, Gio, are the girls supposed to put all their hockey kit when they come back late? And besides, my old friend would stand like a lonely sentry on the landing and the only time you'd see him would be as you passed him on your way out the door. I'm the one who needs the company of my elderly relations, as you put it: you're never here, except to eat whatever it is I've spent my day, alone, preparing." She blows her husband a kiss so that the assembled company will be reassured she is merely poking fun at him.

But it is a poke with barbs, or so Lucas is inclined to believe. As he knows to his cost, the difficulty with playing the role of a spare pair of trousers is that some women are wont to use single, male dinner guests as a fulcrum on which to lever a separation between themselves and their husbands. It is the bachelor's inescapable lot. Lucas assumes the mantel of housewife's choice, a passing preference to a husband and a garish illustration of what the wife would like the husband to become: adoring and faithful, like a puppy, but without both the constant need for walkies and the covering of sofas in hair. It is an often dangerous, if not occasionally lethal, game into which Lucas is being drawn.

He glances up at the longcase clock, but the four cherubs at the spandrels play dumb to his entreaty. They recognise him and are happy, for the moment, to ignore him.

"But it doesn't belong here," the host insists as if he is the only one with 20x20 vision and taste to match.

Lucas knows the clock has been left to Apple by her recently deceased father. Following an unsavoury row with her siblings regarding his estate, the longcase clock is all she is left with to remember him by. Well, the clock and a few million!

Robyn pipes up, "I agree with Giovanni. It upsets the balance of the room." She hopes to curry some sympathy with her Italianate host, thereby making herself look more attractive in his eyes and by so doing improve her chances of gaining the affirmation she so desperately needs from a male — any male except perhaps Lucas. Affirmation comes so much better from a married man. They are not so prone to dishonesty, or so she mistakenly believes; whereas a bachelor may come at her with ulterior, if not sordid, motives.

She is staring intently at Lucas, daring him to disagree in front of so many.

The silence extends. He is not fool enough to respond.

"I shouldn't argue about grandfather clocks while Lucas is around, darling," Apple states, leaping to his defence. "He knows more about antique timepieces than Chronos."

"How so?" Robyn chips in quickly.

"Yes," Giovanni adds, "do tell us how you have such profound knowledge of these things, Lucas."

All eyes are upon him now. The other dinner guests have stubbed out their cigarettes and put down their wine glasses.

"My father," he begins, "as some of you may remember, had an antiques shop on Ebury Street—"

"Same place Lucas has his now," Apple interrupts.

"My father was originally a clock repairer: carriage clocks, longcase clocks, atmospheric and regulator clocks, all types. If a clock was broken, he could fix it. And of an evening I used to watch him — please excuse the pun," but no one picks up on it, "in the workshop downstairs. Over the years, I got to learn the difference between an eight-day clock and a thirty-hour clock—"

"Which is?" Robyn chips in, again.

Lucas pauses, all too aware that now that Apple has sounded his trumpet, there is little more he can do than validate her confidence in him.

He looks very directly at Robyn the Inquisitor.

"Well, a thirty hour-clock usually has a single weight which works both the time and strike mechanisms, and is one which needs to be wound once a day. An eight-day clock, on the other hand, usually has two weights, either of which works the mechanisms individually, so it has two respective keyholes, one for each mechanism which requires winding. These need only be wound every eighth day, or weekly, if you like. They're both, more often than not, cable clocks, whereby they suspend a weight which, as it falls, powers the clock. But there are cable clocks which one winds with a key and others where one pulls on a chain to raise the weight. They're all longcase clocks, so named because they require the length of the case for the pendulum, the seconds pendulum as it is known, to oscillate freely."

James, an avuncular man wearing a jacket more suited to deer stalking than dinner and sitting with the upright military repose of an ex-Guards officer, has passed much of the evening espousing the virtues of the United Kingdom Independence Party. He doubly punctuates Lucas' diatribe by adding, "And all the best of British. Nothing as British as a grandfather clock, eh?"

Apple sniggers into her serviette.

"That's true enough," Lucas agrees, pleasantly, sitting forward to direct his reply. "But the French make them too. They generally call them Comtoise clocks, and the Swedish and Danish call them Mora and Bornholm clocks, named so after where they were made."

However, James-not-Jim, which is how he is known, is not to be cowed. Like the trenchant, political animal that he is, he too leans forward: "But we invented them, didn't we! The grandfather clock: British as boiled beef and carrots."

Apple pales at the idea that she may have cooked an unsuitable meal for such bourgeois palates.

Lucas, however, rises to the bait: "Well, James, as far as we know, Christiaan Huygens, a Dutchman, invented the pendulum clock around the middle of the seventeenth century and some think that either Robert Hook or Richard Harris was responsible for the first of the longcase clocks in Britain. But I would argue that Ahasueras Fromanteel produced the first in London at about the same time as Huygens invented them. Doesn't sound very British, does it, Ahasueras Fromanteel?"

"No," James-not-Jim replies, "it doesn't. Sounds more Flemish. 'Nother bloody immigrant, I suppose." The stale breath of exasperation is exhaled round the table.

"And you'd be wrong." Lucas sits a shade more forward again, his movement designed to draw the attention of the assembled company. "And yet you'd be correct in a way. His parents were Flemish. But, Fromanteel was born in Norwich and had a shop in Southwark. I think that makes him rather British, especially in the 17th century, don't you?"

James-not-Jim chews his moustache. His wife smiles. Apple nudges Lucas gently under the table.

He has, he considers while the rest brood in silence, absolutely no objection to having to sing for his supper as far as his rather birdlike dinner partner goes, but he feels under no such restraint when it comes to the rest, all of whom he considers to be fair game.

Robyn, though, is piqued that he should, whether intentionally or otherwise, belittle the bastion of Little England and continues to peck away at him.

"If you know so much about clocks, Lucas, what can you tell us about Big Ben over here?" She points over her shoulder at Apple's grand inheritance.

"Not much from this range." Although the Regency table is not broad, Lucas pretends his eyesight is not up to in-depth scrutiny from where he sits.

"Oh, come on," she nips at him, "I'm sure you'll be able to beguile us with your knowledge. Come on, indulge us, please."

"Yes, come on, Lucas," James-not-Jim goads.

He smiles, glances at Apple and sits back in an attempt to gain a little perspective from the clock. Lucas narrows his eyes.

"Well, judging by the rise of the hood, the overhanging cornice, the barleytwist columns and the Corinthian capitals, I'd say it is late seventeenth century. It's clearly an eight-day clock as it has two keyholes, although you do find some thirty-hour clocks which have had false holes added: some owners liked their guests to think they were wealthy enough to afford an eight-day model rather than the slightly cheaper thirty-hour clock." He sips his wine; his audience is rapt and rewarded that Apple has the more expensive antiquity.

"Then it has rather jolly, winged cherubs in the spandrels – the space in the four corners around the dial. The dial itself is brass, as most of them were, and shows a Roman chapter ring, half-hour marks and a supplementary seconds dial. Beyond that, the maker's name is probably engraved in some script or other along the lower edge. From where I'm sitting I can't tell you much more than that."

This time, the breath being exhaled around the table is fresh with admiration.

James-not-Jim's wife says, "That's wonderful, Lucas. Apple is right; you are a considerable font of knowledge. I, for one, had no idea they were so complex and so individual. Thank you."

Robyn, not wishing to be confused with the company of the awe-struck, pipes up, "I get the feeling you're hiding your light under a bushel, Lucas. Surely, you can tell us who the maker was. What about the wood panels, aren't they particular?"

He returns his attention to the long trunk door.

"Well, the panels are what one calls bookmatched, which means they are a veneer of two types of wood, probably oak and," he hesitates, narrowing his eyes once more, "some other type of wood, could be apple or pear. But these types of wood were the most commonly used in the seventeenth century. It was only later that the makers began to use mahogany, for obvious reasons."

"Don't see why that's so obvious," she snaps, as though he has just implied his audience is dim.

"I, er, well—"

Fortunately, James-not-Jim takes pity on them both: Lucas for not having to, painfully, point out what he thinks should be obvious, and Robyn for not having to suffer the consequences of being informed the same. And now that Lucas has nailed the bright colours of his knowledge to the mast, James-not-Jim about-faces and steps neatly in line behind him, deciding to throw his lot in with the talking encyclopaedia of the hour glass — longcase clocks being English or otherwise.

He leans forward to address Robyn, who sits at the same side of the table as he: "My dear, mahogany wasn't imported into England until the 1700s. In those days the Bahamas and Jamaica were the only British controlled territories where mahogany was grown."

Lucas glances at James-not-Jim in appreciation.

Robyn says, "Trust you to know all about wood, James. Still, I suppose you ought to, owning half the bloody woodland in Wales." And as if to alleviate her embarrassment, she fixes her evil eye back to her dinner partner. "So, who made it then? Come on, Lucas, let's have an educated guess?"

"Ah," cuts in James-not-Jim, "I predict a wager. Let's see, what will you wager? Port? A bottle of Port wine seems reasonable to me."

Apple, though, has a better idea: "Oh James, speaking strictly for myself I don't like Port. It always makes me feel so sleepy. And besides, shouldn't it be up to Lucas and Robyn to decide? After all, one of them will lose and have to surrender the wager."

Robyn scoffs, "Well, if Lucas can guess who made your grandfather clock from where he's sitting, I'll eat my hat."

Lucas allows the silence to hang for a second or two. Again all eyes are on him.

"I tell you what, Robyn, if I can make an educated guess as to who made this delightful piece of our glorious horological history and guess it right, then I get to give you a lift home. How about that?"

Some nod; others smile. Now that an element of spice has been added to the proceedings those around the table take an even keener interest in the result.

Robyn, much to his surprise, smiles. "And if you're wrong?"

James-not-Jim, grinning like an idiot, offers, "In that unlikely event, Lucas here has to pay for your taxi home and send you a bunch of flowers in the morning. Deal?"

He hesitates, knowing that if he agrees too readily, Robyn will draw from his rapid response that she is coming too cheap.

"Perfect." She leans forward and extends her hand across the table towards him.

Lucas, reluctantly, shakes her hand.

"Come on, then," she follows up quickly.

He demurs, "Don't I get the chance to think about it for a while?" Lucas looks at her across the table and very slowly raises his gaze up at the clock.

"Uh, no peeking."

"I mean, it could be any number of makers: Thomas Tompion, Daniel Quare, Johannes Fromanteel, Edward East. They all made very similar timepieces." He looks up and studies the face of the tall clock.

"I said," Robyn reminds him, grinning at his apparent unease, "no peeking."

"It would be a guess, not much more." He winces and sucks his cheek. "Hard to say."

"Come on, Lucas, don't be coy."

He studies his dinner partner and wonders if he really wants to pay the price of her company all the way home. He lives in Putney; she in Fulham, at least it would be on his way. And the strangest thing is that since she has begun to smile at his discomfort, Robyn has begun to look vaguely human and, as such, far more approachable. But, he reminds himself, it is early days; the sheets of her matrimonial cot will still hold her husband's warmth.

He sighs, surrendering to her insistence. "Edward East, I should think."

Robyn leaps up from her chair, spins round and steps over to the grandfather clock. She has to stand on tip-toe to read the cursive script engraved along the lower edge of the face.

She freezes, "Oh my god! He's right. He's only bloody right. It reads *Eduardus East Londini*," and turns round, her expression a mixture of bemusement, embarrassment and approval.

The diners clap. Lucas colours.

"Well done, Lucas. Knew you could do it," James-not-Jim says, winking slightly lecherously.

"I think after that little drama we could all do with some desert." Apple pats him gently on the shoulder and whispers "Very nice, Lucas. Good boy," in his ear as she rises from the table.

Robyn sits back down, holds his gaze for a few seconds and

then, confusingly, raises her eyebrows at him. "I'll have to think up some more difficult questions for you for the way home, won't I?"

The evening cruises through a sea of Kirsch and Armagnac, and James-not-Jim shrouds the table in cigar smoke. Places are changed and, much to his surprise, Robyn battles for the seat Apple vacates.

"Is it valuable, her clock?" she asks, inclining her head towards it.

"Depends," he replies, mischievously. Now that he has her attention, Lucas decides to make her pay for having been off-hand with him through the early part of the evening.

"On what?" She has cool blue eyes, lips that are a little on the thin side, but not necessarily mean, and her hair is very black; jet black, in fact, and without the slightest trace of grey.

"On the originality of the movement."

She giggles and bites her lip in what he perceives to be a calculated tease. "The movement, huh? How could that not be original."

"Well, the working parts behind the dial — what is called the movement—sometimes get removed and replaced with unoriginal parts. Sometimes it's because they break and need repairing, and sometimes it's because the clock itself is not original and someone is trying to make it look original. The marquetry is not so difficult to reproduce, but the striking barrels, the bell stands, the anchor escapement, the bolt, shutter and brass crutch are not so easy. One often finds at auction a longcase clock which is reputed to be seventeenth century, but is in effect nineteenth century dressed up; faked if you like, to look older. The difference in worth can be profound."

"Brass crutch, eh," Robyn giggles again. She sips her liqueur and lowers her head so that she looks, provocatively, up at him.

"Who'd want one of those?" she asks. But, realising that others around the table are watching her, she reigns herself back from the emancipation lent her by her third glass of Kirsch. "What's a grandfather clock like Apple's worth?"

It is a question that has been troubling Lucas. "Oh, could be anywhere between £20 and a £100,000. It simply depends on the originality."

"Worth a small fortune," Apple shouts, from down the table. "Which reminds me, darling, I need you to drop by and value it for me... for insurance."

The evening slips gently into the wee small hours.

James-not-Jim gives Lucas a hearty slap on the back as they are leaving. "Knew you would guess correctly. If the prize is big enough, the motivation to guess correctly will drive one to the proper conclusion."

Lucas smiles, dishonestly. He is not convinced his prize will turn out to be anything other than a poisoned chalice dressed by L.K. Bennett.

And Apple nuzzles his neck for far too long. "You must come round more often, Lucas. Don't be such a stranger, mm? Remember I need you to give me a valuation sometime soon."

Robyn falls asleep as soon as they turn into the Fulham Road and he is left alone with his thoughts.

Lucas remembers Apple's clock from his father's workshop, thirty years before: a wood-wormed hulk of oak and walnut leaning in a corner; movement plates, suspension springs, blocks, clutch assemblies and support arms all laid out on the workbench; the hour hand missing, the time-wind seized solid and the dial rusted and pitted.

"What can you do with that piece of junk, dad?" he had asked.

His father had stood back from the bench, scratched his stubbly chin and smiled at the young Lucas, "Don't you worry son, we'll have this back up and running in no time. We'll have it looking so fine, even Edward East would have been proud to show it in his shop window in Fleet Street."

"But what about all the broken bits, dad?"

"No matter, Lucas, my boy. I'll find some new ones. No one will know the difference and I won't tell them, if you don't."

GENEVA

Switzerland

Some days are unremarkable. They slide by like driftwood on a broad river and when the light fades I realise they have floated far away, out of sight.

The details of these days are consigned to a file labelled *Not Worth Revisiting*; a file which is subsequently lodged somewhere deep in the cabinet of my memory. Partly, this is because most days follow such a rigid routine that, although they are statistically relevant in their addition, they are consciously irrelevant in their passing. And partly, this is because my mind chooses to retain access only to those days on which something *Worth Revisiting* happens. In this way, my recollections of that happening remain rapid and clear and convenient.

Most days, so many files pass across my desk that even the people to whom the many files belong become unremarkable; they too drift by me, drifting on down to be lost in the crystal clear waters of the great lake that lies just a few minute's walk from my office.

And yet, there are other days.

I sit patiently in the airport concourse and wait for the London flight to be called. When the not unexpected announcement comes that the flight is delayed, I stroll through to the restaurant. The menu promises scallops with endive, a tournedos of guinea fowl or spinach risotto, and a chocolate fondant with raspberries. I like the sound of the fondant; it has been a long week and when I am tired my sweet tooth often gets the better of me. But I have always found food and flying uneasy bedfellows and the yellow windsock out on the runway betrays the stiff breeze funnelling down through the valley between the *Jura* and the Alps.

Pre-flight nerves whisper in my ear that I should surely be better off back in the *Rue de Monbrillant*, sitting in the warm, sifting through yet another batch of archives.

I glance at the wind sock once more. It lies straight out, horizontal with the tarmac, its tail pointing west. My stomach contracts, and the reward offered by the fondant loses its appeal.

Back in the concourse I resolve to make use of the waiting time; I have several papers to read before returning on Monday. The first is a retrospective on the handling of *Displaced Polish Nationals* and the second is a paper entitled simply *Hei Haizi*: a study outlining the difficulties faced by the growing number of Chinese second children not registered at birth due to the fines levied under the One Child System. I am aware that I am painfully ill-equipped to assimilate the sheer number of people who live under a regime callous enough not to recognise their citizens' existence. A vision of eight million people lined up outside my office leaps into my mind and, though I know I cannot deny them their right to apply for my assistance, I pale at the thought of even a small percentage of them turning up at the agency.

So I choose the less demanding option: the retrospective on how my predecessors established *who* belonged *where* in the confusion that followed the Second World War. It explains how so many of those displaced by the war were unwilling to return to the country of their birth, divided up and subsumed as it was by a victorious and increasingly authoritarian Soviet State. Some of the text in the document reminds me of old news-reader-speak; a haughty, clipped staccato of sentences, a language redolent of an era when people's hopes were trodden underfoot like so much gravel on a path.

A few pages later, I shift irritably when I sense a figure orbiting my space.

The minutes pass and I read on. But slowly, inexorably, almost in the way that dawn arrives, I become aware of a new presence nearby.

Then, suddenly, like the dawn, he is there and I can no longer ignore him.

"Excuse me," he says. "Is it history papers you are reading? Or is it law papers?" His pronunciation is middle-eastern and halting, as though he is unsure of his word order.

"In a way both," I reply politely. "But, in essence, history."

His head is round, his hair close cropped and grey, and his skin a mottled olive. And his eyes are thin and a little calculating, but measuring not devious. "Is difficult," he asks, "history? What history is this?"

"Poland," I reply again, expecting him to counter with another question — it is usually the way when strangers bother me. I don't want him to think me bad mannered for not wanting to talk with him and I am considering whether I welcome his diversion, hence my pause. I have time on my hands, but just how much of it he believes my good manners will spare him is quite another matter. He is in no way intimidating or threatening, sitting where he is a couple of seats down, and he has approached the boundary of my bubble courteously, almost reverently, and is now requesting to be granted access to it. There appears no danger in passing a few minutes chatting to a fellow traveller in the airport terminal.

However, I cannot help but harbour a slight, niggling irritation at his unsolicited intrusion. And yet, and perhaps more importantly, I sense no harm in him.

When he doesn't come back at me straight away, I hesitate and so stumble into the hollow I have scooped with my pause. "It... it concerns Poland after the Second World War," I say. "Actually it's more concerned with the Polish people."

"You know the ghatto?" he asks.

"You mean ghetto?" I correct him, perhaps a little too quickly.

"Yes. That is it; ghetto. You know in the ghetto in Warsaw, you know how many people were in the ghetto at the beginning of the war?"

"Something over five hundred thousand, I think." I trawl my memory for the estimate quoted at the beginning of the paper.

"You know, some of the Jewish people were working for the Nazis in the ghetto?"

I turn and weigh him up quickly. He doesn't possess any luggage, or at least nothing of sufficient capacity in which to conceal a bomb, and his torso is lean, clearly not swelled by any explosive waistcoat. But besides that, he exudes casual acceptance, not zealous intention. There is something of the Armenian about him, like a relative of the singer Aznavour.

"Well," I choose my words carefully. "It is true that in the camps they had their *Sonderkommando* and in the ghetto there were Jewish Police. But that doesn't make them extraordinary. The Slovaks had the same. And the *Waffen SS* had French and Russian units."

A grainy, black and white photograph from a history book flashes up on the screen in my head: a middle-aged man, well groomed and attractive but for a livid scar curving across his right cheek. I look for the legend at the foot of the photograph; it is the method by which I have learned to remember the names of faces. Joyce. His name was Joyce, William Joyce. Most people remember him as Lord Haw-

Haw, an Irish-American who broadcast propaganda for the Nazis and who was hanged in Wandsworth prison after the war. And yet, even in America the plague of Nazism drew widespread support from Fritz Kuhn and his *German-American Bund,* and in Britain, Oswald Mosley's *British Union of Fascists* wore black shirts and saluted the same Führer. For their sins, Kuhn spent the war in Sing Sing and Mosley in Holloway Prison. I am reminded of the unpalatable truth that every race has its renegades.

"But, this history you are reading, who has written it?"

"It's a work paper collated by a number of people, mostly Americans I should think, some British, but—"

"Ah!" he interrupts. "Yes, by Americans. You see everything depend on who is writing history and—"

"But this paper," it is my turn to interrupt, "isn't so much about that side of the war. It concerns the Poles who were displaced during the war and how, at the end of it, so many of them required repatriation. None of the major powers come out of it very well; neither the Americans, the British, and certainly not for that matter the Russians."

My criticism of the major powers encourages him. "Please, I think you must mean these people were deported back to their countries?" His accusation, or so the papers in my hand bear out, is well-founded.

"Deported. Repatriated." He pores over the words as though they are both foreign and potentially distasteful liqueurs. His eyes narrow briefly. "These words have similar and yet very different meanings, do they not?"

He possesses an easy charm, disarming perhaps because of his self-depreciative smile, and he reminds me of a stallholder in a bazaar who, knowing he is asking a price wide of the mark, takes it for granted that he will have to barter to make his sale. He is smartly dressed in rather dated, neutral Swiss colours. His trousers hang a little limp on his waist, his worsted jacket looks to be slowly digesting him, and his brown brogues are tidy, if a little past their prime.

"Surely, many of these people did not want to return?" he asks.

I think again about rising and walking away – I am, after all, supposed to be apolitical in my views.

But, I don't.

"You know Shakespeare?"

"Not personally," I jest and immediately regret my patronising humour. However, I realise I have now opened wider the door to conversation.

"You understand," he follows on quickly, "Shakespeare could only write because he was protected by your queen; your queen who watches over all her people."

My mind begins to swim. "I'm not certain he was that controversial."

"And Milton too," he says. "I prefer Milton."

So we sit and talk about the relative merits of Shakespeare and Milton, even though I am not on firm ground with either. Shakespeare, I propose, wrote plays that entertain and nourish the mind. Milton, on the other hand, wrote more for the intellectual spirit.

Shakespeare, he counters, was a great showman, a dramatist. He wrote about humanity, sex, power. Milton, he argues, questioned our attitude to liberty and how we should protect it. As the conversation grows I feel particularly naked in front of this Middle-Eastern man who clearly knows a great deal more about English literature than I do.

Time passes like cooling lava, as it does in an airport concourse, and I glaze over. He talks calmly, yet with some passion for his subject. There is no doubt in my mind he has put his case before; the words come readily to him and his pitch and tone rise and fall with an almost orchestral cadence.

Then I come to, hauled from my woolgathering by the woman opposite coughing.

"I am writing my life story, but it is very difficult," he is saying. "I find English not so difficult to read, but to write... There is some part I have trouble with. Would you look for me? Perhaps correct for me?"

I bridle inside. The departure board lends me no relief.

He catches me looking up. "You are taking plane to England?"

"Yes."

"You live in England?"

"Some of the time in England, some of the time here." I fold my arms across my chest and hope he will pick up on my body language.

He smiles, nods and looks at the floor for a few seconds. His gesture is perhaps a touch too overt, perhaps a shade theatrical. It risks being interpreted as an act of contrition rather than the gracious apology I think he intends it to be.

"I am waiting for friend," he says in exchange. He studies the arrivals board briefly and then produces from the ether a bulging, grey file, which he hands to me so quickly I can't avoid taking it. "See, here..."

I open it carefully. Inside are two hundred or so pages of lined scribble, not all in an identical hand and not all on the same paper. There are small paragraphs, markings in the margin, postscripts, crossings out, corrections, and all in a great variety of pen and colour. There are texts of every nature, some wandering and nonsensical, and yet most considered and well constructed. I read for a while – for too long! Gradually I realise that he is smiling in that way again; that sort of appreciative way, as though he is gaining a fundamental pleasure from my reading his manuscript.

Though I fight it, I find the urge to keep reading irresistible.

He has come to Switzerland as a refugee from Iran; not in flight from the Shah, but from the Ayatollah Khomeini. He was brought to Geneva by a wealthy Lebanese businessman expelled from Iran after the overthrow of the old regime, but his patron has since died. He has a small flat in *Meyrin* – the high rise district behind the airport. There are worse areas; areas the Swiss don't like you to see. He scratches a meagre existence sweeping and cleaning and running errands for local shopkeepers. There is a black man, a neighbour, who plays music loudly all night and who throws stones at his window and bangs on his door and drunkenly rages at him through his letterbox. He is convinced the man is trying to drive him away. But, where should he go?

He moves to the seat beside me, deftly works through the file and pulls out a sheet covered in Pidgin English. Some words are written backwards, some misspelt, and there is no apparent attempt at any structure, grammar or syntax. "You see here," he points. "What I am trying to say is that during revolution, during time of trouble, everyone friend; people like brothers."

I study the text again, slowly trying to draw a common thread from it.

"But, that happy time not last for long. Soon as revolution is over, everyone hate everyone again." He pauses. "You remember Reza Pahlavi?"

"You mean the Shah of Iran?"

"Very good!" He beams at me as though I am his favourite pupil, "Yes, Shah. You know *Savak*?"

"The Shah's secret police?"

He beams again. "Yes. Exactly. Secret police. Well, everyone hate secret police. They do bad things for Shah and for Americans. So people get them out and Shah, he goes too. People are happy. But then we have Ayatollah, and he has religious police."

"*Baseji*? Or is it *Paseji*?" I recall.

"Very good! Yes." His grin grows broader and I am pleased to be getting stars all over my work. "So, when Shah goes, I think life will be good. We will be able to do what we are born to do. When

118

people all believe in same thing, then people are friends. But after, when revolution is over, people have to live in a way they are not born to live. They have to live same way they live before, just like when Shah is boss. So, I come here." There is a pale bitterness, an overwhelming sadness, in his voice and I sense his thoughts have turned to a country on a different continent; a homeland still bright in his memory and a land neither one of us is likely to visit anytime soon.

"And this is what you have written here?" I ask. "And you want me to write it out in correct English for your journal?"

"Yes. Exactly. If you would be so kind." He bows his head slightly, not exactly in obeisance, more in polite request.

He talks and I am obliged to pass my time penning the biography of an Iranian refugee in Geneva airport; a biography, I notice from the preceding pages in the file, many like me have supplemented before.

I finish my task as quickly and diligently as I can, and he is grateful and so touched by the gift of my time that his eyes well with emotion.

"You know," he begins again, "in the war, the Jewish people they come to the border here and Swiss people let them into the country because they have money. More than twenty thousand Jews come here. They let them in even though they have no passports. They—"

I wince when I catch sight of the path down which he wishes to lead our conversation.

"Would you write for me here, please," he points to some unused lines on a page, "about how Jews were permitted to come here because they had money?"

"No," I reply with a well-rehearsed synthesis of horror, umbrage and conviction. "I'm not inclined to write such things. How can I understand what it must have been like to flee from certain death? It's not something I can adequately comprehend."

I am taken with a sudden desire to distance myself from him but realise that, outside of rudely walking away, I have little alternative but to engage him. I am also reminded of the failure of the international conference at Évians-les-Bains, on the southern, French side of the lake in the summer of 1938; a sham of a conference at which all the great nations turned away from their opportunity to resolve the growing refugee crisis. The relief offered by the promise of my flight and the horror aroused by past hypocrisies derail my train of thought.

He smiles the kind of smile a magician bestows on his stooge when he realises he has selected from the audience the perfect patsy on whom to practice his subtle deception.

"People do what they have to do to survive. Besides," I continue, "in England there was considerable indifference to refugees in the months before the war and," I add, "no little Anti-Semitism. In bad times people behave badly. It's not my place to go apportioning blame for the ills that befall others." I say this even though I know it is a trap I fall into every day.

He stays silent for a moment longer. When he judges sufficient time has passed for the both of us to acknowledge the banality of my axiom, he says, "Well, I would like to go to England. But I have no money. And I have no passport. So, when I go to buy ticket they send me away because I can produce no documents. So here I must stay. Here is where I must be. Now I can go nowhere. And always I want to go to England, because in England you can say what you want about people and do what you want. It is a country like no other. You can write what you want, like Shakespeare and Milton, and everyone is protected. You are free."

And that is it. He is silent. A new and satisfied smile spreads across his small round face as though his trick has been nothing more than to demonstrate an uncomfortable logic.

I'm not sure how to respond.

This man, whose name I have not had the grace to ask, is

a Swiss *Hei Haizi*, a grown up child of the *black seed*, as they are known; a division of society denied fundamental human rights by their lack of state-licensed identity.

I glance at the departures screen and am relieved to see my flight has been called. I begin gathering my papers into my briefcase, careful not to pick up any of his by mistake.

"Good luck," I wish him, sincerely.

When I stand, so does he. But he rises slowly and reluctantly and without shifting his gaze from me. Like a lone figure standing in the stalls, he lingers, hoping for just one more glimpse of the stage before he is shown the door of the theatre. He offers me his hand. It is gentle, but not so gentle as to be submissive in its appreciation.

"Thank you. And thank you for helping me. You are kind," he says, as though I have done something far more significant than merely lend him my spare time.

"Well, I don't know about that," I reply. There is a brief and awkward silence. Not stiff, just awkward. "I hope your friend arrives soon."

He frowns at me; he is puzzled by something I have said.

"Your friend; the one you've come to meet?" I smile as broad and warm a smile as I can muster in the hope that my levity will not offend him.

And then, like the spring sun that drives the hoarfrost from the river bank, he beams as he realises that I understand he had no friend to meet in the first place.

I resist the urge to glance back at him as I walk away. I know he is standing where I left him, desperate for the affirmation my acknowledgement would provide. But I do not.

The policeman at immigration barely glances at my passport and the irony of how simple it is for me to pass between countries is not lost on me.

The flight back to London drags. I try to divorce myself

from the proximity of my neighbours, but the violence exacted by the turbulence makes reading impossible and physical contact unavoidable. I am glad I managed to resist the temptation of the fondant.

The tube into the East End rattles and jolts, and I have to steel myself before attempting the steep stairs up to the flat.

Jules opens the door for me and stands back to assess my state. "So how many poor refugees has my angel of mercy plucked from the barren wastes of no man's land this week?"

I am relieved of my case and coat, and presented with a gin-and-tonic, a saucer of peanuts and olives, and my favourite leather wing-chair. Oscar, Jules' West Highland White, weighs my mood and retreats into the kitchen. His finely tuned appreciation of my fatigue tells him that I am not yet long enough through the door to fall for his dishonest affections – his cupboard love.

It is often like this when I get home. Jules knows I am too exhausted for anything other than casual endearments; too dispirited by shuffling the files of the stateless from one department to another, like driving an ever expanding herd of unsaleable cattle from one market to the next.

The first gin panders to my fatigue. The second braces me for conversation.

Jules returns, sits beside me and regales me with some of the more comic moments in the week of an inner-city school teacher. As usual, and particularly when my mood is at its most unyielding, Jules manages to draw a chuckle from me.

In turn I relate the story of the man I met whilst waiting in the airport concourse: the round-faced, politely spoken exile whose comprehensive knowledge of Shakespeare and Milton put me to shame. I explain how this man is imprisoned without any conventional identity in a country without the slightest interest in his welfare. And I describe how countless other unsuspecting travellers have, like me, transcribed the man's very private rendering of Paradise Lost in the jumbled journal of his life.

"You acknowledged him," Jules consoles. "You recognised him for who he is. Most other people would have ignored or rejected him. But, you must learn to leave your work in the office or, as sure as your God made little apples, it will consume you."

It is both too true and too late for that; we both know it. For I have been consumed by my calling — as Jules somewhat mockingly defines my devotion to the *Haut Commissariat des Nations Unies pour les Réfugiers* — ever since my father walked me down to the lake one fine Saturday afternoon and told me of the long and tortuous path by which he and my mother had come to Switzerland all those years ago.

"Dinner is served," Jules announces, getting up and patting my arm in precise imitation of the way I pat Oscar when I feed him my apple core. Pathos! It is one of the many mechanisms Jules employs to humour me when my mood suggests I need anything but. I realise once more how fortunate I am to have someone who cares and who knows me well enough to apply the appropriate balm for my troubled soul.

"Your *ima* called." The announcement from the kitchen is garnished with that harping tone Jules reserves exclusively for delivering my mother's commandments. "She's at the lake house. You didn't tell her you were leaving. She said you *will* be back in time for your niece's *Bat Chayil* next Saturday." A heavily pregnant pause follows and by its duration I understand Jules' next remark will circumscribe the complicated triangle that is our relationship with my mother. "You know she's still in denial, don't you? You do know she'll never entertain the idea that we're anything other than merely flatmates?"

NINE

Kitzbühel, Austria

Charlie and Kurt linger in the shadow of the mountain and gaze down upon the twinkling lights of the medieval walled town. The thunderclap detonations of the New Year's evening celebrations still echo in their ears and the gaudy images of the sparkling fireworks are seared so bright on their eyes they are finding it difficult to pick out the piste in the dark.

Kurt is humming *Stille Nacht*, the Christmas Carol.

That much, Charlie's ears can make out. It is something he has grown used to, the skiing and humming. Kurt maintains it helps his rhythm.

"Gruber is the perfect friend for your last ski of the day. He stops us from skiing too fast. Skiing and singing: they are the same, yes? Like poetry."

Charlie has to agree. His habit is to blitz the last ski down, the odds on wiping out shortening as the temptation to nail one final, memorable run grows.

This evening, though, they've lingered too long drinking

himbeergeist in the *hütte* below the lift station. However, it isn't the lateness of the hour that concerns Kurt; it is the piste.

The *Streif* is a test for the most competent skier even in daylight: the *Startschuss* is steep and the compression out of the *Mausefalle* dizzying. Franz Klammer has won the downhill race three times, consecutively, skiing the three and a half kilometres in just two minutes, so Charlie doesn't understand why he should be wary of skiing the same in ten, even if his route is now lit by the stars.

Kurt is built like *Franz* the *Kaiser* and is just as good-looking. He is shorter than Charlie by a couple of hands, broader in the shoulder and constructed of the same hard clay from which they seem to mould all the local kids. It is impossible to knock Kurt over while he stands on his planks. Charlie knows; he has tried all too often and ended up in a heap. But he likes to remind his companion every now and then that when they ran the first Hahnenkamm races back in 1931 the combined event was won by Gordon Cleaver, an Englishman; though he leaves off the detail that Mouse Cleaver DFC went on to shoot down eight German aircraft during the war. For even though the war has been over for many years and Kurt is 110% Austrian, he's watched Kurt wince every time some drunken Brit can't resist the temptation to rake over the same old coals.

Being an instructor at the *Rote Teufel* ski school pays well – in the winter, but Charlie knows Kurt finds the rest of the year hard. And although there are compensations, they are limited. Quite naturally the women all fall for Kurt, what with his blond hair and blue eyes, but when they go back to his place they learn they have to sleep above the rising odours of the lowing herd in the stall beneath and more often than not they soon run away. Such is Kurt's lot.

However, ten years as an instructor has taught Kurt that the alcohol-fuelled elation and the heady atmosphere of the New Year's celebrations often propel the ordinary skier far beyond the limits of his or her ability, and so the two of them sweep the slope with their eyes and stop every now and then to listen out.

They are standing on the outside of the long right hander that is the first part of the *Steilhang* when they first hear the groan.

Surely, Charlie thinks, there can't be anyone out on the slopes this late?

"From where is it coming?" Kurt asks.

They glance at each other and listen hard for a while.

Surely, it is some furry animal of the forest disturbed in its slumber by the earsplitting fireworks. The silence is vast and eerie.

"Perhaps a trick in the mountain?" Kurt says, craning his neck and frowning in concentration.

"No," Charlie replies, "it was human."

They stand stock still and listen for a further minute or so.

Whatever the noise was, it has ceased.

"It is nothing," Kurt says, "probably a goat, possibly a cow."

"Doubt it; we'd have heard the bell. And aren't most of them locked up for the winter?"

But, just as they are about to set off, they hear another groan from somewhere behind them. Rather reluctantly both young men take off their skis and plant them firmly to the side.

The umbrella of pines cuts out the starlight and the bank beyond the track falls away steeply. They trudge through the deeper snow into the woods, pausing every now and then to listen for the noise that will help them locate its source.

After a time-consuming and energy sapping search they conclude there is no one about and that it probably was, as Kurt suggested, a goat. They decide to return to the piste before the evening gets too much older.

But, just as they set off back up the slope, they hear one final and very low moan; a hopeless and hapless sigh, like that of an insomniac frustrated by his inability to sleep.

They glance at each other, wait and look about once more.

They can neither see nor hear a soul. And then, at the same time, it dawns on the pair of them that they are being watched.

The air stills and drops in temperature. Charlie knows brown bears patrol the Tyrol, but that's mainly in the east. And besides, they've not heard any approach and neither can they smell any strong, noxious scent. Whatever it is they feel, they suddenly come to realise there is a presence lurking in the branches immediately above them.

Kurt shrugs, and ever so slowly they look up.

By some trick of the light and snow, the first thing they notice is the man's shiny, bald pate. He is hanging upside-down, like a bat, just out of reach in the branches of the pine, his arms flopping down.

Clearly, he's attempted the *Steilhang* at too great a pace and has literally flown off the piste into the trees, his skis getting tangled in the branches above his head. He's obviously been trapped in suspended animation for some time and, with his blood draining into his head, he is only semi-conscious.

After some debate as to the best course, they decide they cannot leave him where he is while they go for help; the risk of his freezing to death is too great and if one of them leaves and gets into difficulty, they know they will only compound the problem.

"*Ist alles in ordnung?*" Kurt calls up.

"Thank God!" comes a mumbled reply.

"Are you okay?" Kurt asks, grinning. It is a ridiculous question given the circumstances, but such is his humour.

"Can you release your bindings?" Kurt asks.

"No," the man says, "I can't reach them."

"You know you must have a special permit for night flying on the Hahnenkamm," Kurt sniggers.

The man struggles and a shower of fine snow falls about.

"Stay where you are," Kurt tells him, chuckling. "We will bring you down.

Neither of them is tall enough to grab hold of the man's arms and the branches of the tree start too far up the trunk for them to climb up to him. Kurt waves Charlie over and motions for him to climb up on his shoulders.

Charlie cannot imagine how he is going to support him; in his ski boots and kit he must weigh as much as a small horse.

Kurt braces his back against the tree, slides down into a sitting position and claps his hands together to make a stirrup.

"Come," he says, "you make a step on my hands and I will lift you up. Climb on my shoulder and pull him down. But be careful, if he starts to fall, move out of the way quickly. There is enough snow for a good landing bed for him."

Charlie is hoisted up and, when high enough, he steps clumsily onto Kurt's shoulder, holding on to the tree to steady himself. By stretching up he manages to touch one of the man's hands.

"I can't quite reach him," Charlie says.

Kurt grunts, flexes his legs and begins to inch his back up the trunk of the tree, so lifting Charlie higher; the years of bending his knees to the slope have imbued his legs with an awe-inspiring power.

Charlie tries to relieve him of some of his weight by gripping the tree tight as he grabs the man's wrist.

For a split second Charlie is connected to both Kurt and the man suspended above him. And then he is swinging free, hanging on the man with all his weight as Kurt steps to one side.

The branches creak, the man cries out in pain and their combined weight and the nature of gravity succeeds in breaking the ties about his feet.

The pair of them tumble down into the thick snow in a ragged bundle of arms and legs and skis, one of them clouting Charlie hard on the side of his head.

A meaty paw seizes his jacket and he is hauled upright.

"Have you pain?" Kurt asks.

"No, I'm fine," Charlie replies, shaking the snow out from around his neck.

"And you, *der Flieger*? Are you okay?"

"I'll do," replies the figure half-buried in the drift at the foot of the tree, "Yes, thank you. No complaints. I'm fine; thought I'd be up there all bloody night. Very grateful, naturally, of course!"

Clearly, he is British and, in a manner true to his nationality, profoundly embarrassed that he should need to be rescued from such indignity.

They nurse their prize slowly back up to the *Steilhang* and escort him down to the town. To begin with, the man is unsteady on his skis and Kurt makes him stop every hundred metres or so to gather himself. But by the time they *schuss* the last part of the *Ziel*, he is once more skiing at breakneck pace.

He turns and stops, ignorant that he has sprayed a great curtain of snow over a group of revellers huddled at the bottom of the slope: "Best buy you gentlemen a *glühwein*, if you would join me."

Kurt asks, "Where do you stay?"

"*Tiefenbrunner*," he replies, "See you in the *Goldene Gams* when you're ready." He marches smartly away, skis slung up over his shoulder.

Kurt turns back and shrugs, "Perhaps this is why he did not freeze to death. He already has too much of what the French call *sang froid*.

An hour later, Kurt and Charlie are sitting in the *Goldene Gams* drinking beer when the subject of their conversation strides in, apparently as fresh as *edelweiss*.

He rubs his hands exuberantly. "Now, gentlemen, what can I get you for your trouble? Can't imagine how I'd have got myself down if you two hadn't come along."

"If we had not found you," Kurt replies, "you would have been an icicle by the morning. Perhaps you English should leave *skispringen* to those who understand the aerodynamics of the sport?"

Charlie introduces Kurt and waits for the man to do the same.

"Barclay, with an 'a'," he says and holds out his meaty hand. He wears a *Loden* jacket and corduroys.

Charlie reckons Barclay in his early forties, but might be younger if he's already spent the odd night suspended in a tree.

"What can I get you good gentlemen?"

They settle for more beer, which Barclay orders with a flamboyant wave to the waiter.

Kurt is grinning once more. Charlie knows the look; it means he is up for a little sport. "I have heard your name, *Herr Barclay*. You are an adventurer, yes?"

The split veins of Barclay's nose turn a deeper shade of purple.

Then it comes to Charlie: "You're the fellow who tried to climb the Eiger solo. And didn't you set some kind of record on the Cresta last year."

Barclay studies his hands for a moment. "Mmm! Not the kind one wants to be known for. Least said the better."

They hold thier peace, not wanting to embarrass him into explaining further.

Kurt, however, is not so sensitive. "Ah, yes, *Herr Barclay*. You completed the course three times and every time you finish upside down."

Barclay sniffs and blows his nose.

"And the Eiger?" Kurt continues. "I believe you tried to climb the *Mordwand*, the Murder Wall as some call her, but you had to be rescued by other climbers – climbers who risked their lives to save yours."

Barclay looks up and a forlorn expression sags at the corners of his mouth. "I suppose you'll tell me you've run the Cresta and climbed the Eiger before breakfast?"

Kurt laughs; a deep, guttural, dismissive but fun-poking laugh. "No, of course I have not done these things. To do these things, first you must learn to respect the mountains; something I think you do not. I respect them too much to make fun of them. You must remember, *Herr Barclay*, I have grown up beneath this mountain." He nods at a joyous watercolour of a spring Hahnenkamm beside our table. "I have seen her at her best and at her most unforgiving."

"I can assure you, young man, I have the utmost respect for the mountain," Barclay replies, a winsome, scolded look on his face. "Simply because I like flying down it, doesn't imply I disrespect it."

Kurt laughs again. "So then tell us, *Herr Barclay*, are you accident prone or do you not take the necessary care? Perhaps you are like the cat with many lives. If you are, how many lives do you have left?"

It is too much disdain heaped upon the small hill of his humiliation. Barclay blinks, twitches and colours, throws back his beer and bids them, politely and with hand-pumping grateful thanks, "Goodnight."

On his way out, the boys notice he settles their bill at the bar.

At the end of the week Charlie takes the little train down to Wörgl and as the villages beside the *Brixentaler Ache* interrupt the darkness, he recalls the resigned groan of the curious adventurer hanging upside-down in the tree. For the future, he understands that the sound of the man's surrender will haunt him and hold him back every time he enters the *Steilhang* too fast, and Charlie resigns himself to hearing Kurt tell him it is the reason why he will never manage to ski *der Streif* in under two and a half minutes.

———————

Some years later and the day before Christmas Eve, Charlie is summoned to the offices of a company near Harrogate. The managing director has a pressing need for his financial acumen.

So close to the holidays, Charlie is naturally reluctant to be dragged so far away from what he believes to be the cosy arms of his metropolis, but business is business and he is not the kind to shun opportunity. Besides, he consoles himself, the man's name is familiar, even if he cannot place exactly where in his past it is familiar from.

Not wanting to risk being ridden under in the exodus up the motorway, he takes the train and when he eventually gets to meet the managing director, he is again taken with the feeling that they have met before. Charlie still cannot place him, though, and in case they have met under less pleasant circumstances, he keeps his sense of déjà vu under wraps.

Their meeting runs over and he misses the last train home. But the gentleman is effusively grateful for the benefit of his advice – even if his wooden body language and wearied expression suggest he has heard it all before – and he tells Charlie that he lives locally and offers to put him up for the night. He is, he remarks as though referring to the passing of a pet, recently divorced and will therefore be glad of Charlie's company.

Over dinner, Charlie grows ever more certain that his host's name and face are familiar. Also, it is the man's all too evident impatience which reminds him of someone he has once met. He is not dissimilar to many successful entrepreneurs Charlie has encountered; one never comfortable with the present, preferring instead to talk about how he might finance the next big thing, without actually identifying what the next big thing might be.

"I tell you what," he says, sipping his wine, I'll fly you back tomorrow. I'm going on down to the Channel Islands to spend Christmas at my house near Grouville. I can drop you off on the way: Fairoaks or Biggin Hill, somewhere." And he promises that apart from paying Charlie's fee promptly, he will be sure to need more of his financial advice soon.

"Well," Charlie replies, "It's not every day I get the offer of being flown home in a light plane."

They conclude their business over brandy and the next

morning his host drives him down the Harrogate Road towards Yeadon Airfield.

He drives fast; too fast for Charlie's liking and certainly too fast for the wet and therefore treacherous road.

When he makes a hash of a bend and clips a curb, he groans in frustration.

Charlie had thought his name familiar when his secretary phoned and then again thought his face familiar when they first met, but it is only when he groans that Charlie manages to place him. The sound is unmistakeable.

He is the very same Barclay from Kitzbühel, the man Kurt and he rescued from the branches of the pines beside the *Steilhang* that New Year's evening.

"You like to ski?" Charlie asks, casually.

"Yes," he replies, "You?"

"When I get the time."

The man takes his eyes off the road to glance sideways.

"Where do you ski?" Charlie asks, wishing his driver would resist looking at him every time he speaks.

"Courchevel." He wrestles the car around another corner. "You?"

"Kitzbühel. Ever been there?"

"Ah," he replies, as though his passenger has revealed himself to be a detective come to make an arrest, "I thought I recognised you."

He colours — a reaction Charlie can feel as much as see in the grey light afforded by the heavy cloud cover — and falls silent. But by the time they arrive at Yeadon he's managed to ease the discomfort triggered by the poor card God has dealt him.

Over a coffee in the cafeteria and while they wait for the weather to clear, Barclay thanks Charlie for the trouble Kurt and he went to in rescuing him that evening on the *Streif*. He says he realised soon afterwards that the pine trees had been both his absolute saviour and his potential executioner, for if his skis had not caught in the branches of the tree, he would most likely have been killed by the fall. But, then again, if Kurt and Charlie had not found him, he would without doubt have frozen to death through the night, totally helpless as he was in his state of suspended animation.

Charlie lies, graciously and yet with Kurt's stinging rebuke echoing through his head, that the incident happened a long time ago and that he retains only a vague memory of their meeting. Barclay is relieved. But the more Charlie hears Kurt's voice, the finer the detail he remembers of their conversation with the hapless skier in the *Goldene Gams*. And the more detail he remembers, the more he finds himself glancing out the window of the cafeteria to gauge the weather.

"Bloody meteorologists never get it right, do they?" Barclay mutters, picking up on Charlie's concern, "Shouldn't worry! It'll clear up soon. Just a bit of rain."

But the man's propensity to ignore nature's precocious temperament, mirrored as it is in his own impatience, does not reassure Charlie and in spite of the fact that worrying is not his way, he cannot help but grow concerned. The clouds thicken and the rain falls harder with each glance. The barometer, he imagines, is falling further and further through the floor.

Barclay excuses himself and stomps off for another met-report.

Charlie thinks quickly and acts quicker.

When he returns, Barclay is red-faced and ill-tempered. "Might be a break in about an hour," he states.

Charlie's cellphone rings.

"Excuse me?" he offers, waving his phone at Barclay: "My secretary!"

"What? Oh yes, of course."

"Susan? What's up?"

Charlie pretends to listen.

135

"You mean today?" he asks, ladling his reaction with a generous helping of incredulity. "What now? Well, I don't know. Don't they know it's Christmas Eve? Hold on a minute, I'll find out." He lays his mobile on the table.

"Mr Barclay? Would you mind if I didn't fly back to London with you. My office has had a call from a client in Leeds. They'd like to see me before the company closes down for the Christmas break. I know it sounds a bit strange – last minute and all that, but all I have to do is hop on the train into the city. Would it be a bother to you if I didn't keep you company?"

Barclay fixes him with an amazed, if slightly suspicious stare. "What, Leeds? What, today? Just like that? What a coincidence! Fancy that? No, of course not! Why would it be a bother? Stops me from having to put down at Fairoaks. Saves you the landing fee."

"Well, as long as you don't mind," Charlie replies, reaching for the phone. "No, Susan. Tell them that'll be fine. I should be there just after lunch." He pauses: Susan is rightly bemused – and silent. "Alright. Got that, thank you. Yes, I'll ring you later, when I'm free."

He turns back to Barclay: "That's good of you. And so good of you to offer me the lift back in the first place. I hope the weather clears up soon." Charlie stands, picking up his briefcase with one hand and offering Barclay the other.

"'Course it will," Barclay affirms as though he has a direct line to the weather god. "And if it doesn't clear here, all I have to do is to get up there," he raises his eyebrows and nods towards the heavens, "and get on my way. This front will pass through soon enough. 'Won't last all the way across to Jersey, you'll see."

They shake hands. There is an envelope in Barclay's.

"Thank you, sir," Charlie says, holding the man's gaze. "And thank you for standing me dinner and putting me up last night."

"It's what I owe you for coming up," he says, nodding at the envelope. "I must say I'm impressed, what with you hanging on to see a client up here on Christmas Eve. Committed to your cause! I like that! It's what one needs to succeed: commitment. Not sure the youth of today understand that, eh?"

"Have a good trip," Charlie offers as he turns away.

He leaves Barclay — or *Herr Barclay*, as Kurt had persisted in calling him — standing in the airport concourse, waiting with growing impatience for the weather to clear.

Charlie's journey back to London is minutes short of a four hour bun-fight. The train is late and the passengers peculiarly short tempered: Christmas spirit and seats, it seems, are in equally short supply. And when he finally gets home, he is just in time to catch the end of the ten o'clock news:

"A light plane has gone missing in the channel. The combination of poor weather and bad light has meant that the search for survivors has been called off until tomorrow."

———

Christmas morning, the carol singers from King's College Cambridge accompany Charlie's family lunch preparations with the sepulchral purity of Gruber's *Stille Nacht* and he is reminded of the first time he met Barclay that crisp New Year's evening on the Hahnenkamm.

Charlie steals away to sit briefly at his computer.

Barclay, he learns, has walked the South Pole, rowed the Atlantic and climbed K2 in the years since their first meeting. He is famous, or if not famous then at least a minor celebrity. But he is not renowned so much for his fantastic exploits as he is for the extraordinary circumstances in which he has so often been plucked from disaster, and Charlie wonders what it is that drives such a man to risk his life so often. Is he engaged in some constant and ridiculous struggle to measure up? But to what or to whom?

Adventurers like Shackleton, Blyth and Barrington? Or simply to himself and to what he expects of himself?

He isn't — or perhaps by now wasn't, Charlie thinks — an unpleasant man. There is no denying that Barclay enjoys a love affair with his own sense of bravado, but since their dinner together Charlie has come to understand that Barclay's love does not extend to braggadocio. Barclay's love is for his own adventure, not for a desire to be either recognised or admired.

Later, as Charlie and his family sit round the hearth playing charades, he wonders if the intrepid Barclay has ever known the gentle warmth provided by the congregation of loved ones. Perhaps, he decides, such warmth is not for everyone. Perhaps, for the constant adventurer, a chill and lonely grave is all they can hope for.

When he retires to bed, Charlie is both happy with his lot and quietly sad for the missing adventurer.

———————

Boxing Day morning Charlie is not, if he is honest with himself, surprised to learn from the radio news that *Herr* Barclay is alive and well. He'd ditched in the icy waters south of Jersey only to be fortunate enough — against the very longest of odds — to be picked up by a passing sailboat en route to St-Malo.

Charlie shakes his head in disbelief and wonders whether Barclay's luck will, like the sleeve of his jacket where he tucks his nine lives, ever wear thin.

TRUST

Ollie has no real cause to distrust foreigners but, then again, he has never suffered at the hands of foreigners like his great-grand-father had during the Great War.

In truth, as he sits shading his eyes to peer up at the Gothic façade of Notre Dame, he realises he has precious few memories of his great-grandfather. After all his 'Pop', as the family all called him, was a very, very old man by the time Ollie had been old enough to fully appreciate what he was on about. But the bulk of what Ollie does remember about him centres on a number of conversations in which his grandfather had told him in no uncertain terms that he was never, ever to trust foreigners.

In one of those conversations Pop had told him a story of his time in the trenches of the Ypres Salient. The French, he had maintained, provided the British with false information about the curious mist floating over from the German side. They had said it was only a smokescreen and that it carried with it no physical danger. Well, they had been wrong, fatally wrong, and the British had moved troops up to the front only for them to be asphyxiated in clouds of bluish gas. A lot of his mates had perished that way. Indeed, the names of two of Pop's brothers can be read, chiselled for posterity in the limestone walls of the Menin Gate.

"The French, you see," he'd said, his voice crusty, rasping and hoary, "were the first to use gas. The Boches only gave back what they'd already received."

But it just went to show, that you couldn't trust any of them, German or French. "In those days, the wogs," he used to declare in a tone carefully measured to incense those of a more socially sensitive disposition, "began at Calais."

Ollie doesn't hold to the same, antediluvian view, but he is aware that the garish colours of his forebear's reminiscences are inclined to hold him back from engaging with anyone who isn't British.

Today is Ollie's first visit to Paris – alone. He's been with his parents a number of times, of course. But that was back when his hand had never left his mother's and the buildings had seemed so huge they appeared to be about to fall in on him. And after those early visits, he remembers flying round the *Périphérique* in the back of his father's car, watching out the window in the hope of catching a glimpse of the tall *Tour Eiffel* or the majestic *Sacré-Cœur*. But there had never been talk that he might one day be let loose in the city on his own.

The notion of his absolute freedom to do and go where he pleases comes light and coolly to him, like the spring breeze shepherding the flock of fluffy lambs across the cerulean meadow above him.

The stopping train from Calais had, earlier in the day, eased him haltingly into the Gare du Nord. Others had advised him to take the Eurostar: it would be quicker, easier and cheaper, or so they said. But Ollie had stuck by his guns, telling them he wanted to enter Paris as past travellers would have, with first a view of the countryside, then the suburbs and eventually the heart of the city. His notion, he'd defended, was to follow a trail which would enlighten him as to how the city had formed, organically that is, not to suddenly find himself being digested deep in the bowels of it. And although slow at times, he'd enjoyed his entrée to the sprawling metropolis just as much as he'd hoped he would.

His mother, one who always grew nervy when arranging travel, had impressed upon him the need to collect his ticket for the onward leg of his journey as soon as he arrived at the Gare du Nord. Ollie suspected she harboured a misgiving he would be tempted to squander his travel funds in the fleshpots of Paris and subsequently return home early and with something far more alarming than merely his tail between his legs. It wasn't that she entertained a lack of faith in her son, or so she insisted on telling his friends, so much as a deep-rooted mistrust of the social diaspora of Paris; a view born to the echoes of her grandfather's all too lurid tales. And Ollie had agreed that, yes, it would have been easier and probably cheaper to sort the tickets out online beforehand, but he wanted to experience the process of buying his ticket for each segment of his journey. Ollie wanted to engage with the people, not bypass them. So as soon as he got off the train, and as promised, he queued up to buy his onward ticket to Nice.

Ollie's back pack was a considerable burden to bear and, as he'd already learned, extremely awkward to negotiate through narrow turnstiles. In the queue for the ticket window, he found himself at odds as to whether to keep it on his back or drag it with him as the line shuffled forward.

A short, old lady behind him tut-tutted at his blocking her view. She wore enormous round glasses which magnified her squint and lent her a hostile manner, so he eased out of the straps and set his pack down by his feet.

The station concourse was a feast of colour: the bourgeois of all ages, status and race standing, staring up at the tall departure board, and waiting and watching for a seat to be vacated at the café. The high glass ceiling lent the place an airy capacity and the triumphal arch of the entrance spoke to him of the glories of a republic long put to bed. He decided there must be worse places than the bustling concourse in which to have to wait in a queue, and he passed the time imagining the thousands of troops who must have marched cheerily through the station on their way to the horrors of the Western Front.

As he dragged his pack forwards, the old woman behind him sucked her teeth loudly, clearly resenting his load even more than Ollie.

At the window he asked for a ticket to Nice. Not, he was at pains to point out, for the *TGV* for the whole journey, but only with the *TGV* as far as Lyon. After Lyon, he would like to take the local train the rest of the way.

"*Oui, Monsieur,*" Ollie replied in answer to the clerk's point, "*Je comprends que le TGV est plus vite, mais...*"

The po-faced representative of *Société Nationale de Chemin de Fer* gazed back at him with something approaching astonishment. Did the young man know how long that would take?

Yes, he did.

Did he want a ticket which would allow him to break his journey at more than one stop along the way?

No, he didn't.

Was he sure?

The question and answer session endured for as long as it took most travellers to dunk their *croissant* in their *café au lait* and reduce the residue.

Behind him the old lady scraped her feet like a vexed pony and the expression of the ticket clerk grew increasingly amused.

Eventually, the ticket was slipped almost begrudgingly beneath the glass towards him.

His wallet, though, was in the pocket of his backpack.

He dragged it round in front of him. He struggled with the zip pocket, fiddled with the contents and sorted through his many papers. In short, he hurried.

The old lady scraped and began to mither about the wait.

Eventually he located his wallet, thinking that as long as he kept it so well secured no one was ever going to steal it that easily.

Ollie paid, replaced his wallet in its hidey-hole, hoiked his backpack onto his shoulders and headed for the *Metro*.

Sitting, as he is now, peering up at the great towers of the cathedral, he recalls how the impatient old lady would have made a passable Quasimodo. There was something of the dowager's hump and magnified eye about her which twinned with Hugo's hunch-backed, goggle-eyed ogre and, though probably not unkind, she had seemed no less threatening.

An ice cream vendor is plying his trade on the apron of the cathedral.

Ollie, wonders if he can get over to the stall without taking his cumbersome backpack with him and decides that, although heavy, he doesn't trust those wandering about not to steal it while his back is turned.

He examines the loose change from his pocket and comes to the conclusion his finances will stretch.

When he returns to the stone bench, a family has taken his place. But there is just enough space for him to perch on the end while he eats – if they budge up a bit.

They oblige, but only after he has stood in question for a minute and then only with less fuss than it must have taken Pétain to marshal his troops at the Battle of Verdun.

He sits, carefully, but because of the litter of the family's bags he keeps his backpack on.

Ollie is an eager history student, or leastways he was before he finished school, and he is confident he will be again when he takes up his place at university in the autumn. And he has come to realise recently that he has his crusty old great-grandpop to thank for fostering his interest in the subject. That old man, whom most thought cold and arrogant, would occasionally surprise Ollie with his warmth and gentility, especially when it was announced that some relation had passed, at which point he would take hold of his great-grandson, squeeze him firmly to his bony chest and whisper "Three on a match, eh?" or whenever someone's better health was toasted at a family celebration, he would wink mischievously before saying, "Here's mud in your eye."

Soon enough, these pearls began to reflect the light of his great-grandfather's wisdom through the corridors of Ollie's young, inquiring mind. So was born Ollie's love of, and aptitude for, history and over time he'd learnt to forgive the old man his occasional xenophobic, ethnocentric, misogynistic and generally more morally repugnant outbursts. Pop certainly hadn't been perfect, but what was far more important than his imperfections was the fact that he'd stood up and had been counted when his country had asked it of him.

After working the winter in a supermarket and saving up, Ollie is off to holiday with a friend whose parents have an apartment at Baie des Anges, near Nice. History, he has decided, is his to be made over the next four weeks.

The children of the happy family gawk enviously and endlessly at his ice cream, while the parents try hard to redirect their attention to the cathedral and the *bateaux mouches* passing along the Seine. And all too plainly they make it obvious that they would like Ollie to hurry up and finish his *cornet de glace* before the chorus of their offspring's craving makes it impossible for them to avoid purchasing six of the same.

Ollie sits balancing his backpack on his shoulders and studies the façade of the great cathedral. He wonders at the ornate doors, the trumeau and jamb of which support the lintel and which in turn bears the weight of the intricate tympanum, shrouded within the archivolt. Above that the huge, round Rose Window is set between niches topped by slender, pointy pinnacles decorated with elegant finials.

He gazes further up at the arcade below the twin towers and the exquisitely carved crockets of the gable and-

Ollie is leaning too far back. He flexes his thighs and pushes his feet firmly against the ground to counteract the heavy burden of his backpack. But he is no physicist and does not cater adequately for the vagaries of gravity, and he teeters on the edge of the stone bench as the weight of his backpack suddenly pulls him over backwards.

He topples over as if in slow motion and lands on his back, his calves resting on the flat surface of the bench, his partially eaten ice cream held aloft, like the torch of liberty.

Too late he realises he is beached, like a beetle on its back.

The children giggle and snigger and point. The parents mutter at them to keep quiet before they too realise what has happened. They laugh openly and, Ollie thinks, rather unkindly at his predicament.

He is stranded, helpless and at the mercy of ruffians and pickpockets.

His ice cream begins to melt and drip.

He looks pleadingly for someone to lend him a hand. He cannot right himself without assistance and can only lie and watch the lambs as they saunter across the sky.

The father of the brood — a brood now gathered around him as though they are studying some unfortunate insect, fills the sky, "*Puis-je vous aider, monsieur?*"

As vulnerable as he feels, Ollie rapidly reaches the conclusion that if he doesn't accept the man's offer of assistance, there is every chance he will be marooned as he is until nightfall.

The man barks at one of his children and a happy, smiling, bright-eyed child reaches out for Ollie's ice cream.

He hands it over, knowing it will probably be the last he sees of it. But, if he has to surrender such a prize to regain his equilibrium, then it will be a small price to pay.

The man bends and reaches down to pull him upright, but Ollie's legs lie above him on the bench and for a moment the pair of them resemble an ungainly seesaw as they rock to and fro; Ollie unable to rise and his rescuer confused as to why such a simple feat should make them both look so ridiculous.

He lets go Ollie's hand and calls more troops to his cause.

The children arrive, grab Ollie by his arms and legs and revolve him round, out of the way of the bench. The man then reaches down again and this time hauls Ollie first into a sitting position and second up to his feet.

"*Je suis très reconnaissant, monsieur,*" Ollie says, dusting himself down to mask his embarrassment.

"I am happy to be of service," the man replies, grinning. "It is heavy, eh, this *sac à dos?*"

"*Oui,*" Ollie replies, "*peut-être un peu trop lourd. Je vous remercie, mille fois.*

The children are still giggling. Their mother, though she attempts to conceal her mirth behind her hand in an effort to show good manners, is beside herself with amusement and their father stands proud, both that he has been able to be of some assistance and that, in front of his progeny, his *Anglais* has proved at least as good as the *Français* of the youth before him. The *glace*, however, is gone.

Ollie keeps busy for the rest of the day. There is much to see through such a short window of opportunity: *La Tour Eiffel* dizzying, the *Sacré Cœur* crowded, and the *Louvre* will not permit *monsieur* entry while he has his backpack in place and there is nowhere for him to deposit it.

By late afternoon, he is weary of the many sights and takes a rest in the pretty garden of the *Tuileries*. The cool of the shade beneath the plane trees reminds him of how tired he is, so he lies down and rests his head against his pack. Without knowing it, he falls deeply asleep.

For how long he is dead to the world he isn't sure, but he wakes with a start to find he has rolled over and is now lying properly disconnected, a metre or so away from his pack. Grass is stuck to his face.

He rubs his head. A middle-aged couple sit close by and observe. They could have taken his pack and run off with it, leaving him none the wiser but, Ollie is relieved to find, they haven't.

He drags it closer and checks his watch.

As evening draws in, he makes his way by *Metro* to the Gare de Lyon. He is looking forward to his time on the *TGV* and so arrives early at the platform gate.

"*Billet, s'il vous plait,*" the inspector requests.

"*Un moment,*" Ollie demands, politely.

He searches the pockets of his trousers and then his shirt.

No ticket.

He searches through them again.

Still no ticket!

It must be, he decides, with his wallet in his backpack. He swings it down off his shoulders.

No ticket there, either!

A queue is forming behind him: commuters are keen to get home.

Ollie searches his pockets again, rapidly, patting them as though they are on fire.

Still nothing!

The inspector ushers him aside so that others may make their trains. He drags his pack over.

It makes no sense. He bought the ticket at the Gare du Nord. He recalls distinctly paying for it. Recalls very clearly the po-faced clerk, the impatient woman who reminded him of Quasimodo, the unpacking and repacking of his wallet in his backpack, the-

The one thing he cannot picture is what he did with the ticket. He recalls an image of it lying on the counter. A sickness born of despair immediately infects his stomach.

Did he leave it on the counter?

Ollie checks his watch: the *TGV* leaves in an hour.

Running with the backpack on is not easy. Commuters are surging out of the *Metro* and he has to surrender all his natural courtesies to barge his way down the escalator and into a carriage. Once on the train, he cannot stand still for fear of the clock gaining on him. People jostle and bustle and sway as the tube rattles along, and world-weary straphangers ignore him as they bury their heads in their *journaux*.

At the Gare du Nord, he runs up the escalator into the concourse and sprints to the same ticket window he remembers from the morning.

There is a queue.

Ollie joins it, nervously checking his watch and craning his neck to count how many wait in front.

The queue oozes forward with all the consistency of honey out of a forgotten jar.

There is an argument.

He taps his foot impatiently, screws up his face, hoping that some telepathic, telekinetic force will propel those in front on their way, and above all he hopes — but desperately hopes — that they will have some record of his transaction.

A beggar bothers him.

The commuters shuffle forwards; the last man seeming to take forever with his purchase.

"Haven't you got a home worth going to?" Ollie mutters below his breath.

His turn presents itself. Evidently, the clerk of the morning *had* a home worth going to as the man behind the counter is not the same he remembers.

A black face, no doubt that belonging to a descendant of the Third Republic's colonial ambitions, stares blankly back at him.

"*Monsieur,*" Ollie begins, trying as hard as he can to suppress the urgency in his tone lest he get off on the wrong foot, "*Ce matin j'ai acheté un billet de train, mais je pense que je l'ai laissé ici.*"

The face continues to stare back as though the language of the 10th *arrondissement* is no longer French.

Ollie is at a loss as to how to garner a response. He repeats his introduction, but again he is met with silence and stone. He turns round, expecting to find he has stumbled into a newly written scene from the Hitchhiker's Guide to the Galaxy. Equally bored, but lighter-skinned faces glare back from the line at his heels.

A man is talking to him; who, he cannot work out.

Gradually he recognises the hoary tones of the disembodied voice. It is his great-grandfather, Pop.

"I told you not to trust them," he moans. "I told you the Western Oriental Gentlemen began at Calais. Why didn't you listen, Ollie? That's the trouble with the youth of today; when you bother to give them your advice —"

"*Vous* êtes *Anglais?*" the clerk asks.

"*Oui,*" Ollie replies, browned off yet again that his French has not stood up to the test.

"I told you, Ollie," Pop repeats, "but you didn't li—"

"Shut-up, Pop," he mumbles. "You are not helping."

The clerk blinks, slides open a drawer beneath his counter and removes a small white envelope: "*Où allez vous, monsieur?*"

"*Nice.*"

"*Par TGV?*"

"*Jusqu'à Lyon, oui, mais après ça le train régionaux.*"

The clerk's expression stays cemented, but he slips the envelope under the glass screen.

Ollie opens it, glimpses the slips of paper inside and his eyes well up.

He clutches the envelope to his chest, smiles at the clerk and says, "*Oh, monsieur! Dieu merci! Merci a vous! Je ne sais comment vous remercier.*"

The clerk holds up his hand to stem the flow of Ollie's appreciation. "*Monsieur,*" he points at his wrist, "*vous devez vous dépêcher, eh?* You must hurry, *monsieur.*"

An hour later, Ollie is sipping cool *bière d'alsace*, reclining in the armchair of a *Train à Grande Vitesse* as the champion of French engineering rockets south through the night.

He raises his glass, "Can't trust foreigners, eh Pop? Here's mud in your eye."

A MIXED BAG

A Public School, England

The weight of expectation lies like a suffocating vapour upon the class. Boys cough nervously and Mark is certain he cannot only see the cloud, he can feel it too. It reminds him of the noxious atmosphere of Ralgex in the changing room before a game of rugby.

Mark grows vaguely aware of his own insignificant part in the great formula of the classroom and recognises that he and his classmates are little more than the elixir of youth swilling in a conical flask; a flask held over a flame by a fat man with a purple nose.

Sadly though, the vapour hanging heavy in the chemistry lab isn't that of muscle rub. And neither is it the vapour of scalding steam, nor smelly like that rotten-egg gas. He stares at the array of Bunsen burners, burettes, pipettes, test tubes and tripods on the bench before him.

What was it now? Was it hydrogen something? He said the name of it the other day, didn't he? Now, what was it Popey said? Was it hydrogen sulph—

"Parker? Are you paying attention?" the master calls.

"Hydrogen sulphide, sir. Or should that be sulphate, sir?" he replies, hurriedly.

Ions circle the ceiling, attracting extra electrons each time they skim the sphere of his chemistry master's ego; each one of them destined to bombard the lesser pupil into submission.

The short, porker of a man frowns. "Parker, you haven't been listening to a word I've been saying, have you?"

"Mmm, yes sir. You were saying we had to make sure we knew our periodic, er, table. Yes, sir. The periodic table; we have to know it by heart, sir."

The frown deepens, the glower glows hot and then suddenly fizzes white with fury, smoking and bubbling like potassium in a petri dish.

Or was that in a physics lesson he'd seen that?

"No, Parker, that wasn't what I was saying. We were talking about the periodic table about five minutes ago. Grief, lad! Where have you been this last half hour?"

"Right here, sir."

Some titter. Others snigger.

Mister Pope, a stub of chalk nestling between his fingers like a cigarette, waves the class to hush.

"Parker?"

"Yes, sir."

"Seeing as you find it impossible to concentrate on what I am saying and therefore clearly do not value my time as much as the other boys, would you be kind enough to tell us all the difference between hydrogen sulphide and hydrogen sulphate?"

"Of course, sir. Bad eggs, sir." Mark is certain one of them smells like bad eggs anyway.

"Is that it, Parker?" the bulbous little man wheedles. "Is that the best you can come up with? Bad eggs?" He sighs. "Anyone?"

Few are brave enough to stick their head in the glutton's mouth, lest they end up contributing to Mr Pope's bulging waistline.

Beside Mark Parker a hand gradually gains altitude.

There's a surprise, Mark thinks: *Crispy.*

Crisp is a smart-boy and as such many in the class are jealous of him. They envy him really, even though envy is not yet a recognised presentiment; for envy is a sensual emotion and the class are yet too young to comprehend the delicacy of sensualities. So, jealousy is for the moment how envy manifests itself; jealousy expressed in all too open and often raw resentment.

But Mark gets on with Crisp. In fact, they more than get on, they are friends; that is if one can be friends with a boy as intelligent as Crisp. They are unlike, perhaps poles apart as far as their relative attributes are concerned, but they respect each other's strengths as much as each other's weaknesses. In the balance of things, Mark's modest cerebral ability is not a threat to his friend's superior intellect and, conversely, Crisp's physical frailty means he isn't much of a one for saying boo to a goose. They both know he is never going to threaten Mark's dominance of the sports field; a dominance of which many are jealous, but which few are fool enough to challenge.

"Yes, Crisp?" the master delights.

"Hydrogen sulphate is an ion, sir, H2SO4. Hydrogen sulphide is a compound, H2S, but it does smell of rotten eggs. So Parker was right, sir." He winks, but he winks the eye furthest from the corpulent, ruddy-faced master so that he cannot observe Crisp's slight.

"Yes, Crisp, you are right. And no, Crisp, Parker was not. As usual, Parker was hedging his bets. In your exam tomorrow you may have to choose between two answers which, in your case Parker, means you will only have a fifty per cent chance of choosing the right answer, and that isn't good enough."

Mister Pope glances up at the ceiling of the classroom, as if imploring the gods to aid him in his thankless task.

"Now then," he says, leaning on his desk so that he can get as close to the boys as possible without endangering his respiratory system by breathing in their air, "I hope you have completed your revision and that you are all suitably armed for your exam tomorrow." He pauses, surveying the assembled company in much the same way as would a look out in a crow's nest.

"I hope you gentlemen know all the answers to the questions you get tomorrow. And I hope you get all the questions to which you know the answers. Beyond that I am left only to wish you good luck. Class dismissed! Parker stay behind!"

Usually, at the end of a class, desks are slammed down, books thumped-shut and the din of conversation froth ups like a mixture of baking soda, detergent, water and vinegar.

What is that? Sodium carbonate? Or is it bicarbonate of soda?

But not this time.

Faces turn towards him, some sympathetic, others all too obviously deriving a devilish enjoyment from his discomfort. He glares back at them.

"What have you done now, Marky?" whispers his favourite nerd.

"Beats me, Crispy! Wouldn't be my first private audience with Popey, now would it?"

Mark gets up off his stool slowly, almost reluctantly.

The class file out, many of them unable to resist a backward glance in the hope that this is the last time they see their classmate.

Mister Pope's woodwormy lectern stands up on a raised step; huge sliding blackboards rise up behind it, like the dark halls of hell. The extra height permits the teacher to look down upon his pupils, lending him a false authority.

One winter's afternoon not so long before, the chemistry teacher, Mister Pope, had been standing on the touchline when Mark had executed the perfect flying tackle on an opposing team's winger and, accidentally-on-purpose, collected Mister Pope in his follow through. Since that day, the chemistry teacher has been

154

inclined to maintain a studied distance between them, just as he is now using the lectern as his barrier.

Mark approaches.

"Parker?" The teacher speaks in a low voice to emphasise the gravity of what he is about to say. He tries to smile, too. It is a peculiar look; a look the boys believe Mister Pope practices each night in the mirror and one which he is unlikely to perfect.

"Parker, dear boy, if you could find it within your heart to be absent from the exam room tomorrow, I would take it as a great personal favour."

Mark Parker has fronted up to tougher opponents than this tubby pillock, but—

"Pardon, sir?"

The chemistry master thins his lips and hisses, "You heard, Parker. Find something else to do tomorrow morning and don't darken the doorway of my lab again. You are excused." He begins to marshal his papers.

"Excuse me, Mister Pope," Mark comes again, equally astounded as he is offended. "But did you just suggest I shouldn't turn up for the chemistry exam tomorrow?"

"Yes, boy. I did. That will be all." He tucks his papers under his arm and struts out, leaving his pupil staring up at the dark halls of hell.

Mark Parker wonders how his father – a man who has made a small fortune from sport and yet who dropped out of school early on – would react to Mister Pope's lack of faith in his son. He decides his father would in all probability let it go. As his father has told him on more than one occasion, "There is no profit in violence." And if Mark has to make the choice between being academically competent and being gifted at sport, he has for some time understood that he would rather emulate his father and be good at sport. So he disregards his teacher's request, curses him roundly and leaves.

Outside, a couple of the lads are making themselves busy, colourfully redefining Crisp's character in repayment for his volunteering to answer the teacher's question about the difference between sulphate and sulphide.

Mark marches past: "Leave Crispy alone you tossers. If he hadn't answered Popey's question we'd all still be in there listening to him bang on about how we're going to ruin his grade percentage. Now piss off."

The young bullies do immediately as they are ordered.

"Thanks, Marky. What did old Popey want then?"

"Never you mind, mate. He just wanted to wish me an extra bit of luck, that's all." He makes off towards the geography block, assuming exactly the same demeanour and expression he employs when trundling up to a scrum. Crisp keeps pace, just.

Bentley-Hall, the geography master is pretty much the antithesis of Mister Pope. He is a tall man, rangy of build and, some think, possibly a shade effete. Mark once caught the master staring at him and wondered whether he might not be safe alone in the man's company in the vicinity of the changing rooms after rugby practice. Over time, however, Mark has noticed Bentley-Hall staring at others in just the same manner and realises that he, Mark, does exactly the same when sizing up the opposition players as they get off their bus.

The class turns out to be largely procedural. The teacher runs through a few subjects he thinks might come up, tells them they are all worthy students and wishes them the very best of luck. He then dismisses the class.

"Parker stay behind," he adds, as an afterthought.

For the second time in a day, all eyes turn towards Mark.

"Yes, sir?" he asks, once the last of the class has filed out.

He approaches. "What can I do for you, sir?"

"Everything alright, Parker? You seem a bit despondent; a bit down."

"Er... no, sir." In truth he is thinking of mentioning what Mister Pope has said not forty-five minutes before, but worries, suddenly, that Bentley-Hall might be going to do the same.

What the bloody hell am I going to do if he does?

He seems even taller today, does Mister Bentley-Hall but, unlike the dislikeable Pope, the geography master doesn't lean forward to dominate, rather he leans backwards, resting his elbows on his desk. This pose, carefully designed as it is, draws the boys naturally towards him.

"Look, Parker, I just wanted to give you a small piece of advice about how to approach the geography paper."

Mark sighs, exhaling a couple of cubic metres of stored up, stale air at the floor.

"You sure you're alright, Parker?"

"Yes, sir. It's just that Mister Pope suggested I didn't turn up for the chemistry exam tomorrow and I thought you might be going to do the same."

Mister Bentley-Hall frowns in puzzlement, "Run that by me again, Parker. What did Mister Pope say?"

Mark relates the conversation, careful to repeat exactly the words and tone his chemistry teacher had employed.

"Did he, by Christ?" says Bentley-Hall.

"Yes, sir, he did. Just like that. Thought it was a bit of a strange thing to say."

"Strange, eh? Well, I wouldn't hold too much store by that." He pauses, deep in thought. "But you're right, Parker. Strange it was! Now," he stands up and rubs his face, "I was going to say that when you turn over your paper at the start of the exam, I want you to spend a good couple of minutes reading through all the questions. Don't rush straight in like you rush into a maul or a ruck; take a couple of minutes to read the questions and think about what the examiners are asking. Essentially, what they want to know is how well you know your subject, that's all. It's as simple as that; nothing more. You're not trying to win the ball; all you're trying to do is to convince them you know your subject. So, plan your response to the question before you start writing. Got that? Take your time."

"Yes, sir." Mark smiles, relieved. "And thank you, sir."

"That's alright, Parker. You can do it. You may not reckon yourself to be as bright as Crisp, but I am convinced you know your subject well enough; you've just got to get it down on paper in the right order. Good luck!" Bentley-Hall holds out his giant paw.

At first, Mark is not sure how to react to a gesture no teacher has offered before. But once he recognises the genuine sentiment in his teacher's eyes, he grasps the hand and shakes it firmly.

Outside, the rest of the class have strolled away to the dining hall.

Crisp, however, is waiting. "What was that all about?"

Mark relates his conversation with the geography master, but leaves out the bit about Mister Pope's strange request.

"Favoured status, eh?" Crisp notes, with unconcealed admiration. They slope off to join the others.

The exams are tough: chemistry, everyone agrees, is an absolute bastard, and an awful lot bemoan not having revised the right stuff.

Mark soon sweeps the debris of his exams from his mind and looks forward to receiving the Victor Ludorum for athletics and a special award for scoring more runs in a term than any previous pupil at the school. The accolades, he hopes, will go some way to softening the blow of his academic underachievement; a fact which he is sure will be made all too plain when his exam results arrive.

At Leaver's Day, he notices his wheedling chemistry teacher is sporting a black eye.

The Michaelmas Term comes too soon, and though Mark is pleased to see the same old faces, he is also pleased to see that one or two others haven't made the grade and so have not returned to join the sixth form.

"Good summer?" asks the willowy Crisp.

"So-so, Crispy," he replies, enigmatically. He knows his friend will want to talk about grades and is equally certain his friend will have amassed an army of As. "Go on, then," he instructs.

"Oh, not too bad," the nerd admits, casually. "A few A-stars. Not as many as my parents would have liked. You?"

"Couple of As; mostly Bs," Mark replies, equally as casually. "Funny thing though. Can't understand it. Got an A in geography. Surprised the life out of me. Impressed my parents. My dad even took me to the Oval to watch the last Test as a reward. Flunked chemistry though."

In fact, Mark hadn't really flunked chemistry; he'd got a D, in spite of the fact that he'd tried quite hard. It is part of his nature: trying. He can't help it. But he knows mentioning such a lowly grade will only serve to make him feel reduced in the company of one who will surely have made an A.

"You did, huh," Crisp says. "Funny, so did I."

"You what?" Mark rounds and stares at his friend in astonishment. "Chemistry? You? Crispy? You blew chemistry?"

"Yup! Blew it right out of the water. Not a plank left floating. Got an F. Parents went berserk. Cancelled the summer holiday. Said I didn't deserve a break if I hadn't worked hard enough to warrant it. Brought some tutor in. Told me I would have to resit."

The boys have, fortunately, been assigned to share a study and later that evening they relax and rake over a few coals from the previous term.

"I hear Bentley-Hall hasn't come back after the summer," Mark remarks. "Someone said he'd taken a job at another school. Did you hear that, Crispy?"

"Mmm! Heard the same. Apparently he boshed Popey at the end of last term. Don't know what it was about; nobody seems to: some bloody enormous argument, apparently."

Mark, though tempted, keeps his own counsel. He broods for a while.

Proper bloke, that Bentley-Hall!

"Crispy?"

"Mmm?"

"How come you blew chemistry?" Mark asks, staggered that his friend possesses either the mental acumen or the physical wherewithal to blow anything.

Rex Crisp looks up from his book. Though his hair is ginger, his eyes are almost black. He looks very directly at his able friend.

"Didn't want to pass it, did I?" He pauses, waiting for Mark to take in what he is being told.

"Didn't want to?"

"Uh-huh," Crisp replies. "Didn't want to. You see, my dad wants me to be a bio-chemist like him. Don't misunderstand me, Marky; my dad's not a bad bloke. But I'm buggered if I want to grow up to be like him!"

BY ACCIDENT

Surrey, England

Years later, he teases first-time dinner party couples by asking them how they met. It is a technique he employs to create common ground between those couples who don't know others and these days it is rare for them to have anyone to dinner who isn't married; unless of course it is one of their friends who is recently bereaved. And he knows it will follow that after telling their tale, one of them will be bound to come back and ask him to recall the same.

"Oh, yes. How did you meet? Tell us, please do," a dove will coo.

Abigail, though, will frown in mock disapproval of his coming embellishments and because she knows he will not be able to resist implying that it had been she, on their first meeting, who instantly formed designs on him, rather than the other way round. That is not true, of course, but Abigail has grown to tolerate his adjustment of the facts. She knows all too well that the temptation to gild his lily is far too attractive for him to refuse and it is bound to run away with him, like an insubordinate horse carrying off an inept rider. And she also knows that if he wants to convince himself their liaison was initiated by her, then for a multitude of reasons it is probably better for him to believe so.

Usually, after their guests have left, she pours him a nightcap and abandons him to his favourite armchair where he likes to review the curious circumstances of their introduction.

What intrigues him is the question of whether there was one single cause of it or whether their meeting came about as the result of a whole string of causes; a kind of long, chemical chain reaction or the kind of intricate process similar to that which is required for the American President to detonate an atomic bomb. But whatever its shape or procedure, their meeting brought about a seismic shift in the landscape of both their lives, and in his review lies great, great appreciation.

On this particular evening Bennett — for she addresses him by his surname, as is often the way with older couples — has consumed more wine than Abigail knows is good for him. She has driven him from the kitchen lest, in spite of his good intention, he break some delicate piece of her dinner service, thereby rendering her prized collection of Meissen incomplete and as such worth a good deal less than it might be whole.

The events leading up to their first meeting played out like one of those seventies Hollywood movies in which each individual smaller happening connects with other happenings to form some denouement of consequence; a train wreck or plane crash or something equally tragic.

Bennett lounges and imagines:

The mother of a shop assistant is unwell. A lorry driver sneezes violently. A middle-aged man drops his wallet. A young man stoops to pick it up as the arm of a crane swings through the space he has just vacated, before crashing through a shop front. The pretty shop assistant is taking a telephone call out the back at exactly the moment the store front is demolished.

If the mother had not been such a devout hypochondriac, the doctor would not have had to call the daughter. If the truck driver had not been prone to hay fever, he would not have sneezed and forgotten to secure the arm of the crane to the back of his truck. If the middle-aged man had not been distracted by a glimpse of a friend across the street, he would not have dropped his wallet. If the young man had not bent down to retrieve the wallet, the arm of the crane would have cut him in two. And if the phone had not rung, the pretty shop assistant would have been standing at her counter and she would not only have been killed, but also she would not have required rescuing from the ruins of the shop by the young man.

The curious consequence of the mother's hypochondria and the truck driver's allergic reaction to pollen are manifold. The young man and the pretty assistant marry and move away from the bothersome mother to live happily ever after. The truck driver takes a hay fever cure and his wife, whose sleep is no longer interrupted by his snoring, decides not to run away with the postman. The middle-aged man, whose wallet has been safely returned, can now buy his ticket for the holiday he has been promising himself as a reward for working at a job he hates. Sadly though, his plane is blown up over the Indian Ocean in a terrorist attack and he is no more.

Some you win; some you lose. Bennett chuckles.

"Are you alright in there?" Abigail calls from the kitchen.

"Yes, fine, thank you," Bennett responds.

He thinks he knows why he has had too much to drink: that chirpy gardener. When he'd come in for his morning instructions, the fellow had insisted on calling him *Bazza*, telling him he thought it made him sound more modern than... well, Barry. Bennett understood that the gardener was only trying to be amusing, but the mere idea of it – of being called *Bazza* – dismayed him to such an extent that all day he'd found himself looking forward to when he could weaken the concentration of his dismay by diluting it with copious quantities of red wine. And dinner had provided him with just such an opportunity, which is why he is now floating in a thick, alcoholic haze of obfuscated reflection, wondering why it is that people always try to be so jolly with him.

Like the middle-aged man of his imagination, Barry Bennett has enjoyed mixed fortunes.

He'd been planning his retirement for more years than he cared to remember. Work — for that is how he had come to view his job after he'd realised he would climb no more rungs of the ladder at the firm — had over time lost its impetus and so had he. So when the HR department notified him, not altogether unexpectedly, that he was being offered early retirement, he bit their hand off.

A lump sum and his pension increased in value to reflect the total that would have been achieved had he worked full-term? Well, who would have been stupid enough to refuse that?

His wife had seemed oddly nonplussed at the prospect of having him about the house to do all the little jobs he had put off whenever she mentioned them. Bennett had thought she would be pleased. Or if not pleased, then perhaps he'd hoped she might find it within her gelid heart to express a little gratitude for all the good times he had worked so hard for her to enjoy. But, she didn't. She just said she hoped he wouldn't be in the way and that he was never to ask her what was for lunch.

So, a few weeks before his retirement date, he ordered a new car. Bennett knew full well that he was applying a sticking plaster to the wound she had gashed in his pride; a sort of plug in the breach of his vanity or perhaps, because he hoped she might like the new car, a bridge over the widening cleavage she had wrought in their relationship, such as it was. What else could he have done? Surely a man, after working his fingers to the bone for most of his life, deserved some greater affirmation than that which was to be found in a woman who would willingly hold a ladder steady or pass him a screwdriver when he needed one. Surely if she couldn't see that, then...

"Where are you going?" she asked that first morning. "I thought you said you would be here today; I have a delivery coming."

It was the first day of the rest of his life – the first Monday in god-knows-how-many Mondays that he had not risen at six, been on the train by half-past and been sat at his desk by eight – and all she could care about was that for the first time in thirty years Bennett would be at home to receive a delivery, thus allowing her to go out.

But, in keeping with this new dawn which heralded how different his life was going to be and without wanting to let on about the new car he had to collect, he prevaricated, saying that he had things to do and that he couldn't be sure what his movements were for the day. Couldn't she–

"No, dear," she replied. "I'll be back just after lunch. And I hope you haven't forgotten we are due at the Wardles for Bridge at three."

"But, I– Oh, not the Wardles again, surely?"

"Yes, dear. Don't you remember? We said we'd play Bridge with them on Mondays now that you don't have to go up to town anymore."

He loathed Bridge at the Wardles. He didn't loathe Cynthia Wardle, of course; she was nice. But Jeremy Wardle was smarmy, especially in the lascivious way in which he fawned over his wife – Bennett's wife, that is, not his own. He had often wondered whether his wife resented the prospect of his being at home simply because it made it awkward for her to carry on with what she thought was her clandestine affair with Wardle.

Bennett knew about it, of course. Knew about it, had known about it for some good while and suffered it. Their affair was, after all, his choice. He either put up with it or they parted. So, preferring to have her to come home to as opposed to an empty house, he'd learned to live with it. Bennett had locked the storm of his emotions up in a box labelled *ONLY TO BE OPENED IN EVENT OF RETIREMENT* and tucked it on top of the wardrobe in the spare room.

Divorce? Well, he'd long ago decided that he wasn't going to continue to work if half his wages went to a woman who had the poor taste to indulge in the contents of Jeremy Wardle's underpants. No, divorce could wait until–

The slamming of the front door shattered the fragile ego of his new dawn.

Bennett phoned the garage and offered his apologies for not being able to keep his appointment for ten and would be there by three at the latest. They were polite and suggested he "come whenever it suits".

Fortunately, the package arrived just before one-thirty and he was able to get down the garage by two.

He sips his whisky and chuckles again.

Was that, he wonders, where it all began: the phone call from HR to offer him early retirement; the lump sum which enabled him to order the new car. Or was it long before that? Had his leaving for work every Monday triggered in his wife a necessary predisposition to complete her housework on the same day?

No, it wasn't that. She cleaned and dusted and attended to the laundry every Monday. Always had done! That was how she started her week, with cleaning and dusting and laundry: just like him, starting his week with rising at six, train by half-past and office by eight. That was what he did; that was what she did. That was what they both had done for thirty years.

So was she, like him, entitled to change her routine simply because he had changed his? He supposed she was. He wasn't on the train and she wasn't doing her housework. Instead, she had arranged to play Bridge with the Wardles. Was that her way of setting out the stall of their retirement? Bridge he didn't mind, although he'd only ever played it because he'd considered it healthy for them to share a common recreation. But Wardle? And on a Monday?

When she'd first mooted the idea Bennett had noticed the most unnerving feeling in his water that Bridge at the Wardles was going to prove her next, necessary predisposition for Mondays.

The new, red car proved to be a nest of viperous ergonomics and media interfaces. The salesman insisted on sitting in the passenger seat and forcing upon him a guided tour of the sophisticated workings of the latest technological innovations. He had not felt so disqualified from intelligence since that time the driver told him he couldn't get on the bus without first having bought a ticket. The concept had been anathema to him and on that day his journey had taken him twice as long as expected.

It was the same with the new car; the handover – the driving instructions and reams of paperwork which required signing – took the better part of an hour. At least three times during the lengthy process, he glazed over.

Bennett, glanced at his watch, grew increasingly agitated and urged the young man to bring his education to a conclusion.

Noticing his customer's discomfort, the salesman kindly entered Bennett's home address into the satellite navigation and programmed in from the choices a pleasantly seductive, female voice, assuring him that he would now be certain to get home by the quickest route, one which was not always the shortest.

But it was after three before the salesman had completed his tour of the deck.

Bennett drove swiftly, though not particularly hurriedly. His new car was far quicker than his old one and he hated the idea that he might pick up a speeding ticket on his maiden journey behind the wheel.

He was making good time and quite happy with his progress until the smooth siren of his satellite navigation system ordered him to turn right when he would normally have turned left.

Bennett dithered. Someone hooted. Bennett turned right and followed the road as instructed, the digital clock reminding him just how late he would be getting home.

Soon the siren of his destiny began to adopt the same scolding tones his wife adopted when he arrived home too late to change in time for their leaving to go out to dinner.

He began to fidget in his seat. He clipped a curb, ran the very tail end of an amber light. Bennett swore. He was sure he was being taken down the wrong road.

Then he realised the siren of the navigation system was, truly, taking him the long way round and he capitulated, understanding and begrudgingly admitting that the journey would in all probability be shorter in terms of time, as the roads allowed for more speed and the junctions were fewer.

Now that he was no longer intrigued by the route she had designed for him, he attempted to turn the siren off, thinking the silence might calm his nerves.

He pressed a button on the steering wheel: she grew louder. He pressed an alternative button on the centre console: she instructed him to turn round. He swore, pressed a couple of buttons one after the other and the siren began to shout at him, informing him in no uncertain terms that if he didn't get home on time, she was going to leave him.

The clock began to grin at him with red fiendish eyes: it was after half-past three and he still had a couple of miles to go.

A woman in front was taking her time. She was smoking, talking to her passenger, gesticulating, turning her head from the road, braking whenever she did so.

Bennett saw his chance: mirror, signal and stand on the accelerator pedal.

His new steed shot by the car in front like a Derby winner past a cart horse.

This was it! Bennett was alive! All that work, all those train journeys, all that stuff he'd had to put up with over the years. He was released, let go, an arrow from a bow, no longer just one more of so many languishing in a quiver, waiting to be used.

But the voice kept on.

He was approaching the second last turning from his road, the siren still commanding him to turn round. He glanced once more at the navigation screen and was stunned to see his wife's face mouthing obscenities at him.

Bennett reached over and fumbled for the knob which would surely remove her image from view. He pressed and turned, but still the voice harped on. He looked over at the buttons beside the screen, wondering which one would deliver him the silence he so desperately craved. His first day of retirement and already he was equally as stressed as if he had been at work!

It wasn't supposed to be like this, he thought as he drove straight into the back of the car in front.

The airbag deployed, hitting him on the nose with all the punch of a professional boxer.

———————

At first, Bennett wasn't sure what to think. He'd never been brought to a halt so rapidly in his life. Why, the simple physics of the experience were beyond his grasp! It felt as though all his organs had been wrested from their customary perch, only to slump in a heap somewhere down near his lap.

His nose was wet against the airbag and a second bag pressed against his arm. He eased open the door.

Bennett slid out sideways and, groggily, tried to find his feet. He mustn't think about himself, he told himself; it was far more important and only right for him to direct his concern towards the driver whose car he had run into.

He staggered forwards in the general direction of the car, which was now conjoined to his like an insect in mid-couple.

Blood dripped from his nose and his eyes watered so much it was as if he'd opened them under water. He hesitated, located his handkerchief and, leaning at an angle which he hoped might protect his jacket from the dripping blood, mopped at his top lip.

The car he'd shunted into was black.

Bennett loathed black cars. These days they were all either black or white, neither of which were good colours as far as being recognised in fog was concerned. Only it wasn't foggy; the sun was out and the visibility was as good as it could be.

His wife's car was black, he pondered as he mopped. Just like this one. Dowdy and black, and like his wife. Except that his wife wasn't black and black was fashionable, not like his wife.

Bennett shook his head and immediately wished he hadn't. That wasn't what he meant at all, all that stuff about her being black, and he wondered for a moment whether he might be concussed.

He looked up.

Oh God, he thought. It is my wife's car. Oh God! Oh no! I've run into the back of my wife's car. My wife! Not somebody else's! My own wife's car!

"Barry?" shrieked a voice so disdainful he was sure it couldn't have belonged to a human and therefore assumed it must belong to the siren in his new, bent red car.

"Barry, is that you?" came a second shriek.

"Yes," he mumbled through his now bloodied handkerchief. "I–"

"What the bloody hell are you playing at?" She strutted

towards him. "You've gone into the back of me." The gravity of her tone descended as the pitch of her incredulity soared.

"I–"

"You bloody idiot, Barry!" she stated, and paused. "Is that a new car?" The previously aggravated Mrs Bennett was suddenly consumed by the possibility in her observation.

"I–"

"You bought a new car without discussing it with me first?" she exploded.

"I–"

"And now we'll be late for the Wardles."

Bennett mopped some more. "Well," he mumbled, "one must be thankful for small mercies. Honestly dear, the way you go on about Wardle anybody would think you had a thing for him."

The last thing he saw was his wife's tightly clenched fist sailing towards him and then, very suddenly, the lights went out.

When Bennett came to and his sight returned, he had no real idea of his whereabouts. He identified the fuzzy outline of a person leaning over him and tried to roll onto his side to get some clearer idea of where he was, but he couldn't. His body declined every request he made of it.

He turned his head and saw was his own new, bent red car. The only evidence of his wife's presence was the rear bumper of her black car, which was lying, like him, in the middle of the road.

His nose hurt, a lot, but his jaw hurt too and he couldn't fathom why. Beyond that, nothing at all hurt, which was good but odd, considering?

Hands dabbed at his face.

He hadn't the energy to fight the interference, so he didn't.

Bennett remembered the accident. He remembered his wife and he recalled her anger; the violent sum of all the discontents she had obviously been storing up over all these years while she waited for him to acknowledge her contribution to their life.

Was that, he wondered, her purchase?

Bennett had bought the new car as his reward: had his wife released the sum of her pent-up frustrations on him because she believed she finally deserved to?

Was that her reward?

He remembered her fist. He remembered, vaguely, falling back into the road, a car coming towards him.

"Sir?" asked the voice of an angel. "Sir? Can you hear me? Just lie still, please. You've been hit by a car."

Blood bubbled and popped from his nose as he breathed.

"Sorry about this," he mumbled. "Must look a dreadful mess."

"That's alright, sir. Just you lie still for a minute."

The angel in the bright yellow jacket looked away and said something to someone wearing a green jumpsuit who, in turn, walked away to an ambulance.

An ambulance?

"I'm not that bad that I need an ambulance. It's only my nose." He felt stupid, having caused such a fuss.

She was pretty, though; the police woman. Not young. But pretty all the same. "Can't seem to feel my legs!" Bennett remarked, casually. "Haven't lost them, have I?"

The person in the green jumpsuit returned to view. He was holding some kind of brace and a big board.

"No, sir. They're right where they should be," replied the very pretty policewoman. "Just lie still for a moment, please sir. We'll let the paramedics do their stuff."

She stood up, which made him feel dizzy. She was talking; he knew it because he could see her lips moving.

172

"What was that?"

"We got a call from a member of the public who said she'd seen a man hit by a car. Wouldn't leave her name. Do you know who that might have been, sir?"

Without thinking, Bennett said, "Margaret, probably. Margaret Bennett, my wife."

"And you are, sir?"

"Bennett. Barry Bennett. Who are you?"

"I'm a police woman, sir. My name's Abigail."

GONE

London, England

It is a relief to find the old man in the café just off the Waterloo Road. I use the word *find* in the general sense, because I hope he's going to be there and I am all too aware that one of these days he may not be, and know that when that day comes I will have to go out and look for him just as I did that first time, all those many months ago.

"It's a busy, noisy road, isn't it?" he says through a mouthful of piping-hot baked beans. "If it's like this at midday, you can't imagine how busy it gets during the rush hour."

I don't reply. What's there to say?

He carries on with his concentrations, slowly grinding the beans to a pulp, rolling them around his mouth, savouring every texture and flavour as though they might be his last.

So, what can one say to pass the time?

I suppose one could say the steamed-up double-glazing mutes the road noise sufficiently to permit conversation without having to speak up so much that others have no alternative but to listen

175

to you. I suppose one could point out that one cannot reasonably expect to eat so close to the river without having to put up with the intrusion of the traffic. In fact, as I sit and study him, I realise there is a great deal more one can say about our monthly meeting place and its proximity to the bridge, but I don't; I can see that he's far more interested in his breakfast.

But, like the silence endured by those who live alone, he is keen to engage in conversation.

"As a lad," he begins, "I lived on the approach to a bridge. It was the narrowest, the middle bridge of the three serving our area. The upstream bridge was a grand stone edifice, right slap-bang in the centre of our local market town. The downstream bridge was an old and rickety construction which fed into a village a bit larger than ours; mind you, it was only perceived to be larger because it boasted two supermarkets and not the tiny little one like what we had."

He quiets for a moment to mop his plate, but the fried bread cracks beneath the weight of his fork, so he layers a slab of white bread with hard butter and wipes up with that instead. The metal rack sitting in the middle of our table is arched like the railway tunnel he sometimes sleeps in and for the moment it is heavy with slices of triangular, supermarket-plastic white bread. Soon enough, though, it will be empty.

"More tea, dear?" asks the waitress.

He grins up at her, but is careful not to open his mouth for fear of offending her with his yellow-chequered teeth.

"Guessed as much," she replies and refills his cup with a brew so strong it would surely strip the French polish off my armoire.

"All the three bridges suffer from a terrible weight of traffic," he continues as soon as she has left. "Sixty years ago I'd never have imagined the volume of traffic the bridges have to bear these days. For sure we had a weight restriction back then, probably still is one for all I know, but now it's a wonder how they stand up."

He doesn't look much. But then, neither does he look as bad as some. I have to give him that. It is the attention he pays to his clothing which probably gets him into the café in the first place. Normally, his sort are told to get lost as soon as they open the door.

Imagine that! "Get lost?" How can you tell a man or a woman who is already lost to get lost even further?

To most, the fellow opposite me doesn't conform to the stereotype of the more common urban vagrant. After all, not many of them wear suits. And if they do, not many of them wear jackets that correspond to their trousers. Usually they wear bulky tracksuit bottoms devoid of any particular colour other than the faded manila of the cardboard upon which they sleep. And if they wear jackets, they are usually made from some heavy material like tweed or melton wool, and are worn and creased and often clumsily patched.

But he doesn't. His suit is grey and, if you look closely, still holds a vague chalk-stripe. And whilst not being recently pressed, it presents quite tidily. Not dapper or natty or spruce, you understand, yet somewhere on the bus route to all three. It hangs a little on him, but his blue tie is neatly and tightly knotted and bears the crest of some city institution he used to belong to: a Fleur de Lys, flanked by crowns and masonry hammers. However, it is his shirt that gives him away; the collar and cuffs are frayed and the bright whiteness it must have once possessed has long since faded to the same muddy ochre as that of other's tracksuit pants.

"A blind man would've guessed we lived close by the bridge," he is saying. "You see, it was impossible to get away from the sirens of the emergency services. Although in their defence," he pops another triangle of bread into his mouth and mumbles through it, "they had no alternative other than to use our bridge to reach those in need on the far side of the river."

He quiets, the rotation of his jaw disrupting his progress

through the mist of his memory. But, when he relocates his thread, he continues, "Ambulances were the most common, but that was only because the big hospital stood right behind our house. After them it was the police cars speeding to accidents or robberies: the local villains avoided using the bridges, they presented too much of a bottleneck for their getaways. Well, that and the chance that they might be caught out by the immigration service carrying out one of their spot checks."

He is shaven — up to a point. His cheeks are smooth, but from around and below his bony jawline spring odd tufts of white hair and his neck is reddened and scraped raw in places. You can't blame him; shaving with a blunt razor and without either a mirror or shaving foam is a delicate art and not one many men would want to have to practice.

"And then," he says, "there were the fire engines. They were the loudest. They had a really distinctive siren. They used to wail a strangely quaint, baritone lament; a sort of mournful dirge that wouldn't have been so unattractive if it hadn't been so disturbing. It was sort of earthy, sort of urgent. It reverberated right down in your insides. It left you in no doubt they were hurrying to some awful happening that required their manifold talents."

He slurps his tea and glances nervously round the cafe. Fortunately no one has noticed the slip in his etiquette. And, if they have, the other patrons are far too busy with their own indulgences to make anything of it.

"These days the fire engines give out an ear-piercing European screech," he continues, "which sounds more like a pig being dragged to the slaughterhouse.

"But their noises were not really that much of an intrusion; they were more punctuation marks amongst the continuous racket of the passing cars, the barking dogs and the aeroplanes as they struggled to gain height out of the airport. That's not to mention the high-pitched, nasal whine of the carpenter's saw from the wood yard down the road.

"So, you see, I was brought up in a world of perpetual noise the way those who live farther out in the country are brought up in a world of keen silence. And though I have some memory of feeding at my mother's breast, it is perhaps the hubbub from the bridge that springs to mind when I recall my childhood.

"You know," he follows on quickly, preserving his moment, "even television assisted in my youthful appreciation of bridges. There were bridges at Toko-Ri, Remagen and over the River Kwai, and much later that extremely long bridge that proved too far for all those brave parachutists; all of them bridges in countries I've never visited. There were even some nice photographs of bridges in Madison County, though God alone knows where Madison County is. I was never moved to find out."

He studies his plate for a minute, making sure he has gleaned every last morsel of his Full English from it.

"Yes, my youth was full of bridges of every kind," he goes on, "most real, some imagined. And then there was that awful tune I can remember my mother humming; the one about a bridge being over troubled water. Well," he sits back for a moment and clasps his hands about his stomach, like a vicar finally content with his sermon, "if it wasn't for the water, why the devil would you build a bridge over it in the first place? How anybody ever made a shilling out of pointing out the blinking obvious, I'll never know. It just goes to show how much common sense the record buying public possessed in the sixties, doesn't it? Even that nutter James Brown thought there was some link between being a sex machine and a bridge. Fancy that! Sex and a bridge! I suppose it was the drugs."

He sits forward and examines his empty plate again. When he is certain he has not overlooked the smallest morsel, he stares at the plate, perhaps conjuring a vision of how it had looked before he had cleared it, perhaps commanding his stomach to remember what it has received and so, further on down the road, rest and be grateful.

"To my mind there are two kinds of bridge; there's ones for sleeping under and others for walking over. They're both the same really. I mean you couldn't sleep under one, if you couldn't walk over it in the first place.

"The one for sleeping under isn't so bad, when you come to think of it. It's warm when there are enough people to provide a screen against the mean wind that blows up the river. And it's even better when the soup kitchen turns up round the corner. Although you can't rely on those nice Indian people the way you used to. Sometimes they just don't show up. I don't suppose it's their fault, mind you; it's probably some new EU regulation that stops them from coming regularly.

"'Course, when it really bites you have to move to a vent or a drain or an arch or tunnel or someplace. There's more than a few who think they can brave it out and never wake up. That's when the arches at the station fill up, when it's that cold. But then they're the same as bridges, aren't they, arches; something moving above and us shilly-shallying about underneath.

"Then there's the other kind of bridge; the broad flat one where the wind blows even harder up top than it does down below; not much use that one.

"I remember watching a black and white film as a lad. It was one of my father's favourites. What was it titled now? We used to watch it when my mother had gone to bed. It wasn't rude or anything. It was just that after years of watching films with my dad – mostly war movies, during which my father could never resist pointing out every last lapse in continuity, but of which we were happily ignorant... Well, where was I? Oh, yes. Well after years of watching films with my dad, my mother usually gave up the good fight and went off to lie in the less contentious arms of Morpheus. And my dad? My dad would pour himself another generous measure of whisky and wrestle with the wrapper of another packet of cheese biscuits as he muttered about the lack of detail in the film.

"The lead man was an American; an infantry officer. He spent much of the movie wearing a trench coat; nothing strange in that. But what got my father's goat was the vent in the back of his coat. It was a single-vented trench coat, and according to my father only cavalrymen wore single vents, not infantrymen. Makes sense when you think about it; the sides of the coat falling down on either flank of the horse.

"Then there was the leading lady, the one from *Gone with the Wind*. A right nutcase she was; a wild look in her eyes, like she'd spent too many nights out on the bricks, you might say. Her look was quite disturbing, wasn't it? But that particular woman's dementia was of no lasting concern to my father.

"No, his vociferous censure fell on the fact that the two lovers met on at least three different bridges. Or was it four? London Bridge was definitely in there somewhere. Then there was one with iron girders, probably Hungerford Bridge. And then there was Waterloo Bridge, which was the namesake of the film, of course, and where I have, on more than one occasion, hung my hat, as it were. Funny, how could I forget the name of that film?

"No small wonder though that American fella ended up with London Bridge when he thought he was buying Tower Bridge," he says by way of conclusion.

The waitress, understanding more than simply the simple order of things, asks if dessert is a must.

He stares at me, his blue eyes cloudy and rheumy and weighed with a heavy expectancy. He is waiting to see whether my pocket will stretch to apple crumble and custard.

She asks him again, but looks directly at me.

I nod and he grins, but again without showing many of his teeth.

To fill the time waiting for the order, he goes on a bit about other bridges he has known. I don't really listen; I just sit and search his face for some clue as to how he is in himself.

Crevices of bitter cold are etched in the lines around his eyes. It would be easy to mistake them for smile lines, but I know full well they are not. The cold, once it has taken hold in a man, is unmistakeable. It lives inside him in its many forms, wears many disguises and is always a devious foe. Sometimes, when one starts out warm, the cold comes hard and fast and induces in a man a shivering which is impossible to stop. Sometimes it comes in the guise of a friend, sidling up and gently poisoning you until too late you realise your fingers and toes are numb. And, sometimes, the cold creeps across your skin like the Black Death born upon a breeze. This is when it is most dangerous, for this is when you skin your knuckle or scrape your elbow or graze your knee, and once the first layer of your skin is broken all manner of infection steals in to commence its necrotising. That kind of cold leads only to the mortuary.

He looks across the table at me to check I have not drifted too far from his monologue.

I smile back. I haven't, but I have.

After the bridges will come the river and he will explain to me how the river, though responsible for reducing the temperature beneath the bridge, provides him with direction, and how the constant movement – the flowing of the river – implies progress, and how direction and progress are good for the soul. "We're not suited," he will say, "to standing still. We all need to keep moving, don't we?"

I have, perhaps, heard his diatribe once too often; he rarely deviates from the subject. Clearly he has grown attached to the bridges, which is understandable: they are both his shelter and the roof beneath which he plies his trade, if begging can be defined as a trade.

The apple crumble and custard arrive and he grows confused. Even though it is one of the reasons why we are here in the café, not particularly the apple crumble but whatever sustenance my wallet can stretch to, he knows he must give me something in return for my benevolence, especially if he wants our meetings to continue. But, I wonder, is giving over similar to giving up? Is he prepared to give up the information I have come to obtain? That is what he is thinking.

"What is it you want to ask?" he offers.

"I want to know what brought you to the bridges." It's what I need to know; what I have sat through all his talks for. I couldn't come right out with it the first time; it would have made him too suspicious. He's been gone twenty years, which puts him somewhere around seventy, and when I first found him he proved reluctant to be drawn.

He glances at me and then turns his attention back to the steam curling from his bowl: the chef has been generous with the custard.

"Like all of these things, it's difficult to know the beginning of it," he begins, "Was it the Great Depression of the last century? Was it the great banking crisis earlier on this century? All I know is the unimaginable happened. One minute I was in my office and the next I was out of it. And seeing as I'd spent ten years reassuring my wife that they'd never let me go, that the bank couldn't run without me, I wasn't in the position to turn up at home with my tail between my legs."

The lure of the crumble proves too great for him and he breaks his biography to dive right in.

I wonder if the heat in the food is as fundamental to him as the nourishment it will provide.

"Fortunately, I'd been prudent," he declares between mouthfuls, "There was enough money for the first few years. But I still had to maintain the illusion for her and, if I must be honest, for myself too. So, I'd get up at the same time and get the same train into town, just I had done every working day for thirty years. Only the singular difference was that by then I had no desk to occupy.

Museums and art galleries became my new office, and I became a font of what I'd always thought of as peripheral knowledge. If I didn't know what was painted by whom or when what was made and by whom, then nobody did. I became an encyclopaedia of useless information. I mean, how many of Turner's paintings do you need to sit in front of to know the man loved God but distrusted the sea?

"And, of course, I became quite the liar. Well, you can't sit there at dinner of an evening and relate the truth about what a busy day you've enjoyed at the work when you haven't been anywhere near it, now can you?"

He slows his assault on the crumble, growing aware, like a steam engine stoker, that with each shovel he loads, he is that bit closer to journey's end.

"Then the money started to run low. And, what with that and the lying, I think that was when the last of my dignity deserted me."

"What did you do then?" I ask quickly, allowing him no time to dwell on the darker moments in case it sidetracks his thinking.

"Then?" he doesn't look at me now, "then, one day, I didn't go home. Simple as that, I just didn't go home." He pauses, wondering how to explain the mechanics of it.

"You see, I'd got talking to a few of the others; a few of the ones I'd gotten used to dropping a few coins to when I still had the job. Sometimes, if I had the time, I'd stop off on my way home and talk to them; try to persuade them to spend the money I was giving them on food rather than on booze or meth or drugs or whatever: people like Chalky and Bozo, and Cheeky and Anna or whoever was hanging around the bridge at that time." He scrapes the bowl with his spoon. Every morsel of apple, every crumb of crumble, every smear of custard; no scrap is left behind.

"Then, one day, I simply sat down beside them, and that was

both the end and the beginning of it. It was that easy; though I never got a dog like many of them have. I mean, I know they keep you warm, but it's the responsibility isn't it?" He pauses, indulging in his dessert, but says quietly, "The cold is the worst of it, that and the lack of any real sleep; we're continually being woken up and moved on."

I toy with the teaspoon in my saucer. "And you never went back home after that?"

He wipes his mouth with the paper serviette and examines it to make sure he has deposited nothing of nutritional value on it.

"No," he replies without a trace of sentiment, "I never went back."

"Why?" I ask. "What was so terrible, so wretched that it kept you from going home?"

He studies the ceiling for a while. He wants me to know that his recollection does not come cheap and that I will, in future, be in his debt. It is part of the process which preserves the continuance of our meeting.

But, his eyes no longer seem so distant, so unreachable and rheumy, and his expression softens. Possibly, the happy contentment of his stomach is pricking his memory and slackening his jaw.

"It wasn't her fault, if that's what you're thinking," he begins, "Oh, I could tell what she was going through. I could see it in her eyes; accusation, hurt, pity, and, in the end, a kind of impotence. They were all there. They were all so natural. She couldn't conceal them no matter how hard she tried. Over time, I probably could've learnt to live with the looks, but the problem wasn't with her; the problem was with me. It was around me and within me. And I knew I would never shake it off."

He finishes his tea, gets up and shuffles down the back to the toilets.

I settle up.

He is gone a while, no doubt availing himself fully of the

facilities. But, just when I think I'm going to have to go and see where he has got to, he returns, smiling.

"That was the ticket," he declares. I am not sure whether he is referring to his time in the toilets or his meal. He rubs his clean hands together. "I'm obliged to you."

"Can I do anything for you before you go? Get you anything?" I ask, slipping a fiver onto the table. It is just enough, a fiver; more than that he would refuse.

He gazes down at the picture of the Queen for a couple of seconds before nimbly pocketing the note.

It is as he stands by our table that I notice the cold in his expression. However, it is not a reflection of the knifing wind or the soaking rain, or the glacial concrete beneath the cardboard on which he will lay his bedroll. And neither is it the bitter countenance of rejection that hangs about so many others of his kind. No, his look is not about the temperature. The look that stems from within the man who stoops before me is the damning, unsympathetic frost of self-rejection and the hopeless resignation of that fragile commodity we label self-respect. It is the bough that has broken beneath the weight of ice in the winter of his life. It is the trunk of the once sturdy tree that is now shrivelled and petrified beyond redemption. It is the price he has forced himself to pay for what he believes to be his failure. This is the worst kind of cold, for once a man has surrendered to it there is little chance he will ever find warmth again. He will never banish this cold from his soul, for it is the hoarfrost of guilt; a hoarfrost that persists and which will never thaw.

I sit and watch him tuck his shirt and pullover into his baggy trousers, knowing it will be another week before we meet again.

He shakes my hand and, in spite of his overpowering odour, I am driven to hug him. But I don't. I know that any physical contact will only unravel the knot of my emotions, never mind his. It is better we keep it that I am nothing more to him than a charitable soul with a passing interest in his welfare.

I check my watch: I'm due back at my desk in fifteen minutes.

"Next time," I say and offer him his coat.

The glass door to the street runs down with condensation as I pull it open for him to pass out into the Waterloo Road.

"Sure," he replies, "that'd be nice."

As I stand and watch him shuffle off up the broad pavement beneath the tall buildings, his greatcoat flapping about his heels, I am reminded that my aunt passed away almost ten years ago to the day. The doctor said she died of a broken heart, waiting for him to return from his sudden, self-imposed exile.

I have never had the heart or the ignorant courage to tell him. At her funeral, friends told me that she had hoped every time the phone rang that it might be news of him, or that whenever someone had come to the door her heart had raced at the thought it might be him come home to her at last. But he had never returned. Like the life they had once enjoyed and the hope he had built his dreams upon, he was gone.

THE BACKS OF THE LEAVES

The Drôme, France

He is sitting in the shade of a walnut tree, recording his day's progress in a pocketbook.

COL DE LA VACHE, Dylan writes in one column of the page headed 28th July, and in the adjacent column he adds the altitude, *887m.*

Col de la vache!

He raises his hand to shade his eyes against the glare of the noonday sun.

There are no cows to be seen: they are, probably and sensibly, ruminating in one of the other circles of shade dotted about the high valley.

He glances at the sign once more and wishes it was wooden and weathered, with the name and height of the mountain pass transcribed in a more romantic calligraphy rather than simple, plain white capitals stamped on a black, rectangular metal plate. The rural landscape, he reckons, merits a more fitting symbiosis.

Dylan was never what others alluded to as the athletic type.

It wasn't that he didn't enjoy sport; it was more that his physical attributes had not magnified to the kind of muscular compaction required to compete at any serious level. He was neither tough enough for rugby, nor rough enough for football and whenever he'd tried to muster the wherewithal to join in similar team sports, Dylan had found the boisterous chumminess of it all strangely uninspiring. Running and jumping, he hadn't been bad at — he'd enjoyed the individuality of track and field, but *not bad at* was never going to get him selected to represent the school. So his attitude to sport had lapsed into one of indifference and, eventually, he'd let exercise slip from the menu of his interests.

Cycling, he had come to late on.

The day before, Dylan had cycled the Beast of Provence — *Mont Ventoux*, cycling's Holy Grail. Climbing the initial twenty-odd kilometres up from *Bédoin* had been relatively easy. But after *Saint-Estève* the gradient had steepened to nearly nine per cent, and nine per cent was a good bit more than he was used to. It was not, he'd fallen asleep last night understanding, what his training had prepared him for. It was not like riding Ditchling Beacon, which was how Dylan had, up until now, measured his cycling aptitude. There was, he used to think, Ditchling Beacon and the rest of the world.

He'd first cycled the Beacon as part of a London to Brighton charity bike ride some five or so years before. The climb up the northern side of the South Downs had, on his first attempt, beaten him and he'd had to dismount to catch his breath after only a short way. The next year, he'd got halfway up and the following year, having trained specifically for the climb, he'd made it all the way to the top without stopping.

Dylan had, at the time, considered that something of an achievement and, once he'd sailed sweetly past those walking their bikes up the steep hill, he'd come to the conclusion that if he could ride the Beacon, he could ride anything. Soon enough, he found he looked down on *fat boys*, as he'd heard those who had to push their bikes referred to, and vowed never to number amongst their sorry crew again. Never! Not ever!

If only he'd known *Mont Ventoux* was akin to ten Beacons strung straight out together! Yesterday had hurt and hurt a lot, and he'd had to dismount to rest at least a half dozen times. In that humbling way cycling has of making you feel as though you're playing a protracted game of snakes and ladders, Dylan found himself pushing his bike with the *fat boys* while the more practised *rouleurs* breezed on by.

However, that was history and he now knew he had asked too much of himself by taking on such a climb on his first day. Today's route, though, presents him with yet more challenges: ten or so *cols* which will lead him out of the *Vaucluse* and into the Alps of the *Drôme*; his destination the town of *Die*.

He closes his pocket book and slips it, with his pencil, into the plastic wallet, which he tucks into the back of his vest.

A gigantic bird of prey glides effortlessly on thermals born of the union between the sweltering sun and the intractable mountains, and every now and then a warm wind shoots up from the valley below, crests the *col* and rifles on through the fields of lavender laid out before him. Gaily coloured flowers sway back and forth as invisible artists bless fields with broad brushstrokes of violet, indigo and magenta. A bee buzzes lazily past; a busy bee, but not one that is so busy it must hurry.

Dylan looks at his map and lazily tosses the question of whether he has the time to make a detour down into *St Nazaire-le-Désert* and freshen his feet in the cooling, crystal waters of the *Roanne*.

After a while he spots a lone cyclist approaching up from the south, the way he has come. The rider is lean, like most, and wears a white cap, white singlet and black shorts. He ascends at a smooth and measured pace, much as an escalator ascends and with as much apparent effort. When the rider reaches the top of the *col*, he glances around, notices Dylan and nods courteously, one rider to another in a remote place.

He dismounts, props his bike up against the sign and removes a camera from a small pannier at his rear wheel. He stands back and takes a snapshot, recording the proof of his having attained the *col*.

"*Bonjour, ça va?*" he asks.

"*Oui*," Dylan replies. "*Pas mal. Un peu chaud, mais...*"

"Yes, it is warm," he replies in French-accented English. "Better than rain eh? You have come far?"

Dylan is irked that the Frenchman has picked him for an Englishman but, given the soporific fragrance of the lavender and the welcome opportunity to rest, he dismisses his frustration. "*Beaumont-du-Ventoux*. You?"

"*Bédoin*."

"Didn't see you on the Beast yesterday?"

"No," the stranger hesitates. "This morning."

Dylan gets to his feet. He realises he should have recognised the fellow as a hill-climber — or *grimpeur* as they are known — when he clocked the ease with which the fellow came up the hill.

"You certainly get along. I didn't think I was hanging about. I..." He runs out of words, realising not only how far his fellow cyclist has come in such a short time, but also that if he keeps on marvelling at his accomplishment, Dylan will only be advertising his own shortcomings. "Er, I'm Dylan, pleased to meet you."

"Jean."

Jean removes his short-finger gloves and they shake hands. His grip is vice-like and his hands, like his limbs, are slender and sinewy. His features are sleek, as though his face and his torso have been designed and tested in a wind-tunnel before being commissioned to the road.

"Fabulous scenery up here," Dylan suggests. "A little different to that Bald Mountain, the *Ventoux*."

"Yes, I know what you mean. There are no trees on the *Ventoux*; it is always windy, which makes it difficult. Are you riding far?"

Dylan thinks quickly: if he happens to be heading towards the same night-stop, how embarrassing will it be if he doesn't arrive until a couple of hours after this lean greyhound? The guy will surely suss' Dylan out to be a serious punter.

The *grimpeur's* bike looks to be titanium or carbon fibre or some such exorbitantly priced, lightweight material; nothing like his own cheap and cheerful plodder.

"*Die*," he says, slightly swallowing the name of the town as though it holds some devilish haunting.

"Yes, me too!" Jean replies, studying Dylan's bike for a few seconds. Whatever it is he is weighing up in his mind, it tips the scales positively. "If you like we can ride together for the afternoon?" he adds. "I am pleased to have your company."

They set off together and ride the ups and downs of the *Cols du Portail* and *des Guillens*. At each pass they come to, Jean pauses, props his steed up against the sign and takes a photo. Dylan notes down the name and height of the same in his pocketbook, hurrying so that he is ready to roll in tandem.

"You can have a Garmin or a Raleigh to record the height, gradient and distance you travel," Jean remarks as they cruise off down the slope.

"Sure, I know that. I notice you have one, but you still take a shot of the sign. Why is that?"

"The *Club des Cent Cols* – the *100 Cols Club*. It is a part of the *Vélo Club Annecy*. To join the club you have to ride 100 *cols* and five of them must be above 2000 metres. You are on your honour to achieve this, but I prefer to keep a photographic record. This way, who can argue?"

"Sounds pretty hardcore to me," Dylan says, keeping his sentences short, conserving his energy.

Jean smiles, "Not so difficult, perhaps."

They ride on in silence for a while, immersing themselves in the heady perfumes of the lavender.

Jean keeps glancing at Dylan's bike as though not only is his steed yesteryear's model, but also as if he still can't gauge his companion's proficiency. "You are not interested in how far you ride or how high you climb?" he asks.

Dylan shrugs in response. Or at least he tries to; shrugging is not the easiest of physical expressions when your shoulders feel as though they are welded to the handlebars. The awkward movement causes his bike to wobble momentarily.

"Not really," he replies, trying to sound nonplussed. "I'm not much interested in the statistics of it." And in truth, he isn't.

They drop down to the foot of the *Col de Pennes*, where they pause for water.

Dylan watches nervously.

"Ready?" asks Jean.

He nods and they begin the ascent.

The *Pennes* is different to the last few *cols*. The road steepens very rapidly, as much as twelve per cent in stretches. Unlike yesterday's long, steady climb, though, the road switches back and forth endlessly; the only respite being the bends, where the slope flattens out briefly.

Towards the end of the first kilometre, Dylan's heart and lungs are desperate to vacate his chest cavity and he feels as though he is pedalling squares.

Jean stays with him, breezing up the climb.

Dylan soldiers on; not raising his head, keeping his eyes focussed only a few metres beyond his front wheel.

He creeps round a corner. A sign! They must be nearly there! He glances over at it whilst trying to retain his rhythm and concentration.

Another 3.5 Kms to go! Only halfway! Jesus!

Jean promptly drops him.

The fall-out from having cycled the Beast of Provence only the day before weighs heavily on him. His knuckles burn white against the handlebars. His stomach backs into his spine, his calves strain and his thighs cane. Even the muscles in his neck are yelling their disapproval: they are wrenched wire-tight like twisted cables, bunching in knots and fraying under the strain. He knows he cannot stop when in the company of another rider, imagining and dreading the disgrace it would bring him. He channels the pain, loses his sight and blanks his mind.

There must come an end soon. There must!

And after what seems like a year, he rounds a corner to glimpse Jean taking a snap of his bike up against the sign: *Col de Pennes Alt. 1082m.*

They shake hands and embrace in that peculiarly awkward way men do, looking for all the world as though they are about to be caught holding hands.

Dylan breathes deep. "Quite pleased with that," he remarks, even though he knows he has come up with the laughing group, as those last to arrive are often called.

"Yes," replies Jean, apparently untroubled by the ascent. But, not wanting to be thought uncharitable, he adds, "It is hard. Some longer, some steeper, but not so many so hard. It is a good one to finish, eh?"

They set off again, this time down the hill into the valley of the *Drôme* towards their night stop in *Die.*

Going up, he knows, can be tough, but going down he knows can be plain terrifying.

Jean disappears in a flash of white jersey, whilst Dylan rolls down the mountainside with all the grace and control of an old bucket bouncing down a gulley. By halfway his hands belong to the brake levers, and in the village of *Barnave* he nearly collects an elderly lady, who totters off her top step at exactly the wrong moment. Then there are the few kilometres along the bottom of the valley into *Die* and, fortunately, the other man has not waited.

They pass the night at a small *auberge*. Dylan's bag, he is relieved to find, has been transferred from the previous night's accommodation and he is so cooked from his day's exertions that he barely musters the energy to wash his kit and hang it up to dry.

He sleeps soundly for an hour in a steaming-hot bath before joining Jean for the evening meal.

The lamb is very welcome and proves palatable but, they agree, who amongst the guests would be courageous or stupid enough to complain to the lady of the house if their meal proved anything less. She is formidable and with ease persuades them to share a couple of glasses of *Clairette de Die*.

"People say the *Méthode Dioise* comes before *Champenoise*," Jean says, holding his glass up to the light and examining the liquid's pale translucence. "They chill the wine during the fermentation and the yeast that is left after filtering gives the *Clairette* a very special fizz."

Dylan nods in approval and sips carefully. "It's kind of flowery and grapey and creamy all at once. Kind of refreshing. Bubbly." He knows that in the morning he may pay a high price for introducing alcohol into his system, particularly after so much exercise, but he is heartened by his achievements and bolstered by the company of his new found friend.

"'Nother glass?" Dylan suggests.

Jean shakes his head: "Not for me. I must go back to my room and take on some more food. Fuel for the tank, eh?" he pats his stomach.

"More?" Dylan asks, incredulous. "I'm stuffed. I can't think of anything worse than taking on board more weight only to have to haul it up the road in the morning."

"This is not how it is for me, my friend," Jean replies. "I must eat the calories I will burn. If I don't have 6,000 in my tank, what fuel will I burn? This night I will eat and drink some more protein foods. But I must not stop you." As he gets up from the table, he asks, "Would you like to ride with me a little longer? In the morning? The *Col de Rousset* is interesting."

Interesting!

Dylan turns the adjective over and over, while he stares at his empty glass. A number of similar adjectives leap into his mind: everything from alluring through enthralling to suspicious.

"Sure! That'd be great. But if I hold you up—"

Jean grins, "Okay. Good."

Saturday morning dawns bright and a little too early. Dylan's physical self is in reasonable fettle, but his mental self is somewhat apprehensive; the dubious pleasure of the previous evening's descent served only to provide him with a preview of the climb in store.

They set off while others sleep.

A little way out of town they turn down a road signposted: *Col de Rousset 20Kms.*

Dylan looks up. In front of him rears an uncompromising wall of rock rising almost vertically 1500 metres. The air is cool and beams of misty sunlight breach the teeth of the tall *Vercors.*

The climb begins slowly, almost considerately, with undulations and sweeping curves such as one might expect to enjoy on a merry-go-round. And without really noticing the change in terrain, they are quickly into a succession of long, steady straights broken only by short, tight hairpins. So far, the ride has been unremarkable; it has progressed with ease. But, just as Dylan is about to congratulate himself on attaining that rarefied state of making progress without pain, he finds himself challenged once more.

Five to seven per cent isn't critical; it isn't steep enough to square his pedals as the *Pennes* had done the day before, but the slope is relentless and the work is head-down, perseverant pedal-pushing. Again Dylan finds himself hoping the summit will arrive soon.

"Nearly halfway," Jean notes, his tone casual, his breath plentiful. He dances out of his saddle, weaving back and forth across the road to keep himself in check whilst Dylan labours patiently away.

But Dylan is pleasantly surprised to realise that his own breathing is not as stretched as it had been the day before. The climb is long but his lungs and limbs seem to be handling it, even if his eyes rarely wander from that point of focus ten feet in front of his handlebars.

Jean talks to him, quietly and consistently. And the more he talks, the more his words and sentences seem to overlap; the words joining, rhythmically and poetically, almost musically, to score a soundtrack to Dylan's effort.

He responds only occasionally and only when he feels the need to re-ignite Jean's curious commentary. And very slowly, even more slowly than his advance up the slope, it dawns on Dylan that Jean is talking him up the *col* and the higher they cycle, the more Dylan feels able to talk back.

"Ah, good," says Jean. "The backs of the leaves!"

Dylan thinks about this for a moment. Should he know what his companion is on about? He thinks, but cannot find any explanation for the expression. So, seeing as he is a novice in the land of the crackerjack *grimpeur*, he thinks he might as well ask.

Jean replies, "You know how sometimes when we turn a corner you feel the wind in your face and it is trying to blow you back in the direction you have come."

"Uh-huh!"

"Well, when you can see the backs of the leaves we know the wind is behind us. A leaf always grows with its back to the wind."

"I see," Dylan replies. Or rather he doesn't.

Jean carries on, "So, if you see the backside, the shiny side, of the leaves you know the wind is with you, driving you along the route. Think about it. Feel it. Use it and enjoy it. It is there to help."

The notion that nature is helping him along the route provides Dylan with a much needed boost. He's never entertained the idea that nature might be an integral part of the psychology of cycling. Sure, the road winds down a hill – the easier part in terms of effort – in the same way as it winds up it – the more taxing part. But he's always thought of the mountain as a restive monster in need of taming. That nature, as a primal force, might support him in his quest has until now seemed far too radical to his way of thinking.

What he wonders, if the mountain and the road, and the sun, the wind and the rain, are all a single entity and part of the one same experience? What if it's not about subduing the mountain, he thinks? What if all those elements combine with the rider and his cycle to make up not so much a contest, as one universal and unified journey; a journey sustained by a food of the soul, a food comprised of a blend of achievements, all made possible by a continuous refining of the physical being?

Or is that, he speculates perversely, his pheromones talking? *Pheromones*, he thinks, *that mysterious elixir of extreme exercise that is reputed to anaesthetise the limbs and free the spirit.*

He wrestles with the concept of nature and man's own nurture comingling to create the heady cocktail on which all cyclists depend to nourish their existence.

And–

They arrive at the top of the *col*. Down, far down in the distance, lies their overnight stop of *Die*; it is nothing more than a slight smudge in the fold of a valley far, far away.

Dylan stands awestruck and surveys the climb up which he has just cycled. He marvels at the strange and wonderful contraption that is his mind: for as long as the twenty centimetres between his ears is occupied, he now understands that his physical self will see to the rest.

Well, he decides, perhaps within reason! Although reason, he reckons, really shouldn't be considered or confused when discussing the curious disciplines of the *grimpeur*. His eyes well up and he is relieved his glasses disguise the torrent of emotion swamping him.

"It is a good view, eh?" Jean states.

"Worth every minute," Dylan replies, choking.

After the *Col de Rousset* there is *St Alexis* and after that the road leads them down through *Vassieux*. Jean relates how the Nazis all but wiped the pretty village off the face of the map, townsfolk and all, during the war. Given the peaceful setting, Dylan cannot imagine why anyone would want to.

Up out of *Vassieux*, the *Col de Lachau* is long and straight, a bit steeper than the *Rousset* but, thankfully, a good bit shorter. The difficulty is that the whole slope consists of only two straights broken by one hairpin and when he reaches the top he finds there is yet still more uphill until the intimidating *Col de la Machine*. He rests at a junction in the forest whilst Jean cycles away to bag another *col* up to their left.

"Only a few Ks," the *grimpeur* mutters, as he glides off up the mountainside.

La Machine isn't as bad as the name implies and at the top they pause to rehydrate.

Jean hands him a homemade energy bar of quinoa, dried fruit and honey. As he munches, Dylan understands they are now fairly high up in the *Vercors*. The air is thin and there is no greenery above them, only bare yellow mountain and the vivid blue Alpine heavens.

They come to a man-hewn tunnel in a flat, grey rock face. Passing through the short, cool darkness, they emerge into glaring sunlight and onto a narrow road. On their left the cliff face stretches away, straight-up. On their right, a low wall prevents them from the kilometre drop, straight down into the forested depths of *Combe Laval*. Dylan pedals gingerly along to the *Col de Gaudissart*, hoping the mountain will sleep as he passes.

Down from the *col* the descent is smooth and rapid, the straights longer and the corners less frequent. Even the cars move out of the way of Dylan's flying bicycle. He is at the same time petrified and exhilarated, and judging by the expressions of the drivers he overtakes, so are they.

Once onto the flatter road at the foot of the mountainside, he notices that keeping up is becoming very hard work. Every time Dylan catches Jean and drafts off the back of his bike, he drops him like a stone. He doesn't think the *grimpeur* is doing so out of some form of hubris; rather he reckons his companion is simply that much quicker and is blissfully unaware of the struggle being waged behind him.

Dylan dances to keep up, but his mouth is parched dry and even though his stomach revolves at the thought of liquid, he is criminally thirsty. The sweat at his brow has now evaporated and, he notices, his skin feels oddly dusty.

In *Pont-en-Royans* his joints start to grind as though filled with grit. He pulls up and throws back some water, but finds himself fighting to keep the much needed liquid down. His knee caps would like permission to part company with his shin bones, his calves are cramped with lactic acid and his fingers ache so much he'd like to shake them off.

Jean rides back to see what the trouble is. He is now impatient to get on with his ride.

Dylan is a little confused both mentally and physically. He is at tremendous odds with himself, recognising that he wants more than anything to carry on, but knowing deep down that he will eventually reconcile his leaving the *grimpeur* as the more prudent option. It is decision time. He can't hold the man back: Jean has *cols* to ride, photos to snap.

"It has been very enjoyable riding with you today, Dylan."

"It certainly has been interesting; I'll give you that, Jean. The *Col de Rousset* sure was a long climb. Thanks for talking me up it."

The *grimpeur* frowns, "Talking you up the mountain? I do not think this is possible, talking a bicycle up a mountain."

But Dylan just catches the back end of the *grimpeur's* smile; a fleeting thinning of his lips and the flash of mischief in his eyes, though nothing so overt that a lesser rider might deem his response in any way patronising.

"Sure," Jean adds, "I talked a little. But you were not listening to me, my friend. You were listening to you, to your inner voice."

They shake hands and the *grimpeur* takes off, like an arrow released from a bow, arcing up out of *Pont-en-Royans*, upwards and onwards, dancing out of his saddle, eating up the smooth surface, both ignorant of and completely at one with the massive mountains soaring all around him.

And when he passes the 16km mark, the *grimpeur* will dismount to lean his bike against a metal plate transcribed with the words *Col de Pra d'Étang Alt. 1052m* and he will take a photograph for his record.

LE PLAN

The Haute-Savoie, France

The moment he wakes, he knows it has stopped snowing.

Whereas for the past couple of mornings obfuscated light has muddied the corners of the curtains, now those same edges are set in stark relief and a keen light floods in through the gaps, throwing razor-edged rectangles and slivers of white against the far wall of his bedroom. So, when Atticus draws back the curtains it is no surprise to him that the world beyond the windows is newly redecorated in the brilliant white brightness of snow.

He lies back down, revelling in the changes brought about by a new sun rising in a cold blue sky. The beginnings and subsequent transition to colour never cease to fascinate him. Not since the first fine morning he set eyes on the steep flanks of limestone, which sweep round in a paternal arc from the bald cone of Mt Joly to the jagged peaks of the Aiguille Croche, has Atticus missed the opportunity to indulge himself in the view. And whenever he wakes and the view is obscured by falling snow – snow that is always welcomed by the skier – he still regrets not being able to witness the slender *couloirs* of Les Lanches surrender their shadows.

Away at Rochebrune the gondolas of the lift rise steadily, like pearl-drops on a silver strand, and the drone and buzz of light planes labouring in and out of the Altiport in the cradle of the rocky bowl remind him, gently, that the day is growing old and that it is high time he is out of bed.

He had ventured out early in the heavy snowfall of the previous day in case the expected dump turned out to be nothing more than a flurry. But, with each hour that passed the fall had gathered strength and the increasing lack of visibility and the weighty texture of the squeaky, new snow had clawed back his skis whenever he'd tried to make swift progress. So, at midday he'd surrendered to the elements and returned to the warm confines of his little chalet.

Today, though, will be a good day to ski. If the new snow has frozen over and the *pisteurs* have worked late into the night, the *piste* will be fast and true.

Over breakfast, Atticus considers taking the run over to *Le Refuge de Porcherey* for lunch: the small mountain hut where the old lady cooks up a tasty *Tarte aux Lentilles* is one of the best kept secrets of the Haute-Savoie. However, and if he is honest with himself, it is not the *Tarte* that attracts him so much as the lively, young waitress whose smile and engaging eye contact never fail to lighten his mood. Why, if he was only a few years younger – perhaps only twenty years rather than the thirty-something which separate them, he might ask her whether she would have any objection to meeting up with him one evening. But that is simply a pipe dream; a wistful want and he knows it. It has never been on the cards, no, not really.

Then again, as he waits for the toaster to do its stuff, he notices curled tentacles of spindrift snow licking and dancing off the ridge of Les Lanches du Mt Joly and wonders if *l'epaule*, the shoulder over which he would connect to the long slope down to St Nicolas de Véroce, might be closed due to the wind. He quickly reaches the decision that a day's skiing amongst the trees over at Jaillet will be a safer bet.

Once in the gondola, Atticus sits facing down into the valley. Going up and yet looking down always makes him think of his father. He doesn't know why exactly, but supposes it is the rising in the tiny capsule which causes him to wonder whether the motion is akin to ascending into heaven. Perhaps, he thinks, this was how it had been for his father as he'd travelled towards his next life; a life free from the stresses and strains suffered by lesser mortals. Not that Atticus has ever considered himself hostage to the similar strains and stresses put up with by ordinary people.

No, Atticus does not have to put up with that kind of life. His father, in a round-about way, had seen to that. And though he feels the old man's heavy footprint upon his every day, Atticus understands that he, himself, is as much responsible for his good fortune as anyone else.

He gazes down on the little town and is amazed at just how much individual wealth must be cosseted within the narrow alleys. He doesn't need to marvel at the glittering Swarovski Christmas Tree, which towers outside the Église *Sain-Jean-Baptiste* at Yuletide, nor be acquainted with the name Rothschild to know that Megève is constructed on sound financial footings. It was the money, or the comforting aroma of it, which encouraged him to purchase the chalet in the first place.

His great-grandfather had set up the financial institution which Atticus was smart enough to sell a year in advance of the crisis of 2008. He had seen, to coin the phrase, the writing on the wall long before many of his contemporaries had chosen to entertain even the remote possibility of its writing. And that had been his one, very personal and fundamental contribution to his success.

Atticus didn't like surprises, "No sir," he states, shaking

his head. While others had been watching and reacting to the market, he had been busy looking down the road to see where the market was headed next. Others were paid generous salaries and bonuses to play the market placed in front of them: Atticus' worth had, ultimately, been measured in managing the future; not tomorrow, not next year, but the year after that and further on up the road.

His father's parting shot: "Well, Atticus, we've sailed through a good many miles of choppy water over the last few years. Some we've seen coming and some we haven't. Now you've taken over the helm, don't be caught unawares. Rely on your intuition; it has served you well so far. If you smell the big iceberg coming, don't waste your time rearranging the deckchairs or listening to the orchestra: it'll be too late for lifeboats by the time it hits. Remember: sell while you can, not when you have to."

He had never forgotten that singular piece of advice and it had stood him in good stead. Should he have sold the family firm, though?

Absolutely! But he had been wounded to see the business go and sometimes wondered whether the dark frowns of his father and grandfather — frowns which stared down from their portraits in his dining room — were meant, ultimately, in disapproval. Or was that his conscience harping at him that he had fled when the going had gotten too tough? But Atticus had had a belly-full of the foreclosures and evictions of the early '90s, and besides, the seemingly boundless proceeds of the sale now afforded him a lifestyle most could only dream of.

The gondola lurches and trundles to a halt. He gets out, grabs his skis and poles, and trudges down the steps out onto the white apron, pleased to notice that he has beaten the late-risers to the slopes.

Only the very dedicated are out and about in the crisp, clean air on the crisp, clean snow. He goes through his warm-up routine, wind-milling his arms, flexing his neck and stretching his legs to warm his tendons and muscles. Brushing the snow meticulously off the soles of his boots by running them lightly across the top of his bindings, he steps carefully into his skis.

Atticus once saw a movie on a plane where the protagonist, an elastic-faced individual more suited to gurning than cinema, puts on a crude coconut husk mask he's come across in an old trunk and is instantly transformed into a whirling, womanising devil. The film was vaguely entertaining, if only in the way that it helped pass the time rather than provide great amusement, and it set him to wonder whether something similar might happen to him one day when he clicked his boots into his bindings.

He pauses, expectantly.

But no, his eyes do not pop out of his head, his legs do not elongate and his red ski jacket and black salopettes do not suddenly metamorphose into a Havana nightclub tuxedo and pants.

Oh well, he decides, *perhaps it isn't such a bad thing that I don't assume the features of a lunatic cartoon dog; my looks are rough enough the way they are.*

He sets off down to the *Ravine* for a couple of looseners. The chair back up is long, but it's not cold and the *Gentiane* is broad and deserted and so perfectly pisted that he knows he will enjoy the room to practice without having to worry about getting in the way of other skiers.

An hour later finds Atticus at the top of *Le Christomet*. A stronger breeze blows and across the valley wisps of snow pirouette and waltz about the slopes below Mont Joly. He permits himself a brief, smug smile that he has chosen the right area in which to ski today. But as fast as he congratulates himself, he checks his self-appreciation and lifts his gaze to the great mountain rising so majestically and monumentally away to the east. A vast, swirling ghost of snow obscures the summit; the sight lending Atticus a fleeting guilt that he should feel so good when climbers up on the *Trois Monte Route* of Mont Blanc might be freezing to death.

Thinking it too early for lunch and hoping the breeze might abate if he delays, Atticus cruises over and down the long and winding *Tréfléannaise*, which leads into the pretty hamlet of Le Plan. He loves the pines beside the slender trail; there is something innately comforting about the way they lower their limbs towards him, as if they are bowing before his progress.

But he is skiing swiftly now, the cold air rushing at his face, smarting on his lips.

A train of young skiers, racing suits clinging to their lithe limbs as every one of them mimics the hunched tuck of their instructor, whips in from the *Boënet* on the left and *schusses* across his line.

Of course! It is a challenge and too appealing to refuse. He'll follow them, keep pace with them and then overtake them: show them how it should be done.

But they are gone in the blink of an eye.

Sooner than he thinks decent, he finds himself out of the trees and into Le Plan.

He checks the shadows: it is still early to stop for a coffee and he's enjoyed the run down so much that he thinks perhaps one more run, this time off the top of *Le Torraz*, might be in order.

Atticus slouches on the *Grande Rare* chair and revels in the silence. The pines grow so close to the lift that he reaches out with his pole and knocks the snow off the branches as he sails by.

It is true, the fortune he received from the sale of the family firm affords Atticus so carefree an existence that he can now only just recall the burdens of his former life.

To be gifted the firm was a blessing many were rightly envious of, yet it had come with the odd curse as well. In the early days: getting up in the dark, leaving his wife to the warmth of the sheets, squeezing onto the train and tube. Long days often without a glimpse of the sun. And later on, airline dinners, too much rich food and too much alcohol, soul-less hotel rooms, missed parent-teacher meetings, school plays, sports and speech days, much too much alcohol and then some more, and finally a divorce; the cost of which now seems oddly irrelevant.

Oh, the cost?

He lifts the safety bar up above his head, alights from the chair and slips over to the button-lift of the *Tête du Torraz*. In his dreamy state, the poma jerks him not only rudely awake but also clean off the ground and he spends the first ten metres hanging on like a flailing fish desperate to impale itself on a hook.

Oh, the divorce, he thinks again, as he finally settles.

If only his wife had taken to skiing.

But she didn't. She'd thought it frivolous, an unnecessary indulgence, and so had dismissed it quite early on in their relationship.

Relationship or partnership, he wonders, as he adjusts his seat so that the button does not dig him so unpleasantly.

It was true: he had managed the money and Felicity had managed the children. *Managed? Had that been the problem? Had it been a failure of management or had his attitude towards it being 'a case of management' been the issue?*

"Should have cleared that up at the start, shouldn't I?" he mutters. "Hindsight? Wonderful thing!"

But his love of skiing and her love of surprises had driven a wedge between them; one that he'd been powerless, however hard he'd tried, to withdraw.

Atticus had always liked to get away — and often; about as far away from the pressures, the minutiae and the coat-tails of the firm as he could get. Up in the mountains, with only the snow conditions and the occasional cold to overcome, and with the wind of his own progression blowing through his mind, he'd come upon a peace he'd found he could not replicate in any other holiday destination.

Up here, there are no surprises!

Through the colder months he found he could rely on the snow to be light and fluffy; off-piste a veritable feast of symmetry and rhythm, of leaving fresh tracks through deep drifts of virgin pasture. And as the mountains moved into spring, the icy, compacted snow developed an alternative, but no less reliable character, one demanding hard edges and carving curves which dusted up elegant plumes of abraded snow in one's wake.

Felicity, on the other hand, had not understood — or perhaps had not tried hard enough to understand — the benefits of balancing mind, body and soul in one poetic movement; it had, put simply, not been within her. She'd tried it once and once had been enough.

Such a shame!

And then there had been that day he'd come home from the office for the last time. He'd not mentioned that he was engaged in the process of selling the firm. It wasn't that he didn't trust his family not to let it slip to the press; it was more that he did not want to put himself in the position of worrying about who had informed the press, had they found out. The signing coincided with his forty-fourth birthday.

Was I to know Felicity had planned a birthday party for me?

A surprise party for him on the very evening he had wanted to surprise his own family with the news that they would be financially secure for the rest of their lives — and, if they were smart, the rest of their children's lives, and their children's children too. It was no surprise therefore, that Atticus hated surprises.

The children had seen it coming — the divorce, that is, or so his oldest had remarked a couple of years later. Even *they* had noticed and often opined his unquenchable thirst for Alpine sports. *They*, it seemed, had been all too aware of the unbridgeable gulf yawning between their parents. But *they*, curiously, had taken the separation in their stride.

Odd that, that they should have accepted it so casually!

210

Perhaps the use of the chalet and the house in St Tropez, the constant supply of ridiculously expensive airplane tickets and ready funds for whatever jaunt they had planned next, had proved sufficient to silence their objection to the fracturing within the family home.

But that was some twenty years ago and *they* were all grown up now. Felicity had remarried, although he'd since heard she'd got divorced a second time – or so one of the children had said. He genuinely hoped things would work out well for her.

It wasn't really her fault, now was it?

Atticus hangs on tight as the button-lift inclines almost vertically to drag him up over the crest of the mountain.

He traverses the *Controverse* along the ridge between the peaks of *Le Torraz* and *Le Christomet*, before cutting left down the *Boënet*. The slope is steep, deserted and fabulously well-pisted, and he slaloms in long arcing, carving turns, rolling his ankles and leaning in, keeping his weight over the front of his skis, the G-forces increasing as his speed rises, his outside leg aching in protest every time he asks it to bear the brunt of his exertions and the pain of his pleasure.

Atticus is flying; there is no other way he can think of to describe it. He feels as though his skis no longer adhere to the snow; his limbs feel light, his muscles bubble and bulge. The trees are watching, leaning forward, applauding and encouraging him to even greater elaboration and flamboyance.

God only knows what speed I'm doing?

He tucks through the long left-handed curve where the *Boënet* runs out into the *Tréffléannaise*. He knows he has to hold on and make the turn; to scrub out will mean carnage, serious injury or maybe even death.

As he whistles out onto the flatter trail, the same students, who passed him earlier, fall upon him like a murder of crows and mob him as though he is standing still.

He slows on the trail, his heart pounding in his ears and his hands and legs shaking as though they have, quite literally, turned to jelly.

He slows further, respectfully and grateful for the excuse, as a gaggle of chattering Orientals stand about admiring the frozen waterfall which hangs over the trail just before the *Blanchots* joins from the *Grand Rare*.

A woman stands apart from the gaggle, leaning on her poles. She is wearing a white one-piece ski suit spotted with silver stars, a white helmet, pink goggles and white ski-boots. She is medium in height and her brown hair extends from under the rim of her hat, cascading over the collar of her jacket in much the same way as the ice cascades from the rocks above.

She is crying.

Of course, he can't see her tears; the goggles hide them, as they do most of her face.

She has a reasonable figure, not petite and yet not so full that her suit strains — although he is aware that most ski apparel lends one the latitude of concealing one's true form. All he can tell is that she has a very nice chin; a little small and pointed possibly, but then most chins look small and pointy beneath goggles which resemble huge insect's eyes. It is the contorting of her shoulders and the occasional sniffing sound that alerts him that all is not well.

Atticus glances up and down the trail.

No one!

He pulls across the trail and slides casually up beside her: "Ça va, Madame?"

At first, she doesn't acknowledge him, so he repeats his question a little louder, "Ça va, Madame?"

"What?" She stands up off her poles, as if electrocuted. "Sorry, what did you say?"

"I simply asked if you were alright, that's all. Are you? You seem to be in some distress: have you fallen? Hurt yourself?"

"Yes. No. I mean, yes: it's my knee. But I'll be okay. I'm fine. Really! Thank you," she adds, suddenly remembering her manners.

He is about to turn away but, and he isn't sure what it is that changes his mind, he hesitates. "Look," he begins, "there's a café at the bottom of the trail; perhaps a rest and a cup of coffee might help?"

She studies him nervously, evidently trying to make up her mind whether he is either dangerous or a knight in shining armour, or perhaps both. The woman reaches clumsily into the pocket of her jacket and withdraws a tissue. As she blows her nose, she mumbles, "Well, if you speak English I suppose you must be respectable. And a coffee *does* sound like a good idea."

Atticus usually does his best to avoid people who consider anyone not English to be disreputable; it is a form of bigotry he dislikes intensely. But on this occasion her lack of subtlety appeals to him. Perhaps it is a counterbalance to the disrespect shown him by the all-too-able *étudiants* who blitzed him on the slope a minute or so before.

"Very good! I'll show you where it is. This way," he replies, wondering if it is possible to proceed in any direction other than down to Le Plan.

He waits.

She waits, putting the tissue away and putting on her gloves.

"After you?" Atticus offers.

"Do we have to?"

"Well, there's not much else to do halfway down this track. No coffee shop, if that's what you mean?"

"No," she bridles, as though he is the thickest chamois in the Haute Savoie, "I mean, can't we ski down together; you know, side-by-side? It's not like we're horses and will block the road."

"Very well."

So they set off at a gentle pace, side-by-side.

Her knee, he doubts, is not what is responsible for her tears;

she stands evenly on her skis. But her movements are peculiarly wooden, like that of a puppet, which tells him she is probably one of those who have learnt to ski late in life. She steps a bit in her turns, as opposed to subtly transferring her weight from one ski to the other, and every now and then she wobbles like a blancmange or stills upright like an iron post.

"Actually, *O'Collignon* is an *epicerie*, not a café," he says, by way of not wanting to risk being corrected by someone he has only just met. "But they do snacks and their coffee's awfully good. Try to keep some speed up towards the bottom. There's a tight turn, but it'll help you get over to the houses."

She does as he suggests — *no, there is nothing up with her knee* — and she bumps into his back as they pull up across from the lift station.

"Oops, sorry."

The woman totters alarmingly when she turns to spike her poles into her binding release but, having stepped off her skis, she doesn't pause or show any sign of expecting Atticus to pick them up. Rather, she briskly leans them up against the post and rail fence, marches over to one of the trestle tables and sits down. Her independence appeals to him; his appetite is whetted.

"What can I get you?" he asks, once he's caught her up.

Curiously, she doesn't remove her goggles; she keeps her head down and blows her nose noisily: "A *café crème*, please."

Atticus joins the short queue at the counter.

"How is your knee?" he inquires, placing her coffee before her.

"My knee?" she repeats, as though he has asked after some intensely private part of her anatomy. Her reflective goggles remain in position, making it impossible for him to know whether she is offended or simply poking fun at him.

"My knee, huh? My knee, my hip, my calves, my hamstrings? All black and bloody blue! It isn't easy, is it, this skiing lark? But I'll get the hang of it, don't you worry. And please, please don't bother to ask after my arse?" she suggests rather too loudly for comfort.

But instead of finding her brash candour unsavoury, Atticus is lightly amused, infected as he is by her sense of drollery and her complete disregard for decorum.

Down the valley a team of sledge-dogs are baying for permission to be let loose along the track to La Giettaz.

He doesn't understand why, but somehow the sky very suddenly seems bluer and the snow whiter than he can remember for a long time. The sun is pouring over the ridge into the valley, bathing the woman's white ski suit in a pleasing golden glow. His mouth waters, unexpectedly. He chuckles and stands. He gets the feeling he is going to like this woman in the white suit.

"Oh, sorry," she adds, hurriedly, "I didn't mean to offend. It's just that my *derrière* is so many colours it looks as though I've just planted it on Van Gogh's palette."

Her goggles remain in situ and he resolves to find out what lies beneath.

"You haven't. Offended, I mean. I'm just going to change my tea for something stronger."

Atticus returns with a Ricard and a pichet of water. He can't remember when he last drank before lunch, let alone a glass of the strong, aniseed-flavoured liquid. But right at this moment he can think of no good reason why he shouldn't.

At the very moment he slips his goggles up onto his helmet and raises his glass, the woman does the same.

"Oh, Felicity!"

"Oh, Atticus!"

THE GETAWAY

The Ligurian Coast, Italy

Albert was old before he was young, or so Verity was thinking as she sat watching him from her deckchair.

It wasn't so much that he looked older than his thirty-eight years, which he definitely did what with his little tummy, his grey complexion and receding hairline; it was just that he liked things a certain way.

It wasn't his fault; she was convinced of that.

It was Adolf's.

Well, perhaps more accurately, Adolf Hitler and Albert's father. Why if that wretched German hadn't stirred up all of that mess and, what's more, if Ray Griggs hadn't gone off to clear it all up, then Albert wouldn't have had to've grown up looking after five younger siblings.

It was no surprise to Verity that Albert's father never returned from the war. She'd always thought him an intelligent, if somewhat over-sexed, man. So, what with Albert's mother slaving away in the aircraft factory, it had fallen to her son to ensure that his brothers and sisters got dressed and got off to school on time, and in that way Albert had assumed the mantel of middle age long before his time.

Being part of a large family was never easy, or so he'd told her on more than one occasion: there were always feet banging on the stairs, too many harsh words and too many tears. Oh, and then there was the untidiness; that was just too much to bear. And soon enough Albert had found himself kneeling beside his bed praying for them all to go away and leave him alone.

He knew it hadn't been proper to harbour such selfish feelings and he'd regretted them ever since, but Albert had been one of many and he'd yearned to be singular. To be, as he so often remarked, individual. Not in any stand-out way, he wanted her to know. He hadn't wanted to queue at the bus stop and be singled out as different from his brothers and sisters: he'd wanted, simply, to be recognised as himself and not merely as one of their considerable number.

Over time, his desire to be thought of as individual had mushroomed into a passion and spurred Albert on to do his level best to get away from them. The only reasonable excuse he could find to separate himself from the *Griggs Mob* as they were known, was to absent himself from the house through work. Consequently, as soon as the others were able to look after themselves, he got up early and cycled the paper round, washed up at the local tea-house and later waited table in a restaurant. In short, he kept himself busy. He hadn't liked the paper round, it was too much like hard work, but with every revolution of the pedals he reminded himself that one day, if he was careful with his earnings, he might be able to afford a car and therefore dispense with the pedals.

So Albert, as one might have expected with a child brought up under a cloud of coupons and vouchers, didn't spend the money he earned, he saved it; just like he stored up in his mind all the information he accrued from the many books on accountancy he took out of the library every Saturday.

When Albert finally slipped his mother's apron strings and moved into the flat in Sydenham, he was still supporting his mother and, much to his frustration, three of his sisters, and he spent what little was left of his monthly stipend on the bare necessities.

And so it wasn't until his thirtieth birthday, and his appointment to Manager Accounts of the large department store up the West End, that Albert began to contemplate purchasing any thing that wasn't fundamental to his or his extended family's existence.

He began by purchasing a grey, pin-stripe, worsted wool suit from Anderson and Sheppard, the bespoke tailor in Savile Row where Gary Cooper bought his suits. To complement the suit he also acquired a brace of city-striped shirts from Lewins, three silk ties from Hawes and Curtis, and a pair of brogues from Church's. He wanted to cut a dash. He wanted, subsequent to his promotion, to look every inch the manager and his new sartorial elegance contributed to a lively and very welcome spring in his step.

But, only for a while.

One morning, a junior by the name of Wendell Fitz-Lang strolled into his office wearing an identical tie.

"Hawes and Curtis?" the blond-haired fop piped up, cheerily.

"Pardon?" replied Albert, pretending not to know what the fellow was on about.

"Your tie, Mr Griggs. Hawes and Curtis. They do a marvellous line in silk woven ties don't they?"

"Haven't you finished that balance sheet yet, boy?" he barked.

The young man was the nephew of a main board director, Mr Crosthwaite. He it was who had asked Albert to take Wendell under his wing and show him the many and complex strands of the accounts department.

Then, a few days later, Albert was sat on the bus up from Charing Cross when the same callow youth, Fitz-Lang, leapt on board at the last minute.

"Hello Mr Griggs! I didn't know you took this bus."

Albert took an earlier train from then on and eschewed the bus in favour of a brisk walk up to Oxford Street. And although he remained all too aware of the sea of commuters drifting off to work around him, Albert concluded that the exercise might reduce his thickening waist.

Eventually, he bought a mantel clock from a shop in the Burlington Arcade, the sign on the window of which boasted the owner belonged to the British Horological Society. He didn't really need it, the clock that is, but he felt confident none of his peers would possess such a fine timepiece. And besides, seeing as he never socialised with any of them, there was precious little chance they would ever know he'd splashed out so. He didn't know if it, the clock, was as original as the slick-haired, beady-eyed man said it was, but the Westminster chimes, apart from aiding his punctiliousness, provided Albert's existence with a gentle rhythm; and he tried his best to swing his umbrella in time with his recollection of the clock's pendulum as he walked down Westwood Hill to Sydenham station each and every morning.

Verity often wondered whether Albert was bidding goodbye to the clock rather than her when he closed the door behind him.

Next he acquired a painting: a watercolour of an Italian Riviera scene by a coming artist, or so the vendor in Dover Street informed him: a lithe but shapely woman – the subject of the painting, not the vendor – bathing in an azure sea beneath a pale yellow sun and, in the background, palm trees and bougainvillea gracing a white-washed villa. Albert didn't pretend the painting held any great value; he simply thought of it as a nice thing to have about him. But the more he sat of an evening and gazed at the painting, he came to realise that one day he, or rather they, would have to visit the Italian Riviera.

Verity watched Albert, his trousers rolled up to his knees, as he paddled at the breakwater. In many ways the view before her could have been the very scene the artist of that painting had sought to recreate. She imagined him, brushes and palette in hand, easel leaning before him, dabbing at his canvas: the white-washed villa draped with purple bougainvillea, a single palm standing tall, the flaxen sand, the calm Ligurian sea and the pale disc of the sun suspended high in the cerulean sky. All that was lacking was the shapely woman, or so it occurred to Verity.

"Enjoying yourself?" she asked as he strolled up the beach towards her.

"Marvellous, isn't it?" Albert replied, spreading his arms in appreciation: "The whole beach to ourselves and only ten minutes out of Portofino. Who'd have thought we would be lucky enough to stumble across our very own private beach?"

He stood before her, staring up behind her at their car. Albert had parked it up off the road on a small promontory of rock some fifty yards away.

"Do you know," he said, making a square with his hands as if to frame a photograph, "with the way they've cut the *strada* round that curve and the village... What is it called? Paraggi or something..." Albert paused and scratched his head. "Damn it, I can never get the hang of two blessed 'g's together in the same word." He shakes his head and resumes, "But with that village in the background, I reckon the manufacturers would pay a pretty penny for a photograph of their latest model on tour round the Riviera. Would look great on a poster, wouldn't it? Imagine that on a hoarding down at the station? It would soon thin the numbers on the train, that's for sure."

Inevitably, the trains had grown too crowded for him. He felt, or so he sighed one evening when he'd had to stand all the way home, swamped by the great unwashed, the hoi-polloi, the...

"Yes, I know who you mean," Verity had hurried to finish the sentence before Albert lost his thread.

"There's just," he had moaned, "too many of them."

One October evening, as the carillon chimes of Big Ben heralded his return from work, Albert abandoned his rigid routine of hanging up his overcoat, changing his shoes and fixing himself a whisky before pecking her on the cheek. He simply rushed straight in and kissed her hard on her lips — yes, her lips, his coat and shoes still on.

"You'll never guess where I've been, Verity darling," he said, hugging her as though she'd just rescued him from a hole in the ice. "I've been to the Motor Show at Earl's Court. Mr Crosthwaite was going and invited me along. Wonderful, it was! Saw all the new models: the MG, the Austin and the new touring Rolls Royce Silver Wraith with the coachwork by Park Ward. Mr Crosthwaite ordered one and the best news is so did I."

For a moment Verity wondered if he might crush her beneath the weight of his enthusiasm.

"But I thought you said the new Rolls Royce was going to cost over eight thousand pounds, dear. Wouldn't we be better off buying a house?"

Albert stood back, uncertain as to whether Verity was trying to make a funny; something he'd told her she wasn't awfully good at.

"No, dear," he said, once he'd realised she wasn't joking, "I didn't mean I've ordered a new Rolls Royce. Mr Crosthwaite was also really impressed with the new Rover 90, so I nipped back before I left and ordered one. Do you know they've fitted a switch on the left of the steering column for the Laycock-de Normanville overdrive? And now, when you've engaged the overdrive with the switch, you can re-engage top gear by depressing the throttle pedal. How's that for the latest technology? And they've got separate, pleated leather front seats with folding armrests. Oh, the list goes on way beyond one's imagination."

Albert had hardly drawn breath until it was time for Verity to tip the boiled potatoes into the colander. In fact, he'd been going on about the machine for so long all Verity could think of by way of response was, "I'm sure it'll be a lot of money."

"£1,527.17," he said quickly, sitting down, tucking his napkin into his collar.

Later that night, Verity had lain wondering whether they'd ever be able to afford to extricate themselves from the clutches of grey suburban Sydenham.

He must have heard her thinking, because he rolled over to face her and whispered, "The overdrive's only available on the 90."

At breakfast, aware that he'd committed the cardinal sin of spending their life savings without first consulting Verity, Albert tried hard to pour oil on her troubled waters.

"I've ordered it in a special colour: you know, like the colour of those irises in that painting you like. No one in the world will have one in such a shade of blue. The salesman said it would be the only one of its kind."

But, over dinner that evening, Verity had continued to punish him with her silence. She studied the painting on the wall above his head and wondered whether she'd ever have a holiday, let alone get to bathe in the balmy lotions of the Mediterranean much like the amply proportioned siren pouting down on Albert's balding pate.

"I tell you what, dear," he'd said trying to wrest her gaze from the painting, "How about you and me going for a trip abroad this coming summer? In the new car, I mean. We could take one of those touring drives down to the Italian Riviera, stay in a hotel or two on the way, perhaps even try to find the location of our painting."

So that was how Albert and Verity came to be picnicking on *prosciutto* and *pomodori*, and toasting their luck with tepid *Asti Spumante* as they lounged in their deckchairs on a deserted beach near Portofino.

"No one in the company," he said, "will have ventured to such an exotic location for their holidays."

And Albert repeated once more what he'd told her time and time again when trying to justify the expense of the trip: now, he would be able to relate the adventures of their foreign vacation to his contemporaries safe in the knowledge that this touring holiday was going to crown the zenith of his individuality.

"No one," he added, "but no one, will match this."

Verity was so pleased for him. Finally, she hoped, finally he would be able to stand up, shrug off the mantel of his commonness and distance himself from the herd. No longer would he think of himself as typical. No longer would Albert Griggs suffer from being just another face in the multitude. And now, perhaps at last now, they would be able to get on with their lives without the spectre of his anonymity haunting their every step.

He beamed down at her: "This is it, dear. It can't get much better than this, can it? 1958 is going to be our year, you'll see,"

Verity was about to confirm all her husband's joyous sentiment when she sensed his attention had shifted to the back of the beach.

She twisted round and followed his gaze. A car had pulled up on the promontory of rock beside theirs.

Verity blinked, shaded her eyes and tried hard to focus.

The car, which was now parked slap bang next to theirs, was — was iris blue in colour; similar — no more than similar, it was exactly the same colour blue as theirs. It was a Rover; that much she could see even from where she sat. And the model was, well — the model looked to be identical too.

A tall, fair-haired, young man got out of the car. He stood for a second, surveying the beach, and then waved in their general direction.

Wendell Fitz-Lang! "Well, I say. Hello there Griggs. What an extraordinary coincidence!"

LANDFALL

The Windward Islands, West Indies

His name isn't *Ishmael* or *Santiago* or, for that matter, just plain *Jim*. And he didn't even know that much about sailing when they set out from Spain, but after so many days at sea Charles now feels he's earned the right to be seen as someone who knows perhaps a little more than most.

"So, what do I call you?" she asks, casually.

He's had acres of time in which to read of late, and the only novels of those in the rack on the Eira that appealed to him were Melville's *Moby Dick* and Hemingway's *The Old Man and the Sea*; Conrad's *Lord Jim* he remembers reading at school.

"You can call me Chay," he replies. "And you?"

"Cassandra. Most call me Cassie." She is tall and slender, with sun-deepened freckles and light brown hair, which she ties back off her face with a scrunchy.

"Pleased to meet you, Cassie." And he thinks that if she only knew how pleased he was to meet her, she'd probably slap him.

"And you, Chay."

But, his stare gives him away.

"Just arrived, huh?"

"Is it that obvious?" he asks, colouring slightly.

"Sure," she says. "You don't know it, but you're swaying like a willow in a breeze."

He is sitting, or rather trying to maintain his position, on a bar stool of the *Frangipane* in Port Elizabeth, Bequia. Cassie is standing.

"I wondered why I was feeling a little sea-sick. Strangest thing! To feel sea-sick now, I mean. Didn't feel that way on the trip." Chay is relieved, though; he thought she meant his staring at her.

"Wouldn't worry about it," she replies. "It'll wear off, but you might want to take it easy on the grog for a couple of days: sea-legs and booze don't mix."

"Talking of drink, can I buy you a...?"

"That would be nice, thank you." She waits for the barman's attention.

He smiles at her and, without asking, pours her a Planter's Punch, dressing her glass carefully with nutmeg, chunks of pineapple and slices of lime.

Cassie sips. "Mmm, thank you, Chay. How long was your trip?"

"Twenty-seven days. Funny, it seems longer and yet shorter. It seems like we left only last week, but then I remember the odd hour which seemed to last a whole day. Reminded me of school."

"Much excitement?" Cassie asks.

Chay isn't confident of how he should respond to her question. If he pretends their crossing was so-so, she might think him blasé or might mistake him for one of those salty dogs who roam from boat to boat; a mistake which could lead to him exposing his shallow knowledge of sailing. On the other hand he's aware that if he pours out all the many moments of high drama, she might pick him for the naïve first-timer that he truly is and that's the last thing he wants her to do. Although a good couple of years older than him, she is pretty, if not close to beautiful; a term Chay never in his wildest dreams thought he'd use when describing a woman.

"Some," he replies, nonchalantly.

"Okay?" Cassie watches and waits. When he isn't forthcoming, she says, "Nice ketch, the Eira. She looks easy to handle."

"She is that," Chay replies, with all the assurance of a groom who has come to terms with the unpredictability of a new bride. "She may not be sharp," he says, thinking of her broad beam, "but she's like her name suggests, she's forgiving."

"Is that a Norse name, Eira?"

"So I'm told." He nods. "Although I think Eira means merciful, rather than forgiving. Same thing, I suppose."

Cassie giggles, softly. "Is that how you like your women, Chay, forgiving?"

"Be nice if they were." He replies so quickly that he cannot believe where his observation has come from or why he should be inclined to blurt it out, just like that.

In truth, Chay is feeling a little weird — not sea-sick about to chuck-up weird, more marginally delirious or on the verge of letting loose weird.

She giggles some more and smiles at him. "You're so right, Chay. Women should be forgiving, as long as the kind of forgiving you mean is the kind most men need when they've forgotten how much they had to drink the night before."

"Sorry, you've lost me." He frowns. "Haven't done anything that warrants forgiving, have I?"

Cassie laughs loudly. "Oh, don't worry, kid. The night is yet young."

Her laughter is gentle and refreshing, like the rain of a line squall. She has lines at the corners of her eyes and her lips are full and generous and-

"Your glass is empty," she points out. "'Nother one?"

Windward Island-tanned, professional yacht crews in arrowroot-starched white shirts and shorts, pose earnestly as they swap pleasantries with charterers. Bare-boaters sporting straw hats and sunburnt noses, their pot-bellies proudly protruding over long shorts, prescribe intricate patterns with their fingers as they argue about the inner workings of some mechanical failure. And descendants of white Barbadian settlers sit chatting to locals as though time is theirs to share.

"Good health!" he offers. "Thank you."

"Here's to it," she replies, grinning.

Chay wonders whether the *it* to which she refers is the same *it* of which he is thinking.

"No women on the Eira, then," she states, raising her eyebrow and nudging him with her elbow.

"Sorry?" he replies, suddenly nervous that his subtlety lies sinking somewhere out in the bay.

"Don't be," she winks, clearly enjoying his attention. But equally as clearly, Cassie doesn't appear to feel remotely threatened by his flirting. Her gently amused smile suggests he is her plaything and not the reverse.

"How many on the Eira?" she asks.

An anxious hand grabs and squeezes Chay's stomach. Perhaps Cassie has tired of his company already. Perhaps she wants to know if there are any more attractive crew on board the Eira – any crew more muscular or mature or better looking or capable of easier conversation or...

"Three."

Cassie frowns: "Only three?"

He is again gripped by the same anxious hand, believing she is disheartened to think he may be the best the Eira has to offer.

"Three, huh? That's not many for a fifty footer. You guys must've been busy."

Chay's ego soars like a hawk and he sits up a little squarer. He would offer her his stool, but there is one free behind her and he has just picked up on her accent – Cassie is Australian. If she wants to sit down, she knows where the free chair is.

"We were a couple of times."

"Such as?"

"Oh," he bridles, "bit of a blow coming through the Straits of Gibraltar. You probably know how it is: lots to do one minute, little to do for hours."

"No, I don't. Tell me?"

Some of the traffic, he says, was simply not capable of giving way.

They had left Gibraltar late one afternoon on a freshening breeze. His skipper said the weather was about to close in for a few days and that if they wanted to be in Bequia by New Year, they had better get off to the Canaries while they had the chance.

Chay asked what he could do to hurry them along. If they didn't make it to the Windies for the New Year's jump-up, he was aware he might come to think of their voyage as wasted; the promise of a jump-up being his prime motivation for making the trip in the first place.

"You could go and find Tom," the skipper said. "Tell him we're off and bring him back here soon as you can."

That errand had sounded pretty easy at the time. But after scouring the pubs of Gibraltar, Chay had found the third member of their crew dead drunk on the floor of the pub furthest from the harbour. And by the time he'd staggered and stumbled Tom back to the Eira, the skipper was in the blackest of moods. They tied the idiot to the central leg of the main cabin table and left him there to sober up while they set about leaving.

Then the sun went down and the wind got up. The Levanter blowing out of the east tried to shove them out into the great ocean beyond the Strait and the waves from the great ocean came on to them, like serried rows of tall cavalry. With ten reefs in the main, the Eira ripped up the front of the waves and sidled down the back, the skipper turning her in the troughs in between. Only once did he mistime his turn, both he and the ketch being caught out and confused by a narrow trough with unusually steep sides. The Eira hesitated, the bow wandered, the wave shook them, they heeled over and the top of the main mast slapped over against the coming wave.

Chay remembers holding his breath until the Eira righted herself and he and the skipper glanced at each other and laughed the laugh of lucky men.

Then came the tanker.

They spotted it on the radar. At first it was just a blip like so many others, the only difference that set it apart from the others being that this blip was coming head on and its course was straight and true.

"She's big," the skipper shouted. "She's not for turning."

"Which side do you want to pass her?" Chay shouted back.

Even swamped by his Sou'Wester Chay could make out his skipper's shrug. What with the strong wind directly on their stern and the fast sea coming on before them, he knew they had insufficient steerage with which to make any significant change in course.

So they watched and waited and rode the tall waves like a rodeo rider at the Stampede.

And still the blip grew in size. And it grew and grew in size until its navigation lights glowed bright.

Chay thought it must be two boats the lights were so impossibly far apart.

The skipper glanced at him, caught his nervousness and told him the joke about an American Naval Captain, who persisted in ordering the vessel before him to give way until he realised his aircraft carrier was headed straight at the Fastnet Rock lighthouse. But that didn't help lift his mood.

The leviathan continued remorselessly and inevitably towards them.

Chay remembers looking at the lights of Tangiers off to their port beam and wishing he was sitting, nursing a beer somewhere in the souk.

And still it came on.

The gigantic tanker dwarfed them. It blotted out the starlight, consumed them in its shadow and ploughed them aside, bucking and bouncing them in its foaming bow wave.

Time stood still as Chay gazed up in awe at the mighty black beast that threatened to overwhelm them: four hundred metres and several hundred thousand tons of unstoppable steel and oil that would never know and likely as not care whether they lived or drowned in its wake. The tanker did not blink at their passing.

And then it was behind them and Chay exhaled a sigh of relief so voluminous in its capacity that he hoped he would never have reason to breathe out in such a fashion again.

For twelve hours, the skipper and he sat in the cockpit of the Eira and urged her forward. They drank most of a cask of Pusser's rum, the alcohol rapidly burned away by the intensity of their concentration. But it was all, he tells her, a bit of a storm in a teacup.

"You want another drink?" she asks.

"My shout," he replies and signals in semaphore to the barman.

The skipper, short, stocky and dishevelled, clumps into the bar and plants himself on a stool. His eyes are perfectly rounded pools of swirling colours, his perfume sweet and exotic, his mannerisms slow and robotic. He has been down on the beach indulging in some Colombian Gold and his evening is over even before it has begun.

"I think your skipper is stoned," Cassie remarks.

"I believe you're right," Chay replies. "He deserves to be. He didn't put a foot wrong the whole trip."

After the tanker in the Strait, the voyage down to the Canaries had proved less eventful: dolphins diving in the bow wave, streets of cumulus and a healthy wind herding them on their way.

Cassie seems content. She is a good listener and appears happy to drift in the sea of his conversation.

Chay is growing to like her. He can feel himself starting to unwind and there is now no doubt in his mind that she is one of the most beautiful women he's ever met. There is a worldliness to her and a calm acceptance of him, which is lending the doubt invested in him by his being too long in his own company all the affirmation he desires. Sure, there were Tom and the skipper with him on the Eira, but the hours alone on watch permitted him too much time to think. He'd learned it isn't only the windborne salt that erodes the mariner.

"Was the brush with the tanker the scariest?"

He chuckles. "Nope. The scariest happened when I was on watch one night.

"Rain was falling; couldn't see much. Had my wet weather gear on, but never liked wearing the hood up over my head: didn't like the way it blinkered my vision or smothered my hearing, and I found myself turning round every few seconds to look over my shoulder; like I didn't know what might be coming up behind me. I didn't mind getting my head wet; it wasn't as though the rain was cold.

"So, I was sitting there listening to myself think, when something explodes in the hood of my jacket." He claps his hands together and ducks.

"Frightened the bloody life out of me. I shot halfway up the mizzen mast, just like one of those electrified cartoon cats. The further up the mast I went, the damn thing just kept coming with me, flapping and crashing. I didn't know if it was an albatross or some devil from the deep; took me ages to work up the courage to stick my hand in my hood. And what did I find when I did?

"A flying fish. Not sure who was the more frightened: it or me. I spent the rest of the night walking up and down tossing the bloody things back in the water."

Cassie laughs, openly and loudly.

The skipper turns and stares into space.

"Then on Christmas Eve," he carries right on, "we are becalmed; not a drop of wind, nothing. So, we run up the engine to turn the screw enough to help us make some way.

"During the night, I'm sitting there thinking of my folks back home, putting their presents round the tree. And there's me out in the middle of this limitless ocean, looking up at the stars, thinking of how they're supposed to represent all my friends and relations who're thinking of me. I'm tapping my foot to the slow, regular beat of the engine, when all of a sudden the only thing I can hear is my foot hitting the deck. The engine has stopped.

"Well, I try to get it restarted, but it won't have any of it. So I have to wake up grumpy, here." He nods down the bar where the skipper is still wallowing in his own ocean.

"Anyway, we take up the main cabin floor, bleed the pipes, tinker about a bit, but nothing. And then he says," he points accusingly at his skipper, "There's something wrapped around the propeller." Chay quivers and stares like a madman, or not unlike his skipper.

"As you can imagine, my imagination is running riot. This is it, I think! The Kraken has us. Godzilla has woken. The giant squid has risen from 20,000 leagues. But the skipper simply says, "We'll sort it out in the morning," and goes back to bed. Well, I'm wired so tight I can't do much else but take a flashlight and, approaching the stern with caution, look to see what is wrapped round the propeller." He sips his punch.

Cassie is hanging on his every word. "So, what was it? Come on, what was it?"

Chay assumes a petrified expression. "A couple of hundred

yards of plastic pallet netting," he says, matter-of-factly. "Fallen off some container ship, I suppose.

"The next day, Christmas Day, while everyone at home is tucking into turkey, we're out taking turns to dive down and cut the netting off the propeller shaft.

"Strangest thing," he says, remembering. "I looked down and the blue of the water seemed to go on forever, just down and down and down, without end. I've never seen anything to compare with the way it seemed to go on down. I mean I expected it to end in some kind of darkness, but it doesn't."

Down the bar, his skipper is grinning. He has come to sufficiently to eavesdrop their conversation. "Go on, Chay, tell'er what 'appened next," he pipes up.

"Rather not if you don't mind."

"Oh, come on, Chay. What happened next?" Cassie goads.

"Uh-huh." He shakes his head. "No way. Not happy. Rather forget about it."

"Oh, come on. Be a sport," she continues, provoking him. "Tell you what, if you tell me what happened next, I'll buy you another punch."

"Mmm," he considers, chewing his lip.

"Okay, two punches." Cassie nudges him and her touch immediately unlocks him.

"The next thing, I'm surfacing by the side of the boat and he," he nods again at his skipper, "shouts SHARK! and points somewhere behind me."

One or two have noticed there is a tale being told and have rested their conversation to listen and watch.

Chay steps down off his stool and squats, as though he is treading water. "Say that again? I ask, as I'm taking off my mask." He mimics the movements.

"SHARK!" he screams a second time.

In one swift movement, Chay springs up from his squatting

posture and lands softly and evenly on both feet on the bar, in much the same way a surfer leaps onto his board. It is a feat of considerable physical coordination and agility, and he is surprised to notice that he has not unsettled one glass amongst those lined up beside him.

"And what do I see?" he asks Cassie.

She, like the others in the bar, is both laughing and applauding his gymnastics.

"What do I see?" Chay repeats, not really expecting a response.

"I'll tell you what I see. I see this cretin," he points at his skipper once more, who by now has tears in his eyes as he recalls a picture of the moment, "lying on the deck laughing himself stupid. Funny?" he accuses, shouting. "I didn't think so at the time."

Fortunately, the barman is laughing too.

People clap and whistle their appreciation of his antics.

But, the giant bunny-hop he has so perfectly executed leaves Chay feeling distinctly dizzy; the combination of a good deal more alcohol than he has consumed in over four weeks and the sudden exertion is proving too much for his weary frame.

Cassie reaches out and guides him down off the bar.

"Ah, brilliant," she says. "Fantastic. I bet you couldn't do that again."

He turns to her, readying to her challenge.

"No," she shrieks, "I didn't mean it. Don't you dare!"

The evening draws in. The lights in the bar twinkle, like rows of multi-coloured stars, and Cassie, he finds it hard to believe, is even more beautiful than she was a few minutes before.

A little while later, Chay realises he has now been drinking Planter's Punch for four, or is that five, hours and hasn't eaten since a brief breakfast on the Eira. He grows aware that he is intoxicated by the genial atmosphere, the extra punches Cassie has bought him and the queer sensation of having unmoving ground beneath his feet. Chay has also gained a welcome popularity amongst the assembled host; a popularity that is at the same time heartening and confusing. He is in love with everyone in the bar and the thrill of being so is exhilarating.

He decides it might be best to stand out from the group for a moment before his enthusiasm gets the better of him and steps over by a large bougainvillea bush at the back of the bar.

That he is drunk is not in doubt. The warning signs are everywhere: though the ground is fixed, the room appears to pitch like a heaving deck, his sight sheers and he knows that if Cassie stands any closer to him he will not be able to hold back from kissing her.

Chay turns on his heels, stumbles into the bush and, fighting his way through it, staggers down to the beach. Once there, he pauses for a second before walking, fully clothed, into the dark waters of the Caribbean Sea. It is, his muddled brain tells him, the only way to get back to the Eira and besides, the swim might sober him up and he can always come back later.

The water is warm and he floats easily. He remembers someone telling him the heavy concentration of salt in the sea water encourages buoyancy.

It is true! He laughs, swallows a mouthful of water and gags.

The Eira cannot be far, he thinks. She is moored a hundred metres or so out by a three-masted schooner.

Chay tries the crawl, but the stroke is too urgent, too hurried, so he breast-strokes for a few minutes.

For how long he is swimming, he isn't sure, but by rights he knows he should have been back at the Eira a good while ago and is baffled as to why he isn't.

Whenever his arms and legs grow tired, Chay rolls onto his back and looks up at the stars. They glimmer and shimmer. There are so many and they appear so close, he wants to reach up and touch them. They are beautiful and comforting, like the woman

Cassie he has just met. A twinge of conscience pricks the bubble of his safe-keeping: he shouldn't have deserted her like he did, not after the time and attention she gave him, and he wonders what she must think of him.

He'd been acting, of course, maybe even showing off a little. How could he have been expected to behave otherwise? Chay is so far out of his comfort zone, he has no reference by which to gauge his behaviour. In the same way as when they had set out from Valencia, in Spain, some six or so weeks before and he had no definable idea of what to expect on his trip; equally, he has no idea of how he should be expected to behave in the bar of his landfall. There's no denying the hours of solitude on watch have grown him up a little: they constituted the first period of his life in which he was truly alone. And sure, the skipper was downstairs, ready to be woken at the first sign of danger, but Chay was all on his own, master of the Eira and as such for hours on end the master of his own destiny.

Standing up on watch through the wee small hours, waiting expectantly for the divine incandescence of the sun to rise beyond the horizon and assume the image of a portal into an alternative world, he had begun to feel immortal. And—

Something brushes his leg, making him start and jerk himself upright to look round.

The sweeping bow of a schooner looms above him and he realises he must have touched the anchor chain. He studies the marlin-like bow sprit and the voluptuous maiden staring down at him from the prow.

All those hours on watch: so much time to think! One night, he recalled a film version of Tennessee Williams' *The Glass Menagerie*, in which the supposedly selfish dreamer of a narrator, Tom Wingfield, tells the story of his shy, crippled sister as he stands watch on a tramp steamer. And it had come to Chay that the gods were presenting him with the perfect opportunity to review his life, just like Williams had allowed Wingfield to review his.

Ultimately, though, he'd decided that he was still too young to review a life which had only just begun and that watching the new and beautiful sun free itself from the sticky horizon was to be preferred to hauling over too many so far unsatisfactory coals.

Chay hangs on to the anchor chain of the schooner for a few minutes. His legs, he notices, have assumed the same hard weight as the heavy chain and all too suddenly they don't want to support him anymore, they seem only intent upon tethering him to the bed of Admiralty Bay. And the Caribbean Sea, which earlier on had seemed thickly viscous and vaguely amniotic, is now thin and cold on his skin.

Slowly, like the many dawns he has so recently watched in awe, the realisation comes to him that he is tired and has no idea where the hell the Eira is moored. If he can't find her soon, he will have to make for shore, the few lights of which now seem a long way off. He is alone, just like he was all those nights on watch and it is solely up to him alone to navigate a route home from his current, ridiculous location.

"Chay, is that you?" a siren calls from the dark.

"Yes, it is me," he mutters, quietly, believing that his imagination is getting the better of him and that it is the voluptuous figurehead who speaks.

"Chay, over here!" the siren calls again.

"Oh, bugger off!" he replies, angrily, hoping his ire will still the voice in his head.

A bright light shines on him. A very bright light!

"Swim over here," the woman's voice encourages. "Can you make it over here? Swim towards the light!"

The light? Swim towards the light?

Like that same orange sun which breaks the horizon providing a portal through which he might pass into heaven, Chay is not unnaturally suspicious of the light. Half of him feels inclined to reject it and the other half to accept. The siren's voice is, though, faintly familiar.

"Chay, it's me, Cassie. Can you get over here or do you want me to come get you."

This is, he decides, no time to be stupid. If the hand of rescue is being extended by a beautiful woman, he knows he would have to be pretty stupid to reject it. Besides, he cannot hang on the chain of the schooner all night in the hope they don't weigh anchor before sunup.

He swims towards the light, his strokes laboured and unruly.

The relatively short swim over to Cassie's boat takes him longer and requires a good deal more energy and concentration than he thinks it should. Eventually, he arrives at the step-ladder she has dropped over the side.

At first, he is too tired to climb up but, after some cajoling and cooing from Cassie, he makes it up onto the deck of the sloop and rolls onto his back, exhausted.

"You bloody idiot," Cassie pronounces, looking down at him. "We've been looking for you for the last two hours. Where the hell have you been?"

"Oh," he mutters, pointing to the direction in which he thinks the schooner lies, "there and here." He chuckles.

"Well, as funny as you may think you are, one or two of us have been worried. What the hell do you mean by walking off into the bushes like that?"

She pauses, expecting a reply. When none comes, she continues her scolding, "Not that it matters, but your skipper couldn't be bothered to come look for you; said you'd be alright, didn't seem to give a monkey's."

"Mmm," he mumbles, "probably stoned. Gets like that when he's stoned."

"What was that?" Cassie asks, bending down and straddling him, as though readying to pump seawater from his lungs.

Chay grins, sheepishly: "Didn't want to make a fool out of myself, did I?"

"Well, you've managed that alright. But you weren't making a fool out of yourself in the bar," she says, now rather more sympathetic to his exhaustion and his motive. "You were doing pretty well for a guy who's just come across the pond. Most people don't last half as long as you did." She is sitting on his stomach, trying to work out whether he is soused with alcohol or saltwater.

Although it is dark, her eyes sparkle like the stars crowning her hair.

"I knew," he says, staring up at her, "that if I didn't leave there and then, I wasn't going to be able to stop myself from doing this."

Chay reaches up and pulls her shoulders down so that her face is no more than a small hand's width from his.

He leans his head up and kisses her, slowly and full on her lips.

Cassie struggles, but not violently.

He lets her go and she sits up, giggling.

"You should'n'a done that, mate," says a gruff voice from the darkness.

Chay frowns: "Who the hell said that?"

Cassie grins down at him and replies calmly, "My husband."

"I said you should'n'a done that, mate."

"Why not?" Chay asks, lazily.

"Because now I'm going to have to kill you," Cassie's husband replies. The man heaves into the circle of Chay's vision and stands over him, brandishing an enormous diver's knife, the edge of which gleams.

Murder and hatred are writ large across the man's expression. He holds the diver's knife the same way Chay has seen his father hold a carving knife at Sunday lunch.

"Go on, then," Chay says, his head dropping back with a dull knock on the deck.

"What was that?" replies the man.

Chay rolls his weary head from side to side. "I said, get on with it."

"Chay?" says Cassie, loudly. "He'll kill you."

"I don't care," he replies. "Do what you have to, mate, I'm too bloody knackered to care."

The world lies down beside Chay and waits to see what the man with the knife will do. They both know that over the next few seconds there is the distinct possibility that his life will end. It's not a thought that has ever presented itself to Chay before, except perhaps when the leviathan bore down on them in the straits or perhaps when the skipper shouted "SHARK" and Chay levitated right out of the Atlantic Ocean up onto the deck of the Eira. But, he is simply too tired, as Cassie has just put it, to give a monkey's.

The man chews his lip briefly and says, "He can't say that. That's not what you're supposed to say, you bastard."

The next morning, late morning judging by the height of the sun, Chay and the man wake side-by-side beneath an awning, which a fairy godmother has seen fit to drape over the boom of the sloop. They are covered by individual blankets, too, and between them stand an empty bottle of whisky and two similarly empty glasses. The only water in sight is the Caribbean which shimmers all around them.

"I wondered when you two were going to come up for air," Cassie says, watching them from the hatch.

Chay's mouth reminds him of the last pair of trainers he threw out, and the pounding in his head is relentless. "What year is it?" he asks.

The man, whose name Chay cannot recall, raises his head and groans, "Would've been less messy to've killed you, mate."

241

A while later, Cassie rows Chay over to the Eira and waits for him to smarten up before taking him ashore.

She is, he thinks, even more beautiful in daylight. But, judging by the way she chuckles and grins at him — in exactly the same way he has seen his mother grin at him when he has done something foolish — Cassie has recommissioned her view of him.

They pull up at the jetty, tie up and walk along to the beach.

A shark large enough to swallow a man whole is laid up in the white sand and a group of local fishermen are discussing how to share it out.

Chay and Cassie hesitate.

Noticing them, one of the men turns and grins cheerily, "Caught it in the harbour last night, man. Lucky no one was out for a midnight dip."

APPENDIX

TWO BOOKS

For Betty Chadwick

A couple of years ago we visited our eldest daughter in New Zealand. She has, for some years, been living in the South Island, commuting between there and Utah, in the United States, working as a snow-ski instructor. Skiing is but one of her many passions and I consider myself fortunate enough to share in the same; though not to her standard, I might add.

Most believe her existence idyllic; in many ways it is. But working outdoors, where the temperature can drop very quickly to a deadly twenty below, and in the often unforgiving mountains in which you must above all preserve the physical and mental well-being of your charges, carries with it huge responsibility. And that is not to mention that you have to be a skier of very great ability and aptitude. Through my dedication to her at the beginning of my first novel, *Mazzeri*, I have tried to suggest as much.

Before we left for New Zealand, I received from *Writers and Artists* a copy of *San Miguel* by *TC Boyle*. I read much of this exceptional novel, about three women trapped on an island on the west coast of America in the late nineteenth century, on the plane: I am more than happy to recommend it. The book jacket displays on the front a picture of a woman in white walking away through tussock grass.

In New Zealand, both in the South and North Island, I fished at Lake Taupo, walked the glorious forest paths, navigated the majestic sounds, watched brave and hardy souls compete in an Iron Man challenge, and got to know something of the nature of the mystical countryside and its magical people. I also gave a considerable amount of time over to contemplation, an indulgence which suits the habitat. Probably like most writers, I also took time out to read a novel written by a native of the islands. A friend of mine directed me towards *The Parihaka Woman* by *Witi Ihimaera*, a wonderfully moving account of one native woman's fight against the changing world of late nineteenth century New Zealand.

It was not, though, until I returned home and examined both this book and *San Miguel* that I understood what it was that had been bothering me about them. That they share an equivalent time frame and that they are both written about strong women is obvious, even though the stories are very much unrelated. But aside from the similarities of time and theme, they are alike in one other singular and very remarkable way. The short story, *Two Books*, describes this similarity; not in the way it came to me, but in the way it comes to the two central characters of this story.

I am grateful to Scott Palmer for editing and correcting not only my inclusion of a Maori legend, but also my shallow knowledge of astrology and the fabulous geography and language of New Zealand, as employed here in the telling of Fin and Amy's story. When I bridled at the idea that a lake can breathe, Scott showed me a graph of the variation in the surface level. It appears Lake Wakatipu possesses a tide or standing wave, as some prefer to call it. This variation is translated by the Maori as the giant breathing. Who amongst us is either brave or foolish enough to question such stuff of legend?

I KNOW

For Eileen Morrison

I Know is a variation on several themes.

Whilst writing a scene for one of the characters in *Boarding House Reach*, I came upon the idea for this short story. In the novel, Audrey Poulter comes to the realisation that her marriage has been a sham. Her husband, she learns, has been cheating on her and at his funeral she keeps a sharp eye out for his mistress, all the time hoping upon hope that she will not turn up at the service and in doing so sully the few good memories she holds so dear.

This set me to examine all the various reasons why we go to funerals. Generally we go out of respect for the deceased and out of our very natural desire to show support for and comfort the bereaved. But we go also to recall the many happy memories, or sometimes otherwise, of the person we have lost.

Of late, I have had the sad duty to have to attend too many funerals; it becomes the province of accruing too many years. And on one occasion I set to wonder about those amongst the congregation who may have known the deceased intimately, but

246

who cannot openly mourn them lest they cause upset to the immediate family. More often than not, one has small personal memories, some humorous and others more serious, which are inappropriate to air and which keep us out of, or on the periphery of, the inner circle of mourners. To feel excluded in this manner is to feel very alone.

So, what if not one but two of the mourners hold a similar place in the deceased's history? How would they, could they, articulate the depth of their relationship? What avenue is left open to them through which they can channel their grief without giving up some dark secret?

There exists an old proverb which suggests that *a joy shared is a joy doubled*. This is, perhaps, the reason why we feel compelled to mention happy times when reminiscing about the deceased. It is our hope that we will soften the blow of loss and thereby promote and retain a rose-tinted reflection of our relation or dear friend. In this way we multiply the joy in our memories.

However, the flipside of this proverb suggests that *a sorrow shared is a sorrow halved*. For those who bear a burden of guilt or disappointment regarding some element of their relationship with the deceased, there exists little or no opportunity to reduce their grief. After all, to speak ill of the dead – the measure of that ill being judged by one's peers and not one's self – is bad form.

Just such a story belongs to the narrator of *I Know*.

A Propitious Epiphany
for Padraig

For Dennis Welch

Walking the Camino de Santiago is something more than merely a religious experience. To gauge what it means to those who tread the well-trodden path between Saint-Jean-Pied-de-Port and Santiago de Compostella, or one of the many other trails, one has only to sit by the *Porto do Camino* and watch the beatific expressions of the *peregrinos* as they pass into the city at the end of their pilgrimage.

It was while sitting through mass on the last Sunday of our walk to Santiago de Compostella and wondering whether Saint James would resent an unbeliever in his hallowed house, that I noticed a woman had joined me in the pew. She was middle-aged and dressed for walking; a scallop shell, the symbol of the *peregrino*, hung from her belt. She, I noticed, had removed herself from the company of her family, preferring to sit and contemplate beside someone unfamiliar. She crossed herself and knelt to pray. The mass began, the priests intoned and swung their thuribles of incense, and the atmosphere soon grew so charged that I grew transfixed, occasionally so much so that I had to remind myself to breathe. Partway through the service, the lady next to me rose and left the pew to kneel at one of the confessionals occupied by the priests; these are not closed confessionals, but merely cushions placed at the feet of rather somnambulant figures, sitting at intervals below the Stations of the Cross. They seemed to do little more than listen and absolve, but I guessed that is their purpose.

However, when the woman returned to our pew, I noticed she was in floods of tears. What kind of tears, I could only imagine. Were they tears of joy, sorrow or relief? There was no doubt in my mind that she had unburdened herself of some dreadful weight she'd been bearing for far too long. Her body was wracked with sobs; her anguish, her inner turmoil plain for all to see. And the conflict of her emotions was so palpable that the small distance between us seemed to be bridged by some transcendental arch. I wanted to comfort her in her hour of need, but I was completely aware that only her God was capable of applying the necessary balm. To this day, I often think of that lady and wonder what it could possibly have been that upset her so. I can only hope she received the absolution the Camino is, in many ways, so aptly designed to bring about.

But, to Padraig.

Later on that evening, as we sat at a table in one of the cobbled alleys of the upper city, the piped bands came by. I got talking to a genial Irishman and he told me a story, the seeds of which have blossomed into A Propitious Epiphany for Padraig. The *Scéalaí* are the story-tellers of Ireland and they have a saying that there is no story to be told unless there is a person to listen to it in the first place. I believe it is hard to beat a good meal, good company and a good story, especially one told by a man from Cavan. Appropriately enough, we happened to get into Santiago for the festival of *Día das Letras Galegas*, the Galician celebration day of writers and poets. It is a grand event and an even grander evening; a magical time I wouldn't have missed for the world.

There is undoubtedly something special about the Camino de Santiago; if there wasn't, the *peregrinos* would not keep walking it.

A Shot in the Arm

For Tom Beard

Some bars have *it* and some bars don't. Down the road from where we live, there is a restaurant that upon first glance appears to be as old as Will Shakespeare. In truth it is a recreation of what tourists would like to believe fits the profile of a seventeenth century inn. It isn't a bad spot, but it doesn't, though, have *it*.

The *it* to which I am referring is an atmosphere, a mien, an aura, an ambience or perhaps even a certain social micro-climate. *It* is a bar or restaurant where the odour of hops or the aroma from the kitchen overlays a constant babble of conversation; the kind of place you settle into without feeling, or being made to feel, like a stranger.

There is such a bar in Chamonix. It lies close to the two stations and is generally frequented by the hiking, climbing, skiing fraternity. It caters for most tastes; everything from sausage and egg baguette through nachos to burgers. The menu may not appeal to the more sophisticated palate, but then who wants sophistication when you can have the very best of bourgeois? The beer is cold and refreshing and exactly what one needs after a long walk, and the blackboard boasts more shots than a *Peckinpah* western. The décor is wooden and warm, the music right out of *Rocky Mountain Way*, and the waitresses so charming and easy on the eye that they make it a perfect pleasure for you to part with your money.

Stations, bars, restaurants, cafés, squares are all the kinds of places where one can sit and people watch. It is both a habit and a luxury, and wonderfully time-consuming. And it is whilst watching and wondering what brings people into your sphere of consciousness that many short stories are born. A Shot in the Arm is one such story.

We had taken the little rack railway train up to Montenvers to gaze down upon the *Mer de Glace* and watch the clouds boil up around *Les Drus*. A few late season skiers were traversing off the bottom of the *Vallée Blanche*, the air was cold for May and a few hardy individuals had walked up the path beside the railway line. The view from Montenvers is spectacular, if alarming in as much as it brings home just how far, and how fast, the *Mer de Glace* has receded over the last century.

Back in Chamonix, in this particular restaurant-bar, we sat and ate and drank and talked and listened and looked. And I heard my wife Carol, who was sitting next to me, say, "Don't worry about him; he's probably off writing a short story."

She was absolutely correct. I had departed into that dreamland where stories are brought to life. Matthew's story is about the high mountains, a girl and the bar.

PUDDACIARI

For Chris Otway

Many short stories have grown into significant movies; or if not significant, then at least sizeable movies. One thinks of Ian Fleming, W Somerset Maugham, Graham Greene, Ernest Hemingway, Henry James and Stephen King in the more conventional genres. In the science fiction mould one would put forward Philip K Dick, Arthur C Clarke and H G Wells. And then of the more classical writers we have Rudyard Kipling, Robert Louis Stevenson and Lewis Carroll. The list is extensive. The reasons this is so are twofold. Firstly, the short story is the seed of an even greater story. And secondly, the potency of the short story – or, if you like, the richness of it – permits that seed to geminate. It is what we add to the story – the water and fertilizer of our imagination – which often determines how tall that short story will grow.

Some novelists, though, use short stories as a test bed for their novels. F Scott Fitzgerald in particular was well known for trying out his novel's characters in his short stories. One thinks of Daisy Cary from *The Bowl*, published in the Saturday Evening Post in

January 1928 – a try out for Rosemary Hoyt in *Tender Is the Night*, or Amanthis Powell from *Dice, Brassknuckles and Guitar*, published in Hearst's International in May 1923 – similarly a try out for Nick Carraway in *The Great Gatsby*.

My second novel, *Boarding House Reach*, started out as a collection of character studies. After the essentially historically plot-driven *Mazzeri*, I decided I need to work harder on my characterisation and wrote near-on twenty individual studies. A few months later, I trusted five of those characters enough to want to commit them to a novel and thus *Boarding House Reach* was born.

Puddaciari started as a short story, but evolved into the full-length novel that is now *Ontreto*. It wasn't meant as a rehearsal; it began as a simple story and grew out of my familiarity with the island of Lipari. Lipari is the main island of the Seven Sisters of the Aeolian Islands which lie just off the north coast of Sicily. Though small, at only 38kms round, and an UNESCO World heritage site, Lipari is steeped in history and ranks amongst the most beautiful of the Mediterranean's jewels.

The narrator is clearly similar to the protagonist of my previous novels *Mazzeri* and *Ontreto*, Richard Ross; though I had neither written either or them when I first visited Lipari, nor conjured the central character for the novels. The *escurzionisto*, Sandro, probably glides conveniently from *Puddaciari* onto the pages of *Ontreto*, yet there are a number of crucial differences between the two.

I have grown very fond of not only the island, but also its people and many others I have met who come from Sicily.

A friend of mine comes, originally, from the pretty village of Suteria in the province of Caltanissetta in Sicily. In his youth, he journeyed to England to live with his uncle, an agricultural worker who had come over after the war to escape the deprivations of his home country. My friend studied at Brooklands College in Weybridge and it was there that he was offered an apprenticeship at my father's garage, learning all there was to know about

Mercedes-Benz motorcars. My friend now has his own specialist workshop; his knowledge, particularly of classic Mercedes-Benz, is comprehensive; his work, the very best there is.

Some years ago, he recommended that I visit his friend in Lipari. He said I might like the place. In the event, I fell in love with it and now find it hard to stay away.

His friend has a hotel on Lipari, and his daughter and he have educated me as to the culture, history and ways of the islands. His very charming daughter, Ariana proof read the novel *Ontreto* for me. She corrected my use of the local dialect and proved instrumental in arranging the presentation of *Ontreto* to the island at the *Centro Studi* on the *Via Maurolico* in July this year.

The reason I mention my friend, his friend and his friend's daughter is because without them *Puddaciari* would never have been written, and without *Puddaciari*, *Ontreto* would never have made it off the first page or into print. This is how it works in Sicily: a man knows a man who knows a girl who...

'People watching' is one of my most favourite and most annoying habits, or so those who would like my attention will tell you. Sitting at café *La Precchia*, halfway up the *Corso Vittorio*, or at the bar *Il Gabbiano*, in the beautiful *Marina Corta*, is the perfect place to indulge in just such a practice. Go to Lipari, but keep it a secret.

I See Him Coming

For Sir Gawaine Baillie

Porto in Portugal: a long weekend. Breakfast at the *Majestic Café*, lunch and port tasting at Graham's Port Lodge, a cruise up the *Rio Douro* to the vineyards, dinner al fresco in the *Sebastião*, the sepulchral peace of the *Sé do Porto* cathedral, the cool vapours of the *Jardins do Palácio de Cristal*, the story of Portugal as told on the tiled walls of the *São Bento* station, and lunch on our last day at a restaurant on the bank of the *Douro* overlooking Gaia.

As an itinerary for a few days away, it all sounded pretty idyllic. And it was until that last lunch.

Our second daughter and I are sitting facing my wife and her mother. To our right stands the magnificent span of the *Dom Luis 1 Bridge*; in front of us lies a table laden with fish stew, game sausage, pork and octopus, and glasses of sharp *vinho verde*. By the time the cheese arrives, we have eaten and drunk ourselves to a standstill.

The bridge looms over us. Tourists promenade and trams out of the *São Bento* glide across the upper deck fifty metres above us.

255

Along the low deck, traffic of every size and age crawls between the city and the port wine warehouses of Gaia.

Some movement distracts us and my daughter and I turn to see the last few metres of passage of a body before it hits the surface of the river with an almighty slap.

Kids, lithe and olive-skinned, have been entertaining the tourists by jumping off the lower deck near the rocks on our side; a brave jump of around ten metres. This almighty slap, though, happens right in the middle of the river and belongs not to a child, but to a fully grown.

We look at each other: the shock is written large across her face.

At first, we aren't entirely sure what we've just witnessed. Surely, no one would have jumped off the upper deck expecting to survive?

The body, now a corpse, bobs back to the surface and begins to float along with the swell. Now, there is no longer any doubt about what we have just witnessed.

A fisherman motors his little skiff over to the body and, with the help of another, retrieves the newly departed from the muddy waters of the *Douro*. As he passes back beneath the bridge, he ducks theatrically; a gallows humour I understand, but not one I either sanction or can justify to my daughter, especially one who is studying for her PhD in Autism.

On my return, I google *Suicide* and *Dom Luis 1 Bridge, Porto*: I want to know if there is a report of the incident in the local press. There isn't. Further research leads me to learn that there are far too many suicides from the bridges of Porto; they are in fact so common that they are considered not worth reporting. And besides, who would want such a beautiful city to be notorious for its rate of suicide?

Suicide is ghastly. I can think of no other adjective that better describes it, and since that afternoon in Porto I have given over much thought to the subject and hope with all my heart that there is a guardian angel walking the bridges of Porto. In that hope, *I See Him Coming* was born.

MAURICE AND MIKE

For Tony Williams

1977 was the Queen's Silver Jubilee Year. Virginia Wade won the Women's Ladies Singles Title at Wimbledon, Fleetwood Mac's album *Rumours* was released and, as a twenty year old, I didn't have a bad time of it either. There were, after all, probably worse places to have to pass the summer than the Côte d'Azur.

I worked for most of the season on a large gin palace; I can no longer recall the name clearly. She was large by the standards of the time, over 120 ft, but she would no doubt be considered rather small beer now.

We were berthed in *Port Canto*, the newer marina on the eastern side of the bay of Cannes, and our longest charter was to a lady whose husband, or soon to become ex-husband, was a big player in the Airways. We cruised between those modern Mediterranean dens of opulence and iniquity St Tropez, Portofino, Porto Cervo and Monte Carlo, or Monaco if you feel so inclined. My eyes were opened to the habits of those who could afford to behave badly, and occasionally I found it prudent to look the other way, lest one witnessed something which later on one might have to deny in court.

Whilst we were in port and when we could afford it, we passed our evenings at the *Voile au Vent* on the *Quai St Pierre*. Sadly the *Volly*, as it was known and rather poorly pronounced, is no longer in existence and Cannes has changed beyond all measure. This is no bad thing; I am not one of those who would wish the world to stay the same simply for posterity or to preserve nostalgia. The larger boats now berth round in Antibes, and when I say larger I mean boats of three hundred feet and more: in fact the gin palace belonging to one particular owner of a London football club stretches considerably longer than his team's pitch and is so large it has been barred from entering Antibes.

The boat on which I passed the summer working as a deckhand merited a crew of eight. An engaging New Zealander, who was prone to dance the *Maori Haka* whenever he was a sufficient number of sheets to the wind, was the first mate and my boss. The old chef was... well, the old chef. None of us knew exactly how old he was, but the New Zealander and I thought he must have been the wrong side of seventy. He was a shrunken, wrinkled genius of a man and he could magic *cordon bleu* out of scraps, drink the pair of us under the table and tell better stories than any other sea dog I have ever had the pleasure to listen to. And the old chef had worked many boats, so there was never a shortage of stories.

On returning from charter one day, the first mate, the old chef and I, bereft of much to do and weary after a week without pause, decided to go to the pictures. The film, though I cannot recall its name, was so good we snoozed through it a second time. Later on that warm and sunny afternoon, we strolled down the *Croisette* back to the boat. Outside the Miramar, a taxi pulled up at the kerb and a man and two women alighted: an English girl and her parents. The girl had been commentating on the firework competition of the previous evening; an event her father's company competed in.

Though we had previously been an *item*, as the Americans like to call a relationship, I had not seen her since leaving the UK several months before and was not about to lose the opportunity of rekindling our relationship. In the evening I took her to *La Chunga*, about as upmarket a dive as I could get into in my last pair of clean white jeans and t-shirt. A month's wages soon disappeared over the bar and into the till, but at least I got to walk her back to the hotel. As coincidences go, bumping into her like that out of the blue on the Croisette on a sunny afternoon in August has to be the luckiest in my long list of coincidences. Call it fate. Call it star-crossed. Call it what you will, but five years later, we were married.

I have a great deal to be thankful for, especially to the old chef and the first mate, and hope they will not mind my employing something of their characters in the story.

Some of *Mike and Maurice* is true; some of it is not. I'll leave you to guess which. There is much truth, as the title of this collection of short stories suggests, to be found in fiction.

Towards the end of the summer the boat was sold out from under us, so we jumped. The first mate and I, in company with two others, rented a villa between the *Grande Corniche* and the *Moyenne* overlooking Beaulieu-sur-Mer. We worked in the dry dock down in Villefranche, played chess of an evening in *Les Palmiers* and blew our earnings through the wee small hours at a blackjack table in Monte Carlo. As I said, there were probably worse places to have to pass the summer.

THE LONGCASE

For Norman Webb

This story came to me courtesy of my father.

In the fifties, he was in partnership with a motor-trader and they had a number of premises in the West End of London through which they sold high-end cars.

One day he was summoned to demonstrate a car to a gentleman in Kensington, and by way of demonstration my father offered to collect the gentleman from his flat and drive him to his appointment at the Law Courts. On the way my father learned that the man was being called as an expert witness to verify the originality of an antique longcase clock. The clock in question had been sold by a well-known retailer to an individual, who had subsequently been informed by another expert that his investment was not as original as the vendor had at first purported it to be. The clock was, therefore, not worth the high price the purchaser had paid.

My father asked the expert how he had come to attain such a comprehensive knowledge of antique longcase clocks. The customer related the tale of his apprenticeship, working for a fellow who reproduced counterfeit time pieces, and it was in this way that he had come to learn the difference between an original and a *snide*, as they are called.

The dichotomy was, or so the expert witness went on to explain, that he knew the clock in question was not original because it was one that he had worked on during his apprenticeship.

What, he asked, was he supposed to do? Incriminate himself by explaining that he was intimate with the longcase clock and therefore knew it to be a fake? Or was he to perjure himself by endorsing the provenance of the article?

Whichever option he chose, he knew he would either compromise his reputation, or destroy his standing within the close-knit community of antique longcase clock vendors.

The Longcase is about a young man who comes to realise he may not be able to avoid choosing between the lesser of two such evils.

GENEVA

For Emma Brooks

This story I wrote some years ago, in the days following a business trip to Geneva. At the time my sister-in-law in the States was bravely battling leukaemia and part of her battle revolved around hours of resting, both in and out of hospital. This style of inactivity did not come easily to one who was so normally a whirlwind of activity: the old saying of 'if you want something done, ask a busy person' used to apply.

I'm glad to say that the saying still does apply. Thanks to the incredibly talented doctors and staff at the hospital of the University of California, San Francisco, and the donation of her brother's stem cells, my sister-in-law has survived. Many, as we have had the sad duty to witness so recently, do not.

In order to provide my sister-in-law with some distraction through her long convalescence, I wrote for her this story about my visit to Geneva. It is in the main part true, though I have quite naturally changed the character of the narrator.

So, what was I doing that allowed me so long at Geneva Airport?

I had been contacted by a family who owned an old Mercedes-Benz. They asked if I would buy it and, if we could agree a price, collect it from Geneva. We did and I flew over and was met at the airport by their chauffeur. Their house, across the river, was substantial and surrounded by a high stone wall; the gentleman, or so I was told, had sold his business for such a large figure that he'd bought the bank with whom he kept his account.

The car, a 1965 Mercedes Benz 250SL automatic roadster, with both soft and hardtops, and anthracite in colour, sat on the apron out front. From a distance it looked pretty clean, but when I unlocked the door, I soon realised the look was deceiving. The driver's foot-well was four inches deep with water, the battery was so flat it could not have raised even the faintest glimmer of a smile and the oil in the sump barely registered on the dipstick. An hour later, and bearing in mind I had been told the vehicle was roadworthy and that I was hardly dressed to mechanic, I managed to get her dried out, powered up, oiled up and going, and nursed her down to a fuel station. Sadly, her water pump then gave up the ghost. She never made it down to customs, never mind across the border. The chauffeur took me back to the airport; conversation was not on my itinerary.

Based on the information I had been supplied regarding the roadworthiness of the roadster, I had bought a one-way ticket; perhaps not the brightest move with hindsight. British Airways wanted a fortune for the return trip at such short notice; Easyjet wanted slightly less, but the flight wasn't leaving for another four hours. I debated taking a taxi back into the centre of town, but remembered staying the night in Geneva with my father many years ago and remembered also that the city isn't exactly what my brother would denote as a 'barn burner'. And besides, I had already wasted sufficient funds on my trip and didn't want, now, to throw any more good after bad.

Four hours in the concourse of Geneva Airport! I had thought it was going to drag like a heavy sack. How wrong was I?

Not long after I had spurned lunch, on the basis it was too expensive and I'm not much of a fan of eating alone, a stranger came and perched himself next to me. *Geneva* is his story.

I have also employed a small trick in the construction of this short story. Tell me: what do you think is the gender of the narrator?

You ought also to know that I did end up buying the 250SL, the Pagoda as we know it and the Mistresses Wagon as it is known in Germany, and returned some weeks later with a trailer to collect it. Getting the car out of the country is one whole other story; in Switzerland, the police consider it their duty to be less than helpful and they are incredibly proficient in their duty. I am glad to say, though, that the beautiful 250SL now lives in Bergen, Norway, with a very charming gentleman who loves it very much.

A friend of mine works as part of the UNHCR in Southeast Asia. He deserves our very great admiration and our heartfelt gratitude for trying, everyday, to sole the unsolvable. If I was a refugee, I can think of no better man to turn to.

NINE

For my father

Everyone has their own idea of where the home of their chosen sport lies. For cricketers it is probably the hallowed turf of Lord's cricket ground in St John's Wood, London. For rugby players it is most probably Twickenham in south-west London. Skiers, though, will tell you they prefer such and such a mountain, be it Wengen in the Bernese Oberland, Verbier in the canton of the Vallais, or perhaps Chamonix in the Haute-Savoie – the venue of the first Winter Olympic Games in 1924. But, wherever one perceives the home of a sport to lie, it most probably lies in one's heart.

For me, the cathedral of skiing is undoubtedly Kitzbühel in the Tyrol of Austria. This is not because Kitzbühel was the first place I skied, but because the little medieval, walled town below the Hahnenkamm is the sight of the world's most demanding downhill race course, der *Streif*, and because Franz Klammer, der Kaiser, is for me the greatest of all skiers. Some would argue Jean-Claude Killy is the greatest because he was the most versatile, winning three Olympic gold medals in different disciplines in the

Olympics of 1968. Others would say that Alberto Tomba is the greatest technical skier of all time, winning three Olympic gold medals and two World Championships in slalom and giant slalom. Bode Miller (USA) has an incredible record, so too Kjetil Aamodt (Norway) and Toni Sailer (Austria). But, for me, Klammer surpasses them. It's personal, I understand that.

And it's personal for a number of reasons. Firstly, Kitzbühel was where our daughters learnt to ski. Our eldest, is now a highly qualified instructor and earns her living by teaching the sport. Our second represented her university at the Varsity downhill ski-race championships. And our third is a former five-star Interski winner. The *Jugendgruppe* of Kitzbühel is a hard school in which to learn the subtler arts of skiing, but it is undoubtedly one of the best. And if that isn't enough to draw my vote Kitzbühel's way, my father skied there in the years following the war and I have enjoyed many seasons skiing there since. The *Streif* and the valley below the *Pengelstein* are, in their own way, memorable runs, though the valley is now by-passed by a gondola which saves one the hike over to Wagstätt in order to ski up to Pass Thurn. So who knows, perhaps there is the odd corpuscle of Kitzbühel in my blood. I like to think there is.

The story of Buford Barclay is mired in fact, or so my father led me to believe.

Late one evening, whilst my father and his friend were skiing down the Hahnenkamm, they found a man hanging upside-down in the branches of a pine close to the piste. Clearly, if his progress had not been checked by the forest, the man would have disappeared for good. Equally as clearly, if they had not found him and rescued him from his state of suspended animation, the man would have frozen to death overnight.

There are those, and I probably used to number amongst their group, who ski far too quickly relative to their ability and for their own good. This undeniable foolishness set me to thinking:

why is it that one is driven to ski in such a reckless fashion? Is it the thrill of the speed? Is it the desire to prove one's masculinity or superiority in the face of the mountain? Or is it that certain individuals simply like to live life on the edge and in doing so continuously confront their mortality?

We all like to set ourselves goals, whether it be running the Marathon, climbing Everest or swimming the Channel. But, why do we often choose the most perilous of these options?

Buford Barclay, the subject of *Nine*, is one of these.

I have intentionally left out any solid timeline to the story, for the danger in skiing far above one's ability is still as relevant today as it was sixty years ago, though there now exists a wall of catch-fencing around the *Steilhang* on the *Streif*. Motor-racing is also dangerous, it goes without saying, but skiing, as has been proved recently by one of the best of motor racing drivers, is equally so.

TRUST

For Richard Hawkins

The deep-rooted mistrust of foreigners stems from a basic and very natural fear of the unknown. However, simple common sense dictates that if we get to know someone or something, they are or it is no longer foreign to us.

The word foreign has two generally accepted meanings. Firstly, foreign denotes a character or language not regarded as one's own. And secondly, foreign implies strange or unfamiliar. Then, of course, we have foreign office and foreign affairs, foreign exchange and currency, foreign fighters and films, and even a foreign body in one's eye. There is, therefore, a good deal of the world that we find strange and unfamiliar.

Prejudice is, put simply, a boiled down mistrust of what is foreign. And because the English, by and large, ceased fighting each other in the seventeenth century, it has these days been left to foreign fields in which people must go in order to sate their thirst for aggression. Fortunately most young people are educated as to the perniciousness of prejudice, so this disease of the preconceived opinion or bias is, happily, dying out.

Many older people, though, seek to preserve this antediluvian state of mind because they are anathema or closed to change.

Ollie, the protagonist of *Trust*, is young and educated, but he still finds it hard to divest himself of the prejudices fostered in him by his upbringing. We are all, whether we like it or not and in some small way, given to parrot our forebears. He arrives in Paris not only with time to kill, but also with time to witness at first hand the kindness of strangers. The story of *Trust* is, if you like, a short rite of passage, both physical and metaphorical, given that Ollie is travelling through the city from the *Gare du Nord* to the *Gare de Lyon*.

In May 1977, I hitched to Paris from Le Havre and spent one night in my sleeping bag beneath a mosquito infested hedge in the Normandy *bocage*. I crossed Paris to the *Porte d'Orleans* and stood in a line of similar hopefuls, my thumb out, keen to hitch a lift south out of the city. Hours passed in the heat by the dusty road, during which I watched single female hitchers attract drivers with their provocative poses. What the drivers were not aware of was that the moment they stopped, the male counterpart of the single woman would materialize from his hiding place and present himself at the car. Some drivers would speed off, but mostly the couple would time their ambush so carefully that they made it impossible for the driver to depart once he realised he was the victim of their ruse.

As the evening drew on and the promise of a night's kip on the train appealed more than sleeping rough in the *Tuileries*, I capitulated and traipsed to the station.

Down in the south, I developed a seriously unpleasant ear infection, which forced my return to England. But, not to be deterred, I returned to France some weeks later via the train.

I arrived at the *Gare du Nord* early one morning, my onward train departing from the *Gare de Lyon* later that evening. Some of that day I passed in Paris is represented in *Trust*. The incident of falling off the bench and becoming stranded like an upturned beetle is true, as is the incident with the ticket I had mistakenly not picked up when issued with it in the morning. To me, this was as valuable a lesson in the unfounded mistrust of foreigners as one was likely to receive.

Later the same year, when returning from the Côte d'Azur, I spent the night outside, on the steps of, the *Gare du Nord*. I teamed up with an English girl and a Scots lad who were in the same predicament; for if you had a ticket for the next day's travel, you were allowed to sleep in the station concourse; if, like us, you hadn't, you had to sleep outside.

During the night, we took it in turns to stand sentry while the other two slept. The night was long and full of the most unwelcome interruptions.

The next day, when we disembarked the train at Calais, the Scots lad threw himself at our mercy, telling us he didn't have sufficient funds with which to purchase his ferry ticket and would we, if we had the funds, lend him the money. The girl and I conferred, both deciding that if either of us ever found ourselves in a similar situation, we could only hope that some kind soul might afford us a similar charity. The lad, probably about the same age as the pair of us, was effusively grateful and promised, on receipt of our addresses, to return the money as soon as he could.

My uncle, a wise man, had taught me never to lend money which I could not afford to give away, so I was casually resigned to waving the funds *au revoir*.

Some weeks later, to my great surprise and even greater pleasure, I received a postal order with a letter. The lad, it appeared, had hitched a lift with a lorry driver all the way from Dover to within five miles of his home near Glasgow. He felt like the luckiest man in the world, having run into the girl and me that night outside the *Gare du Nord*. After a less than fulfilling trip round France and Spain, his faith in humanity, he wrote, had been restored.

Trust is a fundamental fragment of that faith; it transcends all borders and boundaries, or so Ollie learns.

A MIXED BAG

For Johnny Lowry

There's a small part of Swede Levov in many of us.

The eponymous and ultimately unsatisfactory champion of Philip Roth's 1997 novel, *American Pastoral*, marches purposefully towards his line of scrimmage just as Mark Parker, in *A Mixed Bag*, marches towards this chemistry teacher's desk the day before his exam. Yet Swede Levov, as perfect a scion of middle America as has ever existed in print, marches through a flawed and brittle world; one that continually throws him a variety of curve balls, if you will excuse me mixing my sporting metaphors.

Mark Parker's world is equally flawed and brittle.

We like to think our teachers are the guardians of our progress, the gatekeepers of our future. In some ways they are. However, in other ways they are most definitely and crucially not.

Our parents liked to think of our teachers as being both intelligent and intellectual – two vastly different yet intertwined attributes – and therefore worthy of their and our respect. Our parents also tended to, at most, deify them and, at the least, put them on a pedestal. Yet what our parents chose to forget, or perhaps conveniently ignore, was that teachers are human, like nearly every one else, and therefore they are, like nearly everyone else, prone to err.

The conversation between Mark Parker and his chemistry teacher, Mister Pope, actually took place, or so my friend told me the day before he sat his A-level Physics exam. I cannot think of anything more disabling or lowering than to be asked, the day before, not to attend an exam purely because a teacher does not want one's failure marked against his record.

There is much to be lauded regarding the Public School system: the competitive ethos, the lofty academic standards, the adherence to certain virtues and the preparation for the adult world to name but a few. There is also much, though, that should be decried.

That, in the early years of the nineteenth century, the Battle of Waterloo was won on the playing-fields of Eton, is very possibly true. But the same could be said for the early years of the twentieth century and the two momentous wars that have bequeathed us a responsibility to ensure so much suffering is not repeated. Sadly, we seem destined not to learn this lesson. Yet many of the boys, now men, I have spoken to since leaving similar schools bear the scars of their experiences concealed deep beneath their weather-beaten exterior.

One can argue until one is blue in the face as to whether elitism, be it sporting or intellectual, is a positive force within education. Many of these arguments are specious and driven by political or social ideology. From a personal perspective, I am inclined to think it is healthy to a degree, if that isn't too much of a contradiction in terms. But when a pupil, whose direction is confused by the fog of adolescence, is informed by his teacher that he is *not up to scratch* as far as his intelligence or intellect is concerned, and when taken in relation to his contemporaries which is what happens to Mark Parker, he is left with two very distinct choices: fight or surrender.

To be informed of one's options the day before an exam, though, is to be compared with telling a soldier that he has no hope but to die when he is ordered over the top of the trench.

In the modern era, the common way is for Public Schools to purge themselves of weaker pupils early on, thus ensuring their institution places higher in the echelons of the A-level league table. Naturally this raises their profile and so furthers the prospects of the school. However, this furtherance comes at the expense of the less-able pupil who is, literally, consigned to the scrap heap or released to wander the no-man's land that exists in being between schools. This distasteful residual of elitism has no place in modern society. Natural selection in the classroom is both archaic in its relevance and offensive to human nature. It deserves censure.

A hundred years ago a less-than-able pupil might have been sent to run a farm in the Outback of Australia or dragooned to guard the passes of the Khyber. Winston Churchill may well have been top of the list of those who have succeeded when others had labelled them for failure, and these days the Empire has, fortunately, metamorphosed into a Commonwealth of greater value.

I was lucky enough to be educated in geography by three gifted and very likeable individuals. Foremost amongst them was the teacher who taught from the text books he had written. The content may have centred on the annual maize crop and how it contributed to the Gross Domestic Product of Nigeria in 1968, but he was no less engaging for it. He was a giant among his peers. The second was a social radical, even though he was known by a hyphenated surname. He was completely unsuited to patrol the rigid corridors of thought advocated by a Public School of the early seventies. But his gift was to teach his pupils how to think, particularly about the broader aspects of socio-economic and political geography. The institution dispensed with his services not long after my departure; that being the pupils' loss. The last of these was the ultimate rugby player if not exactly the ultimate geographer. He was softly spoken, empathetic and inspiring in equal measure. The blend of all these three made for the very best of tutoring. I was lucky.

Mark Parker, a boy of athletic ability but perhaps no great shakes in the academic arena, is one of those who fall between the cracks in the establishment. He is an amalgam of many. His friend Crisp is his counterbalance.

BY ACCIDENT

For Ann Holland

Not long after I left school I found myself working in a pub which belonged to the parents of an acquaintance. The pub, or inn as it was, was set halfway down the south-facing slope of the North Downs and enjoyed fabulous views out across the Weald. The inn was popular with the weekend walkers, who used to infuriate the landlord by bringing their own sandwiches onto his premises, the blue-rinse brigade, who would meet to mither at lunchtime, and a steady crowd of early evening regulars.

This early crowd was made up of an eclectic mix of local artisans, office workers, farm workers, the odd – and I mean odd in both interpretations of the word – musician and artist, and some who would drop in for a quick pint and a chinwag on their way home from the station.

Most evenings the phone at the back of the bar would ring and whoever was working would shout, "Anyone not here?" Many would raise their hands.

This was an accommodation, in the days before the advent of the mobile phone, for those who had promised their wives they would be straight home, but who could not resist the temptation to indulge in a little down-time before facing the trouble-and-strife and ankle-biters back at the castle. This early crowd was supremely entertaining. They were usually larger than life, self-made characters who drank real ale, who were fiercely mindful of the protocols of the bar and who recounted the stories of their working day with liberal doses of irony or some such subtle, and occasionally not so subtle, humour.

Barry Bennett's character was born in the gathering of this great company, as were so many of the characteristics I have relied upon when defining the characters of my novels. He is the hardworking, brow-beaten, white collar breadwinner; the nine-to-five, rat-running, train-taking proletarian who often hurries home to kiss the children goodnight, shine his shoes, make polite conversation over the dining table, sleep and wake, only to rush back to his desk in town. And that, of course, all depended on the trains being on time, which in the days of the nationalised railways many of them weren't.

I didn't get much time to watch television, mostly because in the seventies it finished at midnight which, after I was done clearing up the bar, was about the time I got home; that is to say if I was lucky and there were no late-stayers. So it was only in the eighties when I had a *proper* job, as anything other than working in a bar was perceived to be, that I got to sit down of an evening and chuckle at the shrewd observations of *Cheers*, the television sitcom of the cosy bar in Boston. The writing of this long-running series was inspired. James Burrows, Glen Charles and Les Charles fully deserved all the plaudits the critics heaped upon their gentle comedy of errors.

From my view point, behind the bar of the inn in which I worked through the mid-seventies, I would watch as marriages were both constructed and deconstructed. And some of those relationships were born from the most extraordinary and unlikely of circumstances. Barry's story, though not mired in much truth or fact, is one.

GONE

For Andy Mant

Sleeping rough isn't so bad – as long as you know it's only for one night and that tomorrow night you will lie in a hot bath and, later, clean sheets. I know this because I've tried it, recently.

It was May of 1977 and I hitch-hiked to the South of France with the intention of finding a job working on the *gin palaces* plying their trade out of the Côte d'Azur. The first night I slept by a hedge in the Normandy *bocage*; from broken sleep I awoke sore of limb and covered in mosquito bites. The next night I slept on the train; the hitch-hiking not having progressed as I would have liked. I got a lift to Monte Carlo and tramped from there to Nice. I got assaulted by two old men who should have known better and I got moved on several times by the *gendarmes*. Finally I found a place to hang my hat in Cannes.

The *Hotel des Roches* on the quai of the *Vieux Port* wasn't such a bad spot; it didn't boast any basic amenities: to wash, one used the shower on the beach; for toilets, one used the municipal conveniences at the bus station; and when it rained, you got wet. But it was free and the bands of marauding Algerians only came by once a week. After a while I had nothing left worth stealing.

Fortunately, I found work and stayed the season.

On the way back, in November of that year, I had the misfortune to spend the night outside the *Gare du Nord* in Paris. Bothered by pimps, gigolos, paedophiles, prostitutes and drug addicts, I didn't get much sleep.

Last year, I locked myself out of my hotel in St Malo – a story for another time, perhaps – and slept beneath the ramparts of the walled town. It was September and warm. The bench was fairly agreeable and the *gendarmes* very obviously blinkered. This was relative luxury but, then again, I slept in the promise of a bath and clean sheets.

A close friend of mine with a highly tuned sense of altruism and concern for those less fortunate, recently passed the night under one of the railway arches of Waterloo Station. The exercise was part of a fundraising drive for a homeless charity. I remember asking her what it was like. Her reply was liberally dosed with adjectives the like of wretched, awful, disgusting, humiliating and painful; and this woman, let me tell you, is no shrinking violet. But if I remember rightly, these were the adjectives she employed to describe the mental aspects of sleeping rough; it was only later that she moved on to describe the more physical distress it causes.

But *Gone* isn't simply a story about what happens when a person has nowhere to go; it's more about the cruel forces which drive the being in that direction. Everyone, and I mean anyone who is homeless, has their very own and more often than not intensely personal story of why they are on the streets, whether they qualify as vagrant, hobo, bum, tramp, waif or stray, dosser, pevin, junkie or, as some academics like to call them, as transients, even though they are quite clearly not transient because they have *nowhere* else to go. Some of them even take to the streets of their own volition;

though I have heard this view propounded by those who sit more comfortably with the view that the dispossessed are how and where they are out of choice. But the more common image of the unwashed, unshaven, emaciated Homo not-so-Sapiens, his hand glued to a can of Tennents Extra, smoking a roll-up, a scruffy mongrel nestling beneath his fatigue jacket, only encourages those better off to walk on by.

In *Gone*, I have excluded names for both the narrator and the main character for good reason; the lack of a name depersonalises. When was the last time you asked a homeless person his or her name, or thought of them in terms of being like you, real?

Well, maybe because it's much easier not to know their names; maybe it's easier to appreciate them as tiny specs in an increasingly voluminous diaspora of the dispossessed, rather than as individuals with names, faces and personalities – as, if you like, people.

The main character in the story is a victim of the ever-changing world in which we live. His story is based in solid foundation.

I have found that it is not unusual or strange for people to want to preserve the equilibrium of their lives by convincing those nearest and dearest to them that nothing is wrong and that the world turns today exactly as it turned yesterday.

Sometimes it is easier to lie than to lie down and surrender to change.

THE BACKS OF THE LEAVES

For John Deeker, my father-in-law

There is a gulf of difference in being up to a task and being suited to it. Or so I found out when I offered to accompany my brother-in-law through the last three days of his epic cycle in the Alps, a trip he had planned for celebrating his half century of years.

In the event, he cycled 318 cols in twenty-eight days and along the way amassed three times the vertical climb achieved by the Tour de France, who cycle for twenty-three days. By any stretch of the imagination, this was a remarkable feat of fitness, will-power, endurance and above all mental strength. My brother-in-law now runs the ultimate sportive trial he founded, the *Cents Cols Challenge*. He is the *grimpeur*.

Through the last three days of his ride he battled not only with his own challenge, but also with mine. I had trained, sure. But on one of my training days I took him up Cooper's Hill, near Windsor, informing him that I usually cycled the long climb ten times back-to-back, as I believed it would stand me in good stead for my part in his tour.

He glanced nervously at me and remarked, "Pete, this isn't a hill; it's a slope."

Soon after that, I shifted my training from Cooper's Hill to the North Downs. Cycling up to Newlands Corner ten times back-to-back, I reasoned, must be sufficient preparation for the climbs I would encounter in the Alps.

It wasn't.

In the Alps, I learned a great deal and not simply about cycling. It was never a sport I was drawn to; I had taken it up simply to improve my fitness and raise a little money for a local charity. At 95 kilos, I did not fool myself into believing that cycling in the Alps would be anything other than hard grind.

In a way it was and in a way it wasn't.

Did I come close to understanding the psychology of the *grimpeur*? Perhaps! I certainly grew to understand more about the sport, but I also reached the conclusion that I, at 95 kilos, would never in a million years match the proficiency of the 60 kilo hill-climber.

The greatest lesson I did learn was that the essence of cycling, and particularly hill-climbing, is to be distilled from the battle between the mind and the body. It is waged in the vast vistas of that small distance between one's ears. *The Backs of the Leaves* is a short story about that battle, finding the arms in one's armoury that one never imagined existed, and the manner in which such a battle is fought.

LE PLAN

For Colin Pool

Le Plan is a story ending with what has become known in the trade as an *O Henry twist*.

William Porter, an American writer of the late-nineteenth and early-twentieth century, started out as a bank teller in Austin, Texas. He published a satirical and short-story weekly named *The Rolling Stone* and later wrote for the Houston Post. But, after a scandal in which he was charged with embezzlement at the bank, Porter fled the country, leaving his wife behind. Sadly, his wife fell gravely ill with consumption and Porter returned from his self-imposed exile to be with his wife through her last days. But, on his return he was arrested and sent to jail where he wrote hundreds of short stories and articles under the pen name of O Henry. He became well-known not only for the surprise endings of his stories, but also for his drinking; ultimately passing on from, amongst other ailments, cirrhosis of the liver. *Cabbages and Kings, Roads of Destiny* and *Whirligigs* are but three of his collections of stories. They are fabulous works.

It could be said that Porter was the father of modern short story writing, though that may depend on your interpretation of the word *modern*.

As for Atticus' story, it came to me when sitting on a long chairlift in the *Jaillet* ski field above Megève, in the Haute-Savoie of France.

Small flakes of snow drifted from a misty ceiling and I was wrapped up warm and snug in my jacket, salopettes, suit, helmet and goggles. Four of us were sitting, swinging just slightly as the lift transported us back up the mountain for yet another testing run down. I looked at my fellow travellers and realised that although I knew they were part of our group, I wasn't sure that I recognised any of them individually, concealed as they were, like me, within the confines of their suits, helmets and goggles. Dressed as skiers, one tends to be accepted as nothing more or less than simply a skier; one's identity tends to play second fiddle to one's ability when sweeping down the *piste* at speed.

Also, I wanted to try to describe the atmosphere of Megève to a reader. Though in many ways it is like many other ski resorts, in that it has its fair share of fabulous *pistes* and inviting *auberges*, it is in equally many ways unique. I've heard it said that Mègeve derives much of its ambience from the presence of a certain family of note, vast tracts of local real estate having been granted to the family for financial services rendered to the government of the Third Republic during the various wars — or so, I stress, I have been led to believe.

However, the presence of wealth should not be permitted to colour one's view of staggeringly beautiful mountains, delicious local cuisine, charming hosts and, above all, great, great skiing. These are, of course, the real reasons why Atticus has bought his chalet near the village.

THE GETAWAY

For Gladys Miller

The Getaway is a light-hearted look at social change.

During the years approaching and immediately after the Second World War, Britain underwent a sea-change in attitudes towards both work and play. Nine-to-five became the norm and commuting to one's place of employment took on a new significance. The suburbs assumed the scale of vast dormitories inhabited by workers who left early and arrived home late with the sole intention of grabbing a meal and a few hours of much needed sleep before having to set off again. And in order to get to work, the proletariat found themselves continually rounded up, on and off public transport, in enormous daily cattle drives of humanity. In order to get home, they suffered much the same.

To maintain one's individuality, whilst being guided, goaded, urged and herded with so many thousands of others, must have been incredibly difficult. Things are no different today, except that more of the buses and trains run on time, the rolling stock and carriages are generally of better quality and the advent of the personal computer enables people to work as they travel, or at even home when circumstances allow.

But back then, the accumulation of white goods — machines used for cooking, washing and refrigeration — became an active part of consumerism as one sought to keep up with, if not outdo, the Joneses next door. To have an oven combined with a hob, or a washing machine and/or a tumble dryer, became mandatory if one wanted to be thought of as well to do. One was judged, as far as one's social standing went, by what one had or didn't have about the kitchen.

Once, however, you had acquired all these necessary material benefits and established your status, there were yet other ways in which you could drive your social mobility: a motorcar was one; where you went on holiday another.

In *The Getaway*, I have poked a little fun at social aspiration and used a twist at the end of the story to accentuate the futility of it all. I have to admit to pinching the storyline for *The Getaway* from an incident my father witnessed whilst taking the sun on the Italian Riviera in the fifties.

LANDFALL

For Peter Eaden

Landfall is a short story of coming of age and therefore doesn't
follow the protagonist, Chay, all the way from youth to adulthood.
And neither does it indulge in any lengthy psychological or moral
Bildungsroman; rather it records one small segment of what some
would call a never-ending process.

Sailing the Atlantic is no longer considered exceptional;
rowing across it, maybe. Fewer people have rowed the Atlantic
than have climbed Everest or have, so far, ventured into space.
And historians have argued long and hard about whether or not
Columbus crossed the Atlantic first or whether that honour should
be laid at the feet of the Viking, Erik the Red. I suspect whichever
of the two it was, they both sensed the same relief of any other
sailor who has managed to make it across the *pond* in one piece.

The protagonist of *Landfall* is just such a young man. Through
Chay, we catch a glimpse of the immense relief, the maelstrom
of emotions and the pure joy experienced by one who has just
survived and completed the journey. Dealing with all of these

286

sensations is challenging enough, even for a mature individual, but combine them with the insecurities and naïf ignorance of a certain age and one has a recipe for a cocktail of disaster.

We join Chay on the evening of his arrival in the little island of Bequia, in the Windward Islands of the West Indies. As if completing the voyage isn't exhilarating enough, he meets a woman who appears intent on making his *Landfall* as gentle as possible. Through the evening Chay grows empowered with a sense of his own immortality. After all, he has gone where others fear to tread. He must now be invincible, irresistible and above all else *a man*.

Some of this story is autobiographical; I cannot deny it. How could one begin to describe such emotion if one has not experienced it at first hand? Yet I am not arrogant enough to suggest that all those who have sailed across the pond, either alone or in company, feel exactly as I did. Some sit quietly and thank the gods, others pass it off as if it possesses all the significance of surviving a Saturday morning trip to the supermarket, and one or two get so loud off the back of their arrival that at some stage, and inevitably, they require restraining and a night under watch. I have seen it; it comes to everyone differently.

Chay isn't *everyman*, or *everyboy* for that matter. He may, though, be somewhere in between. During the morning after his *Landfall*, Chay relearns that which he had in his euphoria forgotten; that he is, even after his momentous achievement, still mortal.

About the Author

Peter Crawley was born in Chiswick in 1956. He was educated at Cranleigh School in England and at the Goethe Institut Freiburg-im-Breisgau in Germany. He spent much of his youth in Germany, Austria, France and Corsica. Upon leaving full-time education, and after a short period with the army in Germany, he worked in Stuttgart, as a translator, and on luxury motor-yachts in and around the Mediterranean and the West Indies. *Mazzeri*, his first novel, was published by Matador in 2013, *Boarding House Reach*, his second, in 2014 and *Ontreto*, his third, in 2015. Peter Crawley is a former transatlantic yachtsman and historic motor racing driver. His interests include his family, his research, writing and skiing. He lives in Chertsey, Surrey, with his wife, Carol. They have three daughters.

MAZZERI

Love and Death in Light and Shadow
A novel of Corsica

It is the last summer of the twentieth century in Calvi, Northern Corsica, and an old man sits watching the kites fly. The festival of the wind is a lively and colourful celebration, but the old man's heart is heavy, he has heard the Mazzeri whisper his name. He accepts that people prefer to believe the dream hunters belong to the past and yet he knows only too well that at night they still roam the maquis in search of the faces of those whose time has come.

Ten years later in the high citadel of Bonifacio, in the southern tip of the island, Richard Ross, armed with only the faded photograph of a Legionnaire standing beneath a stone gateway, finds the locals curiously unwilling to help him uncover his family's roots. He rents a villa on the coast and meets the singularly beautiful Manou Pietri, who enchants him with tales of the megalithic isle, its folklore and the Mazzeri – the dream hunters.

For a while Ric's life beneath the Corsican sun is as close to perfect as he could wish. Then a chance encounter with a feral boy turns Ric's life upside down, and he is drawn deep into a tangled web of lies and deceit. On an island where truth and legend meet, where murder is commonplace and most crimes go unsolved, only the Mazzeri know who will live…

Published by Matador June 2013
ISBN 9781780885384 (pb)
ISBN 9781780885814 (eBook)

BOARDING HOUSE REACH

——∞∞∞——

Five strangers come to spend the weekend in a guest house on the Norfolk coast. The Reach offers sanctuary for guests Hacker, Phoebe, Audrey, Philip and the landlady, Stella — all of them drawn together by the secrets of their past.

As the strands of their individual stories are woven together, each guest will confront the painful truths of their personal lives and, as the hours tick away, confess their sins. In a story which encompasses blackmail, rejection, infidelity, redemption and love, the characters of Boarding House Reach know they can run, but will they ever escape the stark reality of their tangled lives?

Published by Matador May 2014
ISBN 9781783063390 (pb)
ISBN 9781783065646 (eBook)

ONTRETO

Arriving on the unspoiled island of Lipari, off the coast of Sicily, Ric Ross carries with him a letter of introduction to Valeria Vaccariello, an aging star of Italian cinema who lives alone in the *La Casa dei Sconosciuti*, the House of Strangers; a woman known locally as *La Strega* – the witch.

Ric is also befriended by *Il Velaccino* – the sailmaker, who seems to know everyone and everything that goes on in the island. But when a politician is shot dead, Ric's search for his family's history soon grows into a quest to prove his innocence.

Told through the eyes of a young man who comes to Lipari in search of his forebears, *Ontreto* is the standalone follow-up to Peter Crawley's first novel, *Mazzeri*.

Published by Matador May 2015
ISBN 9781784622213 (pb)
ISBN 9781784629298 (eBook)